PENGUIN BOOKS

THEN THERE WAS ONE

T0322062

ABOUT THE AUTHOR

Wendy Cross is an young adult author living on the Front Range with her husband and three amazing daughters. After ten years as a copywriter, Wendy became a pseudo-expert on everything from patio furniture to composting toilets. She loves reading and writing YA – especially mysteries – and believes the very best of friends are those who will help you hide the bodies.

WENDY CROSS

THEN THERE WAS ONE

PENGUIN BOOKS

For Jan
Some souls are too beautiful
to remain on Earth

PENGUIN BOOKS

UK | USA | Canada | Ireland | Australia
India | New Zealand | South Africa

Penguin Books is part of the Penguin Random House group of companies
whose addresses can be found at global.penguinrandomhouse.com.

www.penguin.co.uk   www.puffin.co.uk   www.ladybird.co.uk

First published in the UK 2023
This paperback edition published 2024

001

Text copyright © Wendy Cross, 2023
Cover images by Shutterstock

The moral right of the author has been asserted

Set in 10.25/15.25pt SabonLTStd
Typeset by Jouve (UK), Milton Keynes
Printed and bound in Great Britain by Clays Ltd, Elcograf S.p.A.

The authorized representative in the EEA is Penguin Random House Ireland,
Morrison Chambers, 32 Nassau Street, Dublin D02 YH68

A CIP catalogue record for this book is available from the British Library

ISBN: 978–0–241–64157–6

All correspondence to:
Penguin Books
Penguin Random House Children's
One Embassy Gardens, 8 Viaduct Gardens, London SW11 7BW

THE INVITATION

BEX

'You have been chosen.' The courier sets in my palm a small paper mountain, which erupts with engineered snow and holographic fireworks the moment it touches my skin. As the colours fade, the paper neatly unfurls to reveal an envelope, its gold words glinting in the sun:

WELCOME TO *THE PINNACLE*!

'Is this real?' I glance up, but the courier's gone. I jog down the last few metres of the long, sweeping drive and past the privacy bushes that surround our home. Once on the sidewalk, I look up and down the street, but the courier has completely disappeared.

Odd, but it does fit with *The Pinnacle*'s reputation for secrecy. That's the main reason everyone in the Cael Quadrant loves it so much.

The game is pretty normal – contestants compete in physical and mental challenges to win immunity and collude with each other to make sure they aren't the ones advancing to the audience elimination round where someone will be voted off.

And sure, the prize money of five million crians is pretty life-changing – for others anyway. But what gets everyone most excited is that there's no way of applying to be on the show.

The Pinnacle chooses you.

Their method is top secret, and people don't even know they've been selected until a courier hands them an invitation intricately folded into a 3D mountain. Like the one in my hand.

I open the envelope and read the words on the parchment inviting me to compete, fear and hope dancing through me like synchronized swimmers in the middle of a complicated routine. I should go – you only die once, after all. Or is it live? It doesn't matter, because I wouldn't actually perish – it is only a game – but the chances of me losing, well, those are high. Very high.

Or maybe, for once in my life, I would win. When it matters most.

A horn honks, and someone yells out of a speeding car, 'It should've been you!'

I shrink back from the road – why did I venture out so far? I know better than to go beyond our property line.

Clutching the parchment, I race up the drive and slip into the foyer, pausing to make sure Dad's safely ensconced in his office. As I creep towards the closed door, his voice booms through it, magnified by the vaulted ceilings and marble floors.

A sigh of relief escapes me. Running into him now would ruin everything. With one last glance at the office, I dart up the winding staircase to my room.

Then There Was One

I was wrong; the money's important to me too – it can buy my anonymity, something Dad refuses to do.

I'm going.

And he will never know.

ZANE

'Mom!'

I race through the tired hallways of our house, unable to ignore the cracked paint and faded murals that once added life and beauty to our home. No matter how hard Mom tries, this house is way too big for one person to care for. And instead of letting me help, she insists I focus on my studies and my internship.

But neither of those things are going to solve our problems.

'MOM!' I yell again.

'In here!' she calls from the kitchen.

'You'll never believe what just arrived!' I thrust the invitation at her.

Wiping her hands on her apron, she takes it from me. 'What is this?'

I beam. 'It's the answer we've been waiting for.' As Mom reads, her eyes widening with every word, I take her place at the stove.

'I don't know . . .' she says.

I keep stirring, glancing at her as she re-reads the invitation before scanning the paper with information on how to sign the forms giving me permission to compete.

'I'm not sure you should skip school. Plus, you'll miss several matches, not to mention your internship on the council, and –'

'Winning *The Pinnacle* would fix everything,' I interrupt. 'School, sports, the council – none of them pay our bills. But this would.'

She keeps staring at the invitation, the debate she's having in her head flickering across her delicate features.

'Please, Mom. Let me do this. You know I'll win.'

Her eyes don't wander from the parchment. 'But what if it's not safe?'

'Of course it's safe. Besides, we really need the money. We'll –' I catch myself. She doesn't like me to worry even though I know as well as she does that we'll be homeless soon if something doesn't change. But she's determined to take care of it. To take care of me.

Because she believes she has to make up for everything that happened.

'Please. Let me try.' I grip her hands, trying to convey that I don't blame her. That I've never blamed her. She's always been my rock and, for once, I want to be hers. 'Please.'

She hesitates a moment longer before nodding. 'OK – if that's what you want, then you can go. I'm sure I can figure out a way to get enough money to get you to –' she glances at the invitation – 'El Nar.'

'Thank you!' I throw my arms around her. Finally, something I can do to help.

RAYA

I pull the invitation out of my pocket and read it again.

Why the hell would they choose me?

Probably to make themselves look good.

'What do you think, Zircon?' I squat and show my dog the parchment the courier handed me as I left the mine. 'Should I go?'

Zircon gives the invitation a half-hearted sniff before aiming his nose at my pocket.

I laugh and scratch him behind the ears – his favourite spot. 'Don't worry, I got you something. It's good, too. The butcher wasn't watching his dumpsters today.' I pull out a thick bone and give it to Zircon. It's almost as big as he is.

I watch him as I lean against the brick wall of the alley I call home. At least for now. 'You need to learn to control that tail. It isn't smart to let people know what you're feeling all the time.' I'd tried to teach Zircon to not wag his tail when I first got him, but it was like teaching a miner not to steal – pointless.

'If I go it means leaving you on your own for a bit. Can you handle that?' This would be the first time I've left him, and he might worry. I stroke his back. 'You'll be fine if you stay here – catch rodents for food, and don't talk to strangers.' I give him a fierce glare so he knows I'm serious – he likes people a little too much. 'And I promise I'll be back.'

Zircon's too focused on his bone to respond.

I slide down the wall and sit next to him, the cold ground making me shiver. 'I'm going to have to get my hands on some serious money and figure out how to bribe my way on to a shuttle.' He pauses and stares at me, his question obvious. I scratch his head. 'Of course it'd be easier to just buy a ticket, but we miners aren't allowed to leave The Moons. I thought you knew that.' I scan the other paper. 'I'm also going to have to break into someone's house and use their computer so I can send *The Pinnacle* all this information they require. But –' I show Zircon the invitation again – 'did you see the prize? Five million crians! We could leave here forever if I win.'

I pause, taking in the grey dust, bleak sky and red brick walls surrounding me.

'*When* I win.'

DAY ONE

1

BEX

I run a trembling finger down the smooth edge of the gold-lined parchment as I read it for the thousandth time.

> *Bexley Ryker, you are invited to be a participant in the 250th season of*
>
> The Pinnacle
>
> *If you accept, please arrive on El Nar in the Amovi Sector on the 18th and make your way to the transporter hub. Report to the receptionist for your 2:30 transporter ticket to places unknown. You will receive further instructions upon your arrival.*
>
> *All needs will be provided for – bring nothing with you.*
>
> *Sincerely,*
> *Hunter Russo*
> *Producer*

P.S. To celebrate our 250th season, all contestants will be between the ages of sixteen and eighteen. And, in addition to the prize of five million crians, a full scholarship will be awarded to the winner's choice of university.

I fold the parchment along the original creases, which are becoming increasingly thin, and tuck it into my pocket. I cast a furtive glance around the shuttle to make sure none of the other passengers saw, but everyone else is too busy with their own lives to worry about mine. Too bad it's not always like this.

My stomach twists with excitement ... and fear. Maybe being a contestant on the most popular show in the Cael Quadrant isn't the best idea. Especially alongside nine other people who are, undoubtedly, better suited to this type of thing.

But staying home isn't an option any more. And it's not just because access to my trust fund has been blocked.

My hand strays back to my pocket, but I resist the urge to pull out the invitation again. It gives no clues to the competition's location, even though I feel like if I study it long enough, I'll figure it out.

Or figure out why they chose me.

Outside the window of the transport shuttle, stars dart by like startled fireflies as we zoom towards El Nar. Next to me, a petite girl with ghostly white skin, wild dark hair and an impish grin is sketching a picture on a napkin with what looks like a small black rock.

I study the long, bold lines – what is she drawing? I debate whether to ask, but I don't want to insult her or say the wrong thing. I stare longer than I should and realize, as her gaze shifts to me, that she's missing her left forefinger.

Now she's going to think I was staring at her hand.

'Is that your . . . dog?' I blurt out in an effort to make things less awkward.

The girl studies me for a moment, her eyes black and fathomless. She's like one of the wraiths my dad told me haunted the grounds of our estate to ensure I didn't sneak out at night.

'It was going to be,' the girl says. 'But it's not very good.' She speaks with a provincial accent I can't quite place, drawing out her vowels and dropping the g at the end of *going*.

'Oh.' I lace my fingers together, examining the pale pink nail polish I chose for the competition – something that seems foolish now. I want to say more, but my voice is stuck in my throat. What if I say something stupid?

I glance at the girl, the drawing, and back at the girl. 'I used to have a dog,' I finally manage to say. 'His name was Finn.' I can't help but smile at the memory of him – he was the best.

'That's a weird name.'

My cheeks burn, but I force myself to keep talking. 'I, um, love the water, and well, you know – Finn? Like a fish's fin, or a dolphin, or . . .' My voice trails off as she stares at me with her eyebrows raised, amusement playing across her features. 'Anyway . . .' I shift, unsure of where to look or what else to say.

'My dog's name is Zircon, like the stone. He's the same colour.' Her voice is matter-of-fact, as though she doesn't care, but the joy in her eyes gives her away.

'What kind of dog is he?'

She shrugs. 'Normal kind.'

I try again. 'Where'd you get him?'

'Found him.'

'Oh.' Silence stretches between us as I grapple for something else to say. 'Are you going to El Nar?'

'Yup.'

'Me too. I'm Bex Ryker.'

'Raya Quinn.' She nods towards my pocket. 'I saw your invitation.'

'My what?' My voice squeaks, giving away the panic that's been my constant companion since I boarded the shuttle.

'Your invitation for *The Pinnacle*. I got one, too.'

'You did?'

'Yup. Surprised the hell out of me. Never thought they'd invite a poor girl from the Inops Sector. Especially not The Moons. Where you from?'

My mouth opens and closes, but no words come out.

'Don't tell me you're a space pirate.' Raya's eyes dance with mischief.

'N-no!' I splutter. I take in Raya's frayed red shirt, ripped jeans and worn shoes, and hesitate. I could lie – the fact that I live on the wealthiest planet in the wealthiest sector of the whole quadrant could make things awkward. Then again, if *The Pinnacle* announces where I'm from, that'd be even more awkward. 'I'm from the Vauras Sector.'

Far too aware of the small tremor in my voice, I lean back in my seat, struggling to appear nonchalant as I wait for Raya's response. But all Raya says is, 'Which planet?'

I fiddle with the hem of my shirt, stomach twisting from a different kind of fear. 'Rikas.' The word's barely a whisper. Does news from Rikas ever make it to the Inops Sector? If it does . . .

Tension drains from my body when she asks, 'What'd you do there?' She flashes me a mischievous grin, as though the answer's obvious. But of course it is. There's not much else a seventeen-year-old can do.

'School. I'm a senior.'

'Your folks don't care if you skip?'

'No.' I gaze out of the window so she can't see my expression. El Nar looms in the window – yellow and white swirling together like a melted yuzu sundae.

'Lucky you.'

Lucky me. I run my hands over the velvety fabric of my navy leggings – maybe I shouldn't have chosen the ones with the lace detailing. I thought they'd give off an air of sophistication and confidence, but instead I look silly and overdressed.

I swallow hard. Hopefully Raya hasn't noticed.

Struggling to ignore the voice insisting she's not going to like me, I turn back to her, determined to make a friend for once in my life. Or at least gain an ally. 'What did you do on The Moons?'

'Not much. Steal, cheat and fight, mostly. Bet that's why I was chosen – to make things interesting.' She winks.

I try not to gape at her. 'That's definitely . . . interesting.' Is Raya serious? Is that how she lost her finger? Would this make her a good ally . . . or a bad one?

'WE WILL BE ARRIVING IN EL NAR IN THREE MINUTES,' a soothing, robotic voice announces over the intercom. 'PLEASE STAY SEATED UNTIL WE'VE LANDED.'

The panic I've just about managed to ignore rushes back full force, and I dig my fingers into the soft fabric of the armrests.

'Almost there,' Raya says. She carefully folds her drawing and, after a moment's hesitation, places it in the small recycling bin built into her seat. 'I know you don't know me, but want to make an alliance?'

'An alliance?' With a thief? I bite my lip. A maybe thief – she could've been joking. Does it matter either way? Not if I want to win this competition.

'Yup. You've seen the show, right?'

I nod.

'Well, the winners are always part of some sort of alliance.'

'Uh huh.' I clench my teeth so I don't say something idiotic that'll ruin the moment.

'So, whaddya think? Want to be teammates?'

'Sure!' I wince – that came out way too eager, but I'm terrible at making friends. I was convinced I'd be the only person without an ally and the first to leave the game, which would not only be mortifying but also ruin everything. But, with an ally, I could win.

A satisfied expression settles on Raya's face. 'Good. You look smart, and I need smart.'

I flash what I hope is a confident smile. According to my dad, common sense isn't my strong suit, and according to my grades, neither are science, maths, history or anything else, so there's zero chance I'll be winning any of the logic puzzles or trivia games that earn points towards staying in the game. But Raya doesn't need to know that.

'WE WILL BE DOCKING IN THIRTY SECONDS, PREPARE FOR LANDING,' the robotic voice says.

'Ready?' Raya asks as people around us get ready to stand.

I take a deep breath in a futile effort to calm my pounding heart. 'I think so.'

The shuttle shudders to a stop.

'WELCOME TO EL NAR.'

*

Hot air slams into us as we leave the terminal and step on to the streets of El Nar. A small, desert planet in the Amovi Sector, with only one city of the same name, it's home to the largest open-air market in the quadrant, which is popular for its great deals and rare finds. It also boasts the busiest teleport hub with the most inter-sector connections, making it easy for *The Pinnacle* to keep the location of the game a secret. One minute you're in the desert on El Nar and the next you could be freezing in a snowstorm on Gelau or struggling to stay afloat in a lake on Voldivia.

We make our way to the sandy cobblestone streets. Throngs of people surge around us, headed to the market in search of delicacies, treasures and rare artifacts, along with more common items like cleaning bots, clothing or the latest sub-dermal chips that monitor your heartbeat, oxygen saturation levels and micronutrient intake.

Soft fabrics brush against my arms as I weave in and out of the crowd, the smell of citrus, coffee and exotic flowers hanging thick in the air. Voices rise and fall as people barter for jewellery, cotton, decorative copper coins and other expensive things. Vendors underneath bright, colourful tents hold up items, shouting over the clamour as they try to sell their wares: antiques and old books from Earth, or cinnamon, saffron and other rare spices cultivated in special habitats, since they're unable to grow on any of the twelve terraformed planets in the quadrant, nor on any of the moons used for mining.

'You there!' A vendor with dark auburn hair and a bushy beard selects a sparkling green barrette from his table and points at Raya. 'You must try this – it'd look stunning with your complexion. Or perhaps you, my young friend?' He switches his focus to me. 'It would sparkle beautifully against your blonde locks.'

A man in a well-tailored business suit steps between us and the vendor. 'Who created that painting behind you?' His aquiline nose and brown wavy hair remind me of – I gasp and plunge forward, keeping my head down. It's Dad's personal assistant.

A low groan escapes my lips. Why didn't it occur to me I might run into one of Dad's associates? This is his favourite place to find artwork, and he often sends his people here in search of new pieces. What if his assistant sees me? What if he tells Dad I was here? Or perhaps Dad's already figured out I lied and has sent people to find me and bring me home. I quicken my pace, sweat dotting my brow as the sun beats down on us.

Raya doesn't seem to notice my fear as she moves effortlessly between men in crisp, dark suits and women in long, flowing dresses designed to keep them cool. 'So, what are you good at?'

Definitely not planning ahead. I dodge a group of well-dressed teenagers too focused on whatever's happening behind their smart glasses to notice me, my mind racing as I struggle to figure out something I do well. A rack of bikinis catches my eye. 'Swimming and diving.'

'Swimming could be good. Last season, the game was in a desert. Bet we get a lake or ocean or something this time.' She surveys the area. 'I've never been to El Nar. You know your way around?'

'A little. My mom sometimes brings me here to shop. And we stopped here to use the teleporters when my parents took my brother and me to the holo-theatres.'

'Really?' Curiosity and excitement mingle on Raya's face. 'What was it like? What'd you do?'

I hesitate. It was two years ago. We'd gone to experience the new holo-adventure at HoloReel. It'd been a blast, fighting digital bad guys and travelling through different cities and buildings while never leaving the holo-theatre. We even wore Spectra Suits that made us look like the characters we were playing. I'd been a tall, leggy redhead and a surprisingly good shot. Not that it mattered.

'Not much.' It's a lie, but I don't want to explain how I spent hours decoding clues, dodging bullets and outwitting the enemy before Dad kicked me out because I entered the wrong code on the vault.

Raya cocks her eyebrow. 'Not much?'

'No. This way.' I manoeuvre towards a narrow alleyway protected from the sun. Even though it adds a few minutes to our walk it leads to a section of the market designed for the middle class, which means I don't have to worry about running into any more of Dad's people.

We step into the shade where it's at least ten degrees cooler. I run my fingers along the cold, smooth stone walls of the building next to me, leaving behind a trail of hope. We're not that far from the teleporters and freedom.

'Are they safe?' Raya asks.

'The holo-theatres?'

Raya nods.

'Yeah. They're always run in safe mode.'

Raya rolls her eyes as though the idea of safe mode is a bit ridiculous. 'Can you –' She pauses as heavy footsteps echo through the alley. Two huge men are heading straight for us.

Crap! I press myself against the wall, squeezing my eyes shut. I can't believe they found –

'What're you doing?' Raya grips my hand and runs, dragging me behind her. We burst out of the alley, and I slam into a lady with a basket of food. Fruit scatters everywhere.

'I'm sorry –' I bend to help her.

'No time!' Raya grabs my arm and pulls me along. We sprint down the street, dodging shoppers, vendors and animals.

We run block after block until my feet refuse to go any further. 'I – I – can't. Stop!' I double over, chest heaving, sweat pouring down every part of my body.

'You OK?' Raya's not even out of breath.

'F-f-fine,' I stutter between gasps.

'Here.' She shoves a bottle of water at me.

I splash some on my face before taking a drink. It's so cold and delicious, I have to stop myself from chugging it all. 'Thanks.' I hand it back to Raya.

'No prob.' She takes a swig.

I peer over my shoulder. 'Who were those men?' I can't shake the feeling that Dad sent them.

Raya shrugs. 'Thugs, pickpockets, idiots. Who knows? They weren't worth the fight.'

I raise my eyebrows – could she really have fought them and won?

She grins like she can read my mind. 'You don't survive The Moons if you don't know how to fight. Or when to run.'

I nod, still trying to make sense of what happened. 'Where'd you get the water?'

'A lucky find.' She offers me a plump, red apple before taking a bite of her own. 'Which way?'

I stare at her for a moment – she really is a wraith. A smile tugs at my lips. Or a thief. Either way, I'm glad she's on my side. I take a bite of the apple. It's crunchy and sweet, reminding me of the orchards my brother and I played in as kids. We had so much fun pretending we were the explorers who planted the original seedlings brought from Earth to help terraform the quadrant.

For a moment, life seems normal again. I glance behind me one more time, but the men are nowhere to be seen.

'This way.'

2

RAYA

I clench my jaw so I don't gawk, but it doesn't work. The teleporter hub is the size of a mansion, or maybe a castle, or maybe a mansion castle – it's that huge. The white marble walls and polished obsidian floors are so shiny they could be mirrors. And the ceiling's made of gold. Gold! It's got to be worth a fortune. Too bad I can't slip it into my pocket.

I grin – Old George, who watched over all us miner kids, was convinced I could fit anything into my pocket if I tried hard enough. But he never saw anything like this.

'This way.' Bex doesn't notice my shock. Or she's too classy to mention it. She's got this refined way of speaking that's all proper and nice. She says 'cahn't' instead of 'can't' and shit like that. And her clothes are loads fancier than what the Gentry wear, which is saying something because the rich folk who own the mines care way too much about what they wear. But, just like the Gentry, Bex's clothes are useless. All frills and no funtionability. Who thinks it's a good idea to buy trousers with no pockets?

Everything about this girl says rich. Very. Rich.

A tall, skinny lady who's more bones than anything else stands behind a desk made of the same obsidian as the floor. She eyes Bex with the kind of sneer that's normally aimed at folks like me, but Bex doesn't seem to care, even though her hair's a mess from running and sweat's still dripping down her face.

She straightens her shoulders and lifts her chin. 'Hello.'

Skinny raises an eyebrow like she's too good to talk to us.

Anger ripples through me. I change my stance and clench my hands – there's no way Skinny's stopping me from getting to *The Pinnacle*.

But before I can do anything, Bex says, 'I'm Bexley Ryker, and this is Raya Quinn. There are passes waiting for us.'

Skinny peers down her long, thin nose at Bex before switching her gaze to me. 'Are you sure?' she asks, giving me a glare that could freeze molten metal.

Bex doesn't bother to answer – she just holds out her hand. 'The passes.'

Skinny tries to stare Bex down, but Bex isn't taking it. The scared, timid girl from the alleyway's gone. Interesting. I wasn't too sure how good an ally she'd be, but a little bit of stubbornness and a lot of fancy schooling means Bex will probably win all the smart games I'm not so good at.

Skinny glances away first. She taps a few buttons. There's a slight whirring, and she gives Bex two transparent passes.

'Thank you.' Bex obviously doesn't mean it. The woman gives her a short nod and goes back to work.

I shoot Skinny a dirty look and follow Bex, still amazed by the sheer size of the building. 'Where're we headed?'

She gives me my ticket. 'Transporter Four. This way.'

I grip my pass, not bothering to read it, and glance at the huge clock on the wall. It's already 2:25. Shit. 'Come on.' I grab Bex's hand. 'We're going to miss it.'

'We won't – it's nearby.'

She's probably right, seeing how she's been here before, but I'm not risking it. I tug on her hand, and she lets me pull her along as I push past people to the transporter. We enter a small room with a large circular console covered in buttons and screens. In front of it is a raised platform that gleams copper and silver in the light.

'Where is everyone?' I ask.

'I don't know.'

'Well, I'm not waiting – which button is it?'

I go to push a giant green one, but Bex grabs my arm. 'Don't touch that.'

I give her hand a pointed stare, and she drops it with a blush. 'Sorry. I meant to say that you don't need to press any buttons. You just slide your pass into here –' she points to a small slot – 'and stand on the transporter in one of the circles.'

The platform has five circles etched into its silver surface.

'It takes about a minute to charge. Ready?' Her voice trembles on the last word, as if she's not sure she should go through with this. Her loss.

'Yup.' I put my ticket in the slot where it's swallowed whole, then stride to the centre circle, bouncing a little on my toes. Bex hesitates a moment before depositing her own ticket and stepping into the circle next to me.

'Are you nervous?' Bex asks.

'Nope.'

'Not even a little?'

'Life on The Moons sucks, and there's nothing on this show that'll come close to living there.' The circle beneath me starts to glow. 'Besides, it's only a game.'

A game I'm going to win.

A blinding beam of light shoots up around me. When it fades, the transporter room is gone and I'm on the deck of a ship underneath a clear blue sky. Sapphire water stretches out in every direction, sparkling as though it's dotted with diamonds. In the distance is an island covered with trees that shimmers in the sun. I take a deep breath. The air is clean and salty and so much better than The Moons.

I didn't know places like this were real.

'Welcome!' A friendly voice calls from above. 'Take the stairs to the right and join us!'

'Here we go.' I bound up the stairs, not hearing Bex's response. Up top, a bunch of kids are lounging on white chairs, all of them holding fancy drinks.

'And here are our last two contestants.' The owner of the voice flashes us a way-too-white smile and flips his thick, black hair out of his face. He could be on a shampoo commercial.

'I'm Hunter Russo, one of the producers of *The Pinnacle*.' He waves at two empty chairs. 'Please take a seat, and I'll make the introductions.'

I plop into one of the chairs and grin. This shit is super comfortable. Luxurious even. When I win, I'm going to get me and Zircon some of these. Bet he'd love that.

A waiter stuffed into a white coat and black pants gives me a drink with a little pink umbrella sticking out of it.

I'm going to get me one of him, too.

Hunter raises his hands, and the whispers that started when Bex and me showed up stop. I fling my feet on to a stool and chug my drink. It's cold and sweet and fruity . . . I yank the glass away from my mouth, splashing ruby-red liquid on to my hand where it glitters like drops of blood. My heart gives a funny twitch and I set the glass down, ignoring the memories.

'Fabulous, fabulous. The viewers are going to love you.' Hunter claps his hands together, taking us all in. 'Our newcomers are Bexley Ryker and Raya Quinn.' He turns his ridiculous grin on us. 'Next to you are Paloma Bhatt and Evie Valentine.'

I jerk in surprise and lean forward. Evie's coiled in her chair like a snake ready to strike, almost hidden behind Paloma. I can't believe there's members of the Gentry here. And not just any Gentry, but *her*. She turns her head, her clear golden eyes meeting mine.

I hold her gaze. My lips curl into a sneer. She stares at me like I'm just another miner and then looks away, dismissing me.

Bitch never remembers who I am.

'Over there,' Hunter continues, 'you have Zane Wilder, Maria Johnson and Carson Beckett.' There are nods and waves as Hunter says each person's name. He shifts and indicates the people on the other side of me. 'And that's Greyson McKenzie, Oscar Cortés and, finally, Winston Adler.'

Hunter's gaze drifts to the sea for a second before turning his attention back to us. His pupils are huge – he's got to be high on something.

'Since this game is based on surprises, I'm not going to

give you a lot of information before we start. What you need to know is that the competition takes place on that deserted island over there, which is about a hundred kilometres offshore. There'll be a total of nine challenge sets. Each set will contain two physical and two mental challenges that are worth a certain number of points. Some of these will be team challenges, and you'll get to choose your team for the majority of them.'

My gaze slides over the other contestants.

They're all a little pathetic.

Except the really buff guy sitting across from me, confidence oozing off him. I tap my finger on the armrest . . . Zane. Me and Zane need to become friends.

'The total number of points you win in each set determines who gets immunity,' Hunter continues. 'After immunity is awarded, you will vote for two players to move on to the elimination round where one of them will be voted off by the audience. The contestant with immunity cannot be selected for the audience round and immunity resets after every elimination. There is no immunity during the final elimination. The last one remaining wins the game. Understood?'

'Yup!' I say as the others nod, all serious.

'Good. Next, you're completely on your own, with the exception of the other contestants. You're not allowed to ask for help from the crew, the host or myself.'

'What if we get hurt?' Paloma winds a thread from her shirt around her finger so tight her finger turns purple. She's a nervous, jumpy thing. There's no way she's going to win this.

'There will be medics on standby, of course. Any other questions?'

'Which planet are we on?' Zane asks.

'You'll find that out at the end of the competition.' Hunter flashes Zane a sly grin. 'We don't want to inadvertently give anyone an advantage if they're familiar with the planet or its ecology. Now, as I was saying, you may not ask for help. If you cheat or hurt another contestant, you'll be disqualified. Also, you're not permitted to leave the island. Let's see, what else?' Hunter stares at the sky for a moment before snapping his fingers. 'Oh, yes, no technology is allowed, and you'll be responsible for finding your own food and water. Try not to starve, it ruins the fun,' he adds with a wink.

'Starve?' Bex whispers, picking at her pink nail polish. I hide a smirk. There's no way this rich girl's ever gone a day without food. Hell, I bet the most difficult thing she's ever done is decide which outfit to wear.

But she doesn't say anything else, and her mouth's set in a determined line.

Zane seems determined too, but he's not sitting straight as a miner's pick like he's being tested on how good his posture is. Instead, he's leaning back all relaxed and shit, like he's already won. Too bad that's not happening.

I check out the kid nearest Zane. Carter? Carl? Carson? It doesn't matter – there's no way he's going to last. He'll probably be voted out before Paloma, and that's saying something. His freckled skin is pale and puffy, and his hair, which is redder than fire opals, sticks up like it's as scared as its owner.

But I can't read the girl on Zane's other side. Maria? She's long and lean like she's spent her whole life running, but her face don't give anything away. She could be scared, bored, excited or a million other things. She might be a good ally – but I don't like people I can't read. And there aren't many.

'I think that's it.'

My head snaps up at Hunter's words. 'What'd I miss?' I ask Bex.

'There's a small storm predicted for tomorrow morning, which might delay the crew an hour or two. And we're to follow him to the top deck.'

'One more thing.' Hunter pauses at the bottom of the stairs, facing us. 'We don't officially start until tomorrow, but to get everyone into the competitive spirit, you're going to race to the island.'

Carson's eyes bulge. 'What do you mean?'

'This yacht is modelled after Old Earth-style boats to keep with the theme of *The Pinnacle*, so the water's too shallow for it to get much closer to shore. You'll have to swim. And, to make it more interesting, the winner gets these.' Hunter holds up a small box.

'What are those?' Evie asks.

'Matches.' Hunter turns the box around, studying them. 'They're an old-fashioned way of starting a fire.'

'But natural fires have been banned since –' Winston begins.

'Since the wildfire that destroyed hundreds of terraforming modules when the endeavour to settle the Cael Quadrant began,' Hunter finishes. 'However, as you undoubtedly already know, *The Pinnacle* is about celebrating those intrepid explorers who set out into the unknown to test the limits of space and humanity. This year, one of the ways we're paying homage to those who came before us is by using natural fire to cook, sterilize water and stay warm.'

Paloma furrows her brow. 'But –'

'Don't worry, we obtained all the proper permits.' He flashes us another smile and shakes the box. 'Make sure you do everything you can to win these matches. Let's go.'

I follow the others to the stairs at the back of the boat, my mouth dry. I haven't been swimming since I was ten. It was hot out, hot for The Moons anyways, and I'd snuck out of the mines early so I could get the dirty lake us miner kids swam in all to myself. I was about to get into the water when a large van with no windows pulled up on the opposite side. Two men got out and began hauling long, black bags out of the back.

I hid behind some old junk as they flung the bags into the water, marking where they hit. There might be something good in them – food or clothing. Maybe even shoes. Hopefully some without holes.

I waited for them to finish, not daring to move until they left. In the middle of the lake, one bag kept breaking the surface, bobbing up and down like a fish.

I paddled out to it and lugged it back behind the junk. It wasn't too heavy, which was nice. Making sure I was still alone, I unzipped it, and a small, pale hand flopped out. I stared at it a moment. Then poked it.

It was cold and wet and real.

I took off across the dirt plains, leaving my shoes and coat behind. Not even Old George could make me feel better about what I'd seen, and boy did he try.

I eye the sparkling ocean, that ghostly hand floating in my memory. But the shore of the island's only about twenty metres away. I can make that.

I hook my thumbs through my belt loops, but my hands don't stop shaking.

'Don't worry.' Bex breaks into my thoughts. 'I'm on the deep water swim team in school and an alternate on the high dive team. Those matches are ours.'

'If I don't drown. If I do, they're all yours.' I'm only kind of joking.

'I'll come to your rescue if you sink. I also own the unofficial school record for holding my breath the longest. Seven minutes and thirty-three seconds – and that was in real water, like this, not some virtual reality program with the oxygen turned off.'

I can tell she's proud of that fact, but who cares if it was real water or not?

'I'll make it.' Even though I can swim twenty metres without some rich girl's help, there's no way I'm fast enough to win those matches. But if I help Bex win instead, she'll share. Who am I kidding? She'll share even if I don't help. Nice people are stupid like that.

On the upper deck, Hunter's barking directions, all signs of his earlier charm gone. 'Line up,' he says. 'Right there.' He points to the smooth, white wall where the other contestants are standing, nervous eyes fixed on the ocean. A long platform with no railings stretches out over the water.

My heart starts working double-time. It's at least a six-metre jump.

'Ready?' Hunter holds up his arm.

I shove my hand into my pocket and make sure my switchblade is secure – don't want to lose that. I don't go anywhere without it.

Hunter drops his arm. 'Go!'

Giving the kid next to me a swift elbow to the stomach, I race forward and, before I can stop myself, leap off the edge. For a few, wonderful seconds I'm flying through the air. Then cold water greets me with a smack, and the ocean closes over my head as I sink.

Kicking to the surface, I scan the area. Four kids are ahead of me but Bex is in front of them all. I grin. That girl wasn't kidding when she said she could swim.

A wave crashes into me. Spluttering, I start paddling as Hunter zooms by us in a small hover boat. Evie passes me, helping Paloma make it to shore. One kid swims up next to me, and I push them underwater to give myself a nice boost.

The beach shines in the distance and I can't help but admire it. It's more beautiful than anything I've ever seen. When I win *The Pinnacle*, I'm building a house on that beach with a giant window that faces the water. Hell, I'll build two – one for me and one for Zircon. He'd love having a place of his own. I'll even get him his own waiter in a white coat. Nothing but the best for us.

I keep on paddling, not bothering to try to win the race. There's more important battles ahead.

A tall, lanky guy rises out of the ocean and races through the shallow water, Bex on his heels. I let out a whoop of excitement and swallow salt water. Gagging and spitting, I yell again. Bex has almost got him.

Those matches are ours.

3

ZANE

I leap back into the waves and offer my hand to a floundering contestant.

The gangly girl coughs her thanks as I pull her on to dry land. Loose strands of raven-black hair cling to her face and make-up streaks down her brown cheeks. Pavani ... Padma?

A petite girl glides out of the water after us, her face twisted with annoyance. 'We don't need your help.'

I raise an eyebrow but don't respond.

She's silent as well, sizing me up as though deciding whether or not I'm worth her time. 'I'm Evie,' she finally says. 'And that's Paloma.' She motions to the tall girl who's re-braiding her hair with trembling hands.

'Zane.' I turn back to the water where the last person is making her way in. I hold my hand out again, but she marches past it without a second glance and joins the others.

I grin as I do the same, my feet sinking into the soft sand, the sun warm on my back.

I like her even more than I did when she elbowed me in the stomach on the boat. She's scrappy and tough – the perfect ally. What's her name? Raya? Yes, Raya.

'And the winner is . . .' Hunter eyes us for a second, building up the moment. 'Greyson McKenzie! Congratulations!'

Greyson waves the matches over his head while letting out a triumphant whoop and yelling, 'That's how you do it!'

He surveys us with a smirk, arrogance pouring off him like sweat after a game.

Damn it. He seems worse than Evie from the way he was boasting when we first arrived on the boat, but matches are matches and fire guarantees hot food and clean water. So I flash a smile when Greyson's eyes meet mine and discreetly point to my chest. 'Allies?' I mouth. He gives me a quick nod.

Good. That's one down, even if it's temporary.

'I'm sorry,' the curvy girl next to me – Becca? – whispers to Raya. I didn't want her on my team either, but for the exact opposite reason I didn't want to team up with Greyson. She seems nice enough, but nice doesn't win games. However, if she and Raya come as a pair, I'll take them both. At least for now.

'All right,' Hunter says. 'That's it for tonight. But before I leave, we've prepared one more surprise.'

I rub my hands together, adrenaline pumping through my veins. It doesn't matter if I'm not the fastest swimmer, I excel at a lot of other things.

Hunter points down the beach. 'We've decided to treat you to one last meal.'

In the distance, a long table is set up in the sand. My smile slips. Another challenge would've brought me even with Greyson and given me an edge in choosing the perfect team. But, judging from the murmurs of excitement running through the group, I'm the only one who's disappointed.

'Go ahead and eat, and we'll start filming tomorrow. And remember,' Hunter gives us all a pointed look. 'Choose your friends – and enemies – wisely. Good luck!' With an exaggerated salute, he strides to the small hover boat sitting on the beach and pushes it over the water.

As the others watch Hunter speed back towards the anchored yacht, I survey the smooth, sandy beach with the same vigilance I use when checking out a track, court or field.

You can't win if you don't understand the arena.

My gaze strays to the wall of tropical trees about fifteen metres inland, standing tall and proud like a line of cadets at the Vauras Military Academy. According to the many videos I watched after receiving my invitation – videos that included how to build sand huts, water retreats and ice houses, so I'd be prepared no matter what – we can use their branches, bark and leaves to construct an A-frame or lean-to shelter on the beach while using any leftovers as fuel.

However, the beach is severely lacking – there are only a few pieces of driftwood, some rocks and shells scattered about. But that doesn't stop the island from being a great location overall – tropical, plenty of wood, and I bet there's fruit in the . . . I check out the trees again. It's not quite a jungle, but it doesn't seem like a normal forest either. Maybe a hybrid jungle? Either way, there'll be food and clean water somewhere in its depths.

And I bet we can come up with a way to collect rain if necessary. Now that would be a good bargaining tool.

My stomach rumbles, and I glance at the table. I suppose a last meal isn't the worst surprise in the quadrant.

'Guess we should eat,' I say into the silence. Everyone surges forward and I fall into step with Raya, who barely reaches my bicep. 'I'm Zane.'

'Raya.' Her eyes rake over me, deep and penetrating, like she can see what I'm made of. I straighten my shoulders and lift my chin, meeting her gaze.

'And this is Bex Ryker,' she adds.

I stumble, staring at the girl. Her cheeks deepen into a bright, fiery red that glows against her ivory skin.

'Bexley Ryker?' I didn't catch her last name on the boat.

'Yeah.' Her gaze shifts to the table, body rigid as though she's preparing for me to out her in front of everyone, which, even if it'd help me win the game, I'm not sure I could do.

Hoping to put her at ease, I focus on Raya. 'So, what do you think of this place?'

'I think I've hit the mother lode.'

'Agreed.' I've been to a lot of beaches in the Asa and Varaus Sectors, but this one's different. It's more pristine, the air is cleaner, the colours brighter, the white sand fine and soft. And from what I've seen of pictures of the Lake Cities in the Amovi Sector and the cold, barren wastelands that make up the Outer Planets just outside the boundaries of the quadrant, there's nothing that comes close to this place. It's beautiful enough to be an island resort but, from what Hunter said, it's not. So where are we?

'Where're you from?' Raya asks.

Her tone, which suggests she's not just asking a simple question but is instead sizing me up, reminds me I'm playing a game and figuring out where we are isn't part of it. 'The Vauras Sector.'

Bex's head shoots up, eyes wide. 'Which planet?'

There are only two, and I don't think she's going to like my answer. 'Rikas.'

Bex stops. 'Wait. Are you Councilman Wilder's son?'

'Yeah.' I brace for the next line, dreading the words that always follow this revelation.

'I'm sorry for your loss. My dad said he was a great man.'

Most people thought he was a great man. 'Thanks.' I turn to Raya. 'He passed away about a year ago.' I pause, a thin thread of fear weaving its way through me, but Bex doesn't jump in and explain what happened. Instead she keeps her head down, her expression hidden from view.

'That sucks,' Raya says, but I get the distinct impression she doesn't care whether my dad is dead or alive.

Thank goodness.

I cast another look at Bex, but now she's staring into the distance, as though deep in thought. My heart skips a beat. Is she planning on using what she knows against me? Would she do that? Would I retaliate?

Pretending I'm not concerned, I motion to the long, rectangular table with plates and bowls crowding the surface, almost hiding the red-chequered tablecloth underneath. A line's already formed. 'Shall we?'

'We shall,' Raya says in a slightly mocking tone before rushing ahead of us like she hasn't eaten in days.

I take in her ragged clothes and slight frame; maybe she hasn't. Struggling to ignore the uncomfortable thought, I focus on the smoky smell of grilled meat, silently thanking our ancestors for bringing livestock from Earth when they settled the quadrant all those years ago.

Leaving Earth was an experiment, designed to test the limits of humanity. As soon as the international efforts to terraform the moon and Mars were declared the 'Achievement of the Millennium' and 'A Tribute to the Human Spirit', world leaders came up with the idea to terraform other planets across the Milky Way, starting with the Cael Quadrant.

Not everything survived the journey, or flourished in the environments of the new planets, but the cows did. Mom and I used to joke that we'd make the move back to Earth if the cows ever went extinct – we both love steak that much.

Assuming there are still cows on Earth, that is. Once people had successfully settled into life in the Cael Quadrant, they made the long journey back to Earth less and less until most of our ties vanished and we became our own people.

Or, as Mom would say, 'We are no longer Earthlings, we're aliens who love cows.'

Chuckling at the memory, I cast a hungry eye at the platters piled high with hot dogs, hamburgers and cheeseburgers. Several colourful bowls filled with small bags of crisps dot the table, along with a stack of compostable plates on each end.

Off to the side, full of bottled water, is a red cryogel cooler that'll keep the drinks cold for days. Nice.

'Why does *The Pinnacle* still do everything Old Earth-style?' Maria dangles a bag of crisps between her thumb and forefinger and wrinkles her nose. 'This is hardly the type of nutrition we need for a competition as gruelling as this one.'

'I think it's kind of quaint they use Old Earth norms as their standard,' Oscar says. 'Plus, it adds to the challenge.'

'I'd prefer healthy to quaint.' Maria drops the crisps back in the bowl.

'Here you go.' The short, scrawny guy loading plates with food gives Raya a hot dog and a bag of spiced crisps before handing me a plate with a hot dog as well. He grabs another plate as Raya snatches two more bags.

'I'll get my own.' Greyson reaches over Bex's head for a burger instead of the hot dog the kid is holding.

'Here.' Evie plucks the plate off the table and hands it to Greyson. 'Enjoy.' The disdain in her voice at having to serve someone is palpable, but her gold eyes track the matches in Greyson's other hand like a cat stalking its prey. There's no doubt Evie's clever and probably manipulative. Two things I need to remember.

'Hot dog?' The boy offers Bex a plate.

'Thanks.'

'You're welcome,' he squeaks. 'I'm Winston, by the way. I'm sixteen and I know I look young but I'm not. My dad says I'll grow, but we'll see. I don't know anyone here so I thought I'd hand out food so I could meet people. Do you know anyone?' He gazes at Bex with wide, nervous eyes. I bet he's never approached a girl, much less spoken to one.

'Only a little bit. I'm Bex. It's nice to meet you.'

'Very nice.' Raya rolls her eyes and pulls Bex away.

Bex regards her plate with distaste as she stumbles after Raya. 'I really don't like hot dogs.'

'Go ask for a hamburger instead. Or I can do it for you.' I hold out my hand to take her plate.

'No, it's OK. Thanks, though.'

I drop my hand, confused. 'All right.'

Everything I thought I knew about Bex is proving to be wrong. The newsfeeds portrayed her as boisterous and confident, a real party girl. But she seems shy and timid. She also seems a little lost, like she's not quite sure how she ended up here.

Compassion tugs at me as she settles in the sand and lifts her plate in a gesture of thanks towards Winston, who's still watching her like he has a schoolboy crush. I sit next to her. Part of me longs to make her a permanent part of my team, to help her across the finish line. But I won't risk losing the prize money. I can't do that to Mom.

Raya plops down on the other side of Bex and takes a huge, enthusiastic bite of her hot dog, shattering the melancholy that's settled over me. I watch as she devours it in seconds.

Bex glances at me and mouths, 'She's from The Moons.'

My heart sinks. Mining operations run on thirty-three of the moons that orbit the single gas giant in the Inops Sector. They're known collectively as The Moons, even though they each have their own designated number. There are rampant rumours about how poorly the miners are treated by the Gentry, who control everything out there.

Raya stuffs crisps in her mouth like she may never eat again, and guilt pierces me like an arrow hitting the bullseye – I'd never given much thought to the rumours.

'Aren't there ten contestants?' Bex is surveying the beach, a crisp halfway to her mouth.

I glance around. Evie's prattling on to Paloma about the new vintage-style Model T and coordinating goggles her mom's buying her, while Oscar, Maria and Greyson huddle in a group, whispering, their food largely ignored. Winston's sitting a metre or so outside their circle, watching in earnest.

'I –'

'Greetings, my most intrepid contestants.' We all jump as a voice booms through the sky. 'Welcome to The Island . . .'

I scan the area, but don't see any sonic broadcasters.

'. . . where you will find the justice you attempted to evade.'

An unnatural silence sweeps across the beach. I stare at the sky as though a face will appear to condemn me, unease making it impossible to move.

The voice continues, eerily monotone:

'Greyson McKenzie, you abandoned your schoolmates Ace Yarrow, Cal Wixx and Shaw Hawthorne on the Argos Peaks, where they were later found dead.

'Carson Beckett, you fell asleep at the wheel, causing an accident that killed five-year-old Addie Blair and eight-year-old Thomas Blair.

'Paloma Bhatt, you left two-year-old Rebecca Bones locked in a closet while your boyfriend was visiting you, resulting in Rebecca's death.

'Evie Valentine, you killed a homeless man, Enzo Casal, and streamed it for all to see.

'Winston Adler, you gave your father, a respected judge, false evidence to ensure Lucas Evers was sentenced to death.

'Raya Quinn, you stabbed Josephine Harris to death over a sack of food.

'Maria Johnson, you purposely gave London Weeks synthetic nuts to prevent her from competing against you, causing a fatal allergic reaction.

'Zane Wilder, you shot and killed your father, Reddin Wilder.

'Oscar Cortés, you poisoned your grandfather, Arvin Cortés, so you'd have access to your inheritance.

'Bexley Ryker, you purposely drove your solar cruising yacht into a motorboat, killing Olivia Adams and her three-year-old son, Samuel.'

A pause thick with violent promise hangs over us. I hold my breath, my stomach threatening to send its contents back up.

And then: 'Let the games begin.'

The voice cuts off, its last words lingering in the air. Nobody moves. Not even the wind blows. It's as though time itself has stopped, waiting to see what'll happen next.

'I didn't do that,' Winston's high voice breaks the stunned silence. 'I never gave my dad anything. Nothing. I wouldn't do that. Ever. And even if I'd tried, he wouldn't have let me. He –'

'I didn't kill my grandfather,' Oscar interrupts in a panicked voice. 'He raised me. I would never hurt him.'

I run a shaking hand over my head, anger reverberating through me. What kind of sick joke is this?

'I didn't kill nobody,' Raya declares before taking another bite of her crisps.

'Obviously,' Evie drawls from behind me, her voice rising above the clamour, 'this is all part of the game.'

'What do you mean?' Maria voices my question, her tone and dark eyes suspicious.

Evie sweeps her arm in an arc. 'Isn't it obvious? The producers want to create some sort of distrust between us, something that'll affect the way we see each other. It makes for good television.' She leans back on her elbows, legs stretched out in front of her, feet crossed at the ankles. 'I can tell you with absolute certainty I didn't kill a homeless man.'

'I saw the video,' Oscar says.

'What video?' Evie takes a sip of water, thin eyebrows raised like a referee waiting to hear some ridiculous argument about how pushing another player wasn't actually a foul.

'The one where the homeless man was beaten to death on The Moons. It actually happened.' Oscar frowns. 'I can't be the only one who saw it.'

He's not. I remember the video well. From the expression on Raya's face, she does too.

Evie sniffs. 'It may have actually happened. But I didn't do it.'

'Then why would they say those things?' Bex asks in a low voice. She's hugging her knees to her chest, face pale. I meet her terrified gaze.

Not everything the voice said was a lie.

'I told you why.' Evie's narrowed eyes land on each of us in turn. 'Did any of you do what that voice said?'

Everyone shakes their head, including me and, after a brief pause, Bex. Her gaze meets mine, her fear obvious. I give her a quick nod of reassurance – her secret's safe with me. She nods back, relief flooding her features. My stomach stops churning at her silent promise, and I take a long, deep breath to calm my nerves.

'Then we can ignore it and finish dinner.'

'Evie's right.' Greyson's arrogant voice breaks the tension stretching over the beach. 'They want to raise the ratings. I'd never abandon anyone on a mountain peak, especially my friends. Heck, I haven't even been there, wherever it was.'

Oscar stares at Greyson, eyebrows raised, but doesn't say anything.

Greyson takes a swig of water, seeming not to notice. 'Let's finish eating. After that, we can build some shelters. I'll share my matches with whoever constructs the best one for me to use.' He reaches for his hamburger.

'I bet I can build you a great shelter.' Winston inches closer to Greyson but still keeps his distance. 'I mean, I've read . . .'

Tuning out Winston's ingratiating babble, I turn back to my plate, but I'm too angry to eat. The producers had no right to make that recording. *The Pinnacle* is already the most watched show in the quadrant, it's not like they needed to come up with something new to up the ratings.

Raya rips open another bag of crisps and pops one into her mouth, seemingly unbothered by the whole thing. 'I bet –'

'HELP!' Maria's pointing at Greyson. 'He's choking!'

I jump to my feet, slipping in the sand as I race across the small swathe of beach separating us. Greyson's on his knees, clawing at his throat.

'Can you breathe?' I ask. Greyson shakes his head, lips turning blue, eyes wide with panic.

Manoeuvering behind him, I wrap my arms around his ribcage and thrust upwards. Nothing happens. I thrust again.

'Come on,' Bex begs. 'Spit it out.'

'Help him!' Maria cries.

'What do you think he's doing?' Raya snaps.

I try again. Greyson leans forward, toppling over my arms, heavy and limp.

'Is he breathing?' someone asks.

'No.' I yank Greyson into an upright position, my breath coming out in ragged gasps as his head flops forward. 'Breathe!' I shove my fist against Greyson's upper abdomen again and again and again.

'He's dead,' Paloma moans, covering her mouth. 'He's dead.'

'No. He's. Not.' I punctuate each word with an upward thrust.

Someone grabs my arm. 'Stop.'

I jerk free. Rolling Greyson over, I press my fingers against his neck, searching for a pulse, dread overcoming me. He can't be dead – not like this. I push harder against his skin even though his eyes stare unseeing at the sky and small pools of foam dot the corners of his mouth. The box of matches is still clenched in his fist.

The colour drains from Oscar's face. 'He's . . . he's gone?'

'Yeah.' I swallow hard, unable to tear my eyes away from Greyson's still form. Not willing to believe he died. That I failed to save him.

Paloma tilts her head towards the sky. 'Do you think . . .'

'No. No way.' Oscar backs away from Greyson, every word infused with panic. 'There's no way that voice had anything to do with this.'

Paloma doesn't move. 'But it said we're here to be served justice, like it's going to make us pay for our crimes.'

'So you did kill that kid?' Raya asks.

Paloma rubs her arms, colour draining from her face, eyes darting to Evie. 'No, of course not.'

I almost believe her.

Raya rounds on Maria. 'What happened to Greyson?'

'I don't know.' Maria shrinks under Raya's glare. 'He was eating his hamburger and he choked. You saw the rest.'

'And you?' Raya's liquid black eyes bore into Oscar.

'Greyson choked and that guy did the Heimlich manoeuvre.' Oscar points at me.

Raya spins so we're facing each other. 'Were you really trying to help?'

I stare at her in shock, heart hammering at her accusation. 'Of course I was.'

'Raya,' Bex says, as though soothing a child. 'It was an accident.'

Raya surveys us. 'Where's that red-headed kid? What's-his-name?'

'Carson?' Oscar says.

'Yeah, him! I haven't seen him since the boat. Maybe it was him.'

I scan the group, but he's not there. My stomach clenches as I double-check, counting each person.

Nine.

Bex was right. It's supposed to be ten.

Remorse pricks at me like a thousand darts. I didn't notice Carson was missing because I'd dismissed him the moment I saw him. Nothing about him inspired confidence.

I glance at Raya, a question hovering on my lips. I could've sworn . . . I rub the back of my neck. I'm not one hundred per cent sure what I saw. 'Has anyone else seen Carson?' I ask instead.

'Not since the boat when he told me he didn't want to be on the show,' Oscar says.

'What?' Raya says in disbelief. 'There's no way he dropped out. No one's that stupid.'

'He said he couldn't swim. He was going to ask Hunter if he could go home.' Oscar backs away from Raya, as though he expects her to pounce on him for what he said. I don't blame him. I bet she could best any of us in a fight.

'Idiot,' Raya mutters.

'Look,' I say, with as much confidence as I can muster. 'I'm sure Greyson's death was an accident and that Carson had nothing to do with it. He's probably back on the boat with Hunter as we speak.'

Raya eyes me like I'm stupid. 'Hell of an accident.'

'Did anyone else have a hamburger?' Bex asks in a quiet, quavering voice. There's a chorus of noes as we shake our heads. 'What about the medics? Are their supplies here? Or maybe we could signal Hunter.'

'I'll look!' Winston starts searching the beach.

'It's not like you can bring someone back from the dead,' Raya calls after him, but no one responds.

'I can't see the yacht,' I say. 'Maybe Hunter already left in preparation for the storm.'

Winston rejoins the group. 'I didn't see any medical supplies.'

Paloma shudders. 'Do you think it was done on purpose?'

An exasperated sigh escapes my lips. 'How did someone make him choke?' I ask. 'Tell me that.'

'Maybe they . . .' Bex's voice trails off, her eyes locked on Greyson's body. She shakes her head slowly. 'I don't know.'

'The probability of making someone choke on food is pretty much zero,' Winston says. 'Unless someone hit him on the back or jarred him, then it has to be –'

'Did any of you do that?' Raya demands. 'Knock him around in some way?'

'No. We didn't.' Evie glares at Raya. 'For the millionth time, it was an accident.'

'How would you know? You weren't even sitting next to him,' Raya says.

'I was,' Oscar says. 'We were talking about ...' He hesitates, eyes darting towards Maria. 'Plans,' he finishes, as though realizing it doesn't matter any more. 'For the game. Greyson took a bite of his hamburger and started choking.' Oscar raises his hand half-heartedly in the air and drops it back to his side as though that explains everything.

'That's when I called for help,' Maria says. 'You know the rest.'

I meet Raya's skeptical gaze. 'It all sounds rather straightforward to me,' I say. But doubt gnaws at me. That voice ... and the timing ...

'I'm not buying it,' Raya says. 'It don't make sense.'

'So you think someone choked him on purpose?' Evie drawls. 'You're dumber than you look.'

'But still not as dumb as you,' Raya retorts. 'He could've been poisoned.'

'Poisoned?' Paloma covers her mouth, eyes wide with horror. 'What if we were all poisoned?'

Raya rolls her eyes. 'Then we'd all be dead.'

'But we aren't.' Evie shoots Raya a withering glare. 'Because it was an accident.'

'Or maybe it was an allergic reaction?' Paloma sounds almost hopeful.

'I've never seen someone foam at the mouth when they had a reaction.' Maria crosses her arms in a way that would imply confidence if it wasn't for the way she keeps shifting her stance.

Evie plants her hands on her hips. 'You would know.'

'This isn't getting us anywhere,' I interject, tired of the back and forth.

'What do you think we should we do?' Bex twists her hands together so violently I'm sure she's going to rub the skin right off.

'We definitely shouldn't eat any more hamburgers,' Winston says. 'I mean, we don't know if that was the only one that was poisoned, assuming it was poisoned, but it's better to not take any chances.'

'Obviously.' Raya's voice is thick with sarcasm.

'We'll avoid the burgers and wait until Hunter and the crew get here tomorrow,' I say. 'In the meantime, we should move the body.'

'Move him?' Evie wrinkles her nose. 'Why?'

I throw my arms up in the air. 'Because it's the right thing to do.'

'Besides,' Winston says, 'his body will start to decompose and smell and . . .' His voice trails off as his gaze drifts towards Greyson. 'Maybe we should put him under the trees so he's out of the sun, or bury him . . . ?'

'I don't know if we should touch him.' Paloma's dark eyes dart between the sky and Greyson. 'What if whatever happened to him is contagious?'

Evie snorts. "'Cause choking is contagious.'

Paloma glares at Evie. 'Just –'

'Stop,' I snap. 'There's no point arguing.'

Paloma stumbles as though I've slapped her. As though I'm the reason Greyson's lying dead on the beach. But I tried to save him – they all saw me try.

I swallow hard. Why didn't it work? I take rescue classes every year so I can lifeguard at the pool. I should've been able to save him.

Weariness washes over me. 'I'm sorry. I didn't mean to snap.' We all huddle there, shaken and scared, except Raya and Evie – they're too busy glaring at each other to notice anything else.

'Come on,' I say. 'Let's move the body.'

4

BEX

Zane shifts closer to Greyson. 'Who wants to help?'

I link my fingers together and stare at the sand.

I should say something, do something, but my body refuses to cooperate as fear and uncertainty ripple through me. I close my eyes, but flashes of that sunny day at the lake and the green dinosaur t-shirt force them open again.

No one else has moved either.

Evie crosses her arms and wrinkles her small, pert nose. 'I'm not touching that thing.'

'Me either.' Paloma backs further away from Greyson.

'It's not a "thing", it's a person.' Zane's scorn is obvious, but he manages to keep his tone neutral as he asks Oscar for help.

Oscar frowns and shakes his head.

'I'll help.' Winston's whole body shakes under his over-sized, short-sleeved red plaid button-down shirt and khaki cargo shorts. He's so small I doubt he can lift Greyson, who's at least double his size.

Or was.

I study my feet, an unexpected tear tracing a path down my cheek. I swipe it away.

'Thanks,' Zane says. 'I'll grab his shoulders.'

'I'm in.' Raya positions herself at Greyson's feet. 'I'll take a leg.'

'I'll take the other one.' Winston's voice cracks like he's on the cusp of puberty.

'On three,' Zane says.

'Wait.' My mouth is dry, and it takes me a moment to ask, 'Where are you going to put him?'

'Over there, under the trees.' Zane points to a spot about ten metres away from the food. 'And we can use the tablecloth to cover him.' He looks at Evie and Paloma. 'Would you please grab some rocks to weigh the tablecloth down?'

'Not my problem,' Evie says.

Paloma sidles closer to her, like a mouse seeking cover behind a pebble. 'Or mine.'

Fighting the urge to fade into the background, I take a tentative step forward. 'I'll do it.' My voice quivers and my gaze keeps darting to Greyson without my permission. His sandy skin has a strange, pale pink hue to it that's unsettling.

What if he was poisoned?

But if he was . . . I swallow hard, unable to dislodge the lump of dread that's settled in my throat. I had wanted a hamburger. What if I'd asked for that instead? What if –

'I'll help.' Maria interrupts my thoughts. She sounds confident, but her fingers shake as she smooths back her short hair. She gives me a defiant glare when she catches me staring, as though daring me to say something, and strides off. 'Let's go.'

I scurry after her, struggling to tamp down my fear. What if she's the murderer? What if it's one of the other contestants? Except that's stupid. Greyson choked, nothing more.

'I'll grab the tablecloth,' Oscar says.

I glance over my shoulder – Oscar's headed towards the table, uncertainty marring his chiselled features as he stares at a platter of hamburgers.

A few metres away, Winston, Raya and Zane grapple with Greyson's body – Winston keeps dropping a leg and apologizing in long, breathless sentences – while Evie and Paloma watch and whisper to each other. They don't seem to care that a person died. Perhaps because they're – no, stop thinking about it. It was an accident. It doesn't matter what the voice . . . that voice . . .

Surely it knows what I did was an accident? Even the Justice Seekers said I was innocent.

A cauldron of fear, guilt and anger bubbles inside me; it takes everything I've got to keep walking.

Maria scans the beach for stones, the late afternoon sun casting her in shadow. 'It's weird to think Greyson was alive less than thirty minutes ago.'

'Yeah.' The waves crawl up the sand and back again, high tide changing to low, the only sign of life on this stretch of beach. The emptiness is disconcerting – almost like the island's hiding something.

I glance at the tall, lush trees forming a barrier along the beach, their leaves rustling in the breeze.

Or hiding someone.

I take a deep breath to calm myself, but the air carries the scent of saltwater and grilled meat, making my stomach twist and turn. I rub my arms, shivering even though it's warm – something isn't right. The timing of that voice was too perfect.

Was Greyson guilty? Or was his crime only half-true, like with Zane and me? And what about the others? Murder carries the death penalty on Rikas. And justice is swift. Often too swift. But is it like that elsewhere?

I study Maria as we continue down the beach. Her posture is self-assured, her strides long and confident, almost like she knows she's not in danger. Or maybe it's because the further we get from Greyson's body, the more surreal it all seems, like some nightmare. She doesn't even look like a murderer.

Of course, when I think of a murderer, I picture ugly, hunched men with pockmarked faces and filthy clothes, not normal, everyday kind of girls. Doubt digs its claws into me, clinging to my mind like a drowning man clings to a raft.

Would Maria really give some girl nuts to win a competition?

She scoops up a rock. 'I wonder how long they'll delay the game. It'd better not be more than a day or two.'

I don't respond. I'd rather not think about it.

'Don't you want to play?' She scrutinizes me with her big, brown eyes, her tone incredulous.

I grab a stick half-buried in the sand and snap it into little pieces. Of course I want to play. I want to play, I want to win, and I want to break free from my father and escape the stares and whispers that follow me wherever I go.

I squeeze the small, wooden pieces, their sharp edges cutting into my skin. I was going to win this game, take the money and vanish from society. But then Greyson died and ruined everything.

Fury, quick and hot, floods through me, followed by shame. An unexpected sob rises in my throat and I struggle to push it away.

'Well,' Maria says, 'don't you?'

'No.' I toss the remains of the stick into the ocean. 'I don't. But it doesn't matter either way, they're going to cancel it.'

'Why?'

'Because a boy died,' I snap. 'And then there's that voice,' I add with more composure.

Maria waves her hand as though dismissing the idea. 'I agree with Evie – the voice has to be part of the game. Unless you actually killed those people?'

'N-no. It was just . . . unnerving.'

Unnerving how they knew. Then again, it makes sense the producers would know about the accident. It was on every newsfeed, after all. Perhaps they decided to do something new with the show? Or maybe they always looked for dirt on everyone to heighten the tension and distrust between the contestants, like Evie said. But it's not like they could make someone choke on their food.

A chill creeps down my spine.

Could they?

'They'll cancel the game,' I say again, having to fill the silence that's settled over us. 'Out of respect for Greyson and his family.'

'Oh puh-lease. There's no way they're going to cancel it – *The Pinnacle*'s too popular. Besides, they haven't even begun filming, so it's not like they even have to edit him out.'

'They still might cancel . . .' And they should. I know they should, even if I'm desperate for them to continue.

'You keep telling yourself that.' Maria strides away without another word.

I grab a rock and trudge back the way we came, longing to be far away from this place. It's probably for the best if *The Pinnacle* is cancelled. There's no doubt I'd make a fool of myself and prove once and for all, in front of the entire quadrant, that Dad's right about me.

His words from our last fight still echo in my ears.

'You're an embarrassment to this family and the Ryker name!' he yells, gripping the edge of his graphene desk, face red with rage. 'When will you grow up?'

Recoiling at the vitriol in his words, I stammer an apology.

But how do you apologize for killing someone? How do you ever make that OK?

'And you're lucky the Brentleys didn't call off the engagement to their son. We need that alliance.'

'But I don't want to marry –'

'If you want your inheritance you'll marry that boy. And since the family business is going to your brother –'

His words hit me with the force of a cannon, shattering me into a million pieces as he takes the one thing I have left. The family business always passes to the eldest child. It is the law. For Dad to petition to have that annulled . . . everyone would know exactly what he thinks of me.

And they'd have to agree.

I stare at the floor, blinking fast. But the tears still fall.

'– you'll need someone who can take care of you,' he finishes. 'Because I'm done.'

'Arthur.' Mom slips into the study. 'That's enough.'

Taking my hand, she guides me out of his office and into my bedroom before pulling me into her arms. The comforting scent of her citrus-and-ginger perfume curls around me while I sob into her shoulder, tears doing nothing to wash away the pain, the grief, the embarrassment that is my life.

When I finally pull back, she gazes at me with such love I have to look away.

I don't deserve it.

She gently lifts my face, and I raise my eyes to meet hers. 'You are so much more than your father says you are. You're smart, kind, giving, compassionate and beautiful – inside and out.'

She wipes my tears with her thumbs. 'It was an accident, Bexley. A horrible accident, which doesn't change the fact that I'm lucky to have you as a daughter.'

I scuff my toe in the sand. Mom isn't lucky to have me as a daughter. Whenever I try to make her proud, I end up mortifying her instead.

The wind whips my hair across my face, and I swipe it and the memories away. If Maria's right then I still have to play the game. And there's no way I'm going to win on my own, that much is obvious.

I have Raya, but that's not enough. We need at least one more person. Two would be better. As I stop near the area where Greyson was announced the winner, my stomach sinks. I dread the thought of convincing people to be on my team, but there's no other choice.

I watch Zane as he pulls the tablecloth over Greyson with great care, as though they're good friends.

Were good friends.

Swallowing hard, I jog over before I can talk myself out of speaking to him. 'Need some help?'

'Only those rocks.'

'Here.' I give him the one I'm still gripping.

Zane sits back on his heels, amusement playing across his features. 'I'm afraid I'll need more than one.'

Heat creeps up my face. 'Sorry. I'll find more.'

'No need.' Maria joins us and lets go of her mint-green tank top, the rocks cradled there tumbling to the ground like a stone waterfall.

Dimples appear in Zane's cheeks. 'Thanks.'

Turning my head so he can't see my embarrassment, I start placing rocks on the red-chequered tablecloth. At this rate, it's guaranteed I'll be the first one out, even with Raya's help, unless I figure something out.

Maria's watching Zane's every move as though she's plotting the best way to approach him as well. I can't let her have him. He's strong, good in a crisis and a natural leader. I only need to convince him I'm valuable. Or useful. Or at least likable. Something.

I pull the tablecloth tight and set a rock on it, disgusted with myself. I can't believe I'm strategizing over a dead body.

'I'm sorry,' I whisper to Greyson, before turning back to Zane and opening my mouth to say something impressive. Nothing comes out.

The corners of his mouth tilt up. 'Yes?'

I bite my lip. Apparently humiliating myself is going to be my main accomplishment the short time I'm here. 'Nothing.'

I place another rock, mind racing. I can't afford to let

things end here. I gather what little courage I have and force myself to make eye contact with Zane again. 'I mean, not nothing. We should figure out where to sleep. The sun's going to set soon, and I read once that if you want to stay warm, you should build a bed first and then something for over your head.'

Maria snorts. 'It's supposed to rain – shelter's probably more important than a bed.'

'There's no clouds,' Raya says from behind me.

'Doesn't mean there won't be,' Maria retorts.

Raya crosses her arms. 'Doesn't mean there will.'

I flash her a grateful smile.

'I think we read the same book,' Zane says to me. 'Raya, want to grab some palm fronds with Bex? I can finish up here.'

'Sure.' Raya grabs my arm and pulls me away. 'Whatcha doing?' she practically hisses when we're out of earshot.

'Getting Zane on our side. He's the strongest guy here, we could use him.'

Raya grins. 'I didn't think you had it in you.'

My face flushes for the millionth time today. 'That's not what I meant. Besides, it may all be for nothing – I doubt the game's going to continue.'

'It will.' Winston falls into step with us.

'How do you know?' Raya picks up her pace, and Winston jogs to keep up.

'My brother used to be in the business – only a production assistant, nothing big or exciting. It's not like he was a director or an executive producer or –'

'You got a point?' Raya asks.

The tips of Winston's ears turn pink. 'Sorry. Anyway, it takes an act of the universe to cancel a show. Especially when it's as popular as this one. There's not enough time to find a new cast before the season premieres. They'll postpone it a day or two, probably find replacements for Greyson and Carson, and then start filming.'

Raya casts me a sidelong glance, and I can see her planning and scheming, but all she says is, 'Guess I got plenty of time to work on my tan.'

'You'll burn,' Winston says. 'You're like me, super pale. I should've gone to the doctor for a NoBurn treatment before I came here, but I bet Hunter has some regular sun protection we can use. Some of us are really pale. Not everyone, but . . .'

Raya drags me away, calling over her shoulder, 'We're going to search for palm leaves.'

'Fronds,' I say.

'What?'

'They're palm fronds, not leaves.'

'Whatevs. As long as we're ditching the kid.'

I peek at Winston, who's standing alone on the beach like a little boy who's lost his parents, the sunlight making his dark brown hair flicker with shades of red.

He doesn't fit in here.

My heart gives a sympathetic lurch. 'He seems OK. Some of the challenges involve logic, and he seems really smart, and . . .' I close my eyes and blurt out the next sentence, hoping Raya doesn't laugh at me. 'We should have him on our team.'

'Are you kidding me? There's no chance in hell I'm doing anything with that boy. Besides, you're smart.'

'He's smarter. Think about it. Zane's super strong, you know how to fight, and I'm a good swimmer. Winston's intelligence is the perfect finishing touch. We'd make a great team. Please.' I hold back a groan – I sound like I'm begging. Which I kind of am.

Raya eyes Winston as he ambles towards Oscar. 'If we take Winston, then I guess we don't need you. We've already done the swimming part.'

My mouth drops open, and I struggle to find the words to defend myself. Why did I say anything? I know better . . .

Raya slaps me on the shoulder. 'I'm only joking.'

'Really?'

She snorts. 'Yeah, really.'

I take a deep breath, willing myself to believe that Raya joking with me is a good sign and not a bad omen. 'Then you want him?'

Raya shrugs. 'Might as well.' I can't help but smile as she yells, 'Hey, kid!'

Winston points at his chest.

'Yeah! You. Come here.'

Winston runs over, skinny arms pumping in an awkward rhythm at his sides. 'Yes?'

'Wanna be teammates?' Raya asks.

Winston starts to nod, but stops, giving her a dubious stare. 'Why?'

'Are you smart?'

'Yeah.'

'Are you lying?'

'No. I've been a member of Scitus since I was five.'

Raya crosses her arms. 'So?'

'It's an interplanetary organization for exceptionally bright students.' I quote the brochure I've read a thousand times with the vain hope I might be offered a slot. 'My brother's a member.'

Raya studies Winston with a new appreciation. 'So how about it? You wanna be the brains of this operation?'

Winston bounces from foot to foot as though he's trying to contain his excitement. I bet he was always picked last. 'Yes! Absolutely!'

'Great,' Raya says. 'Go find some palm leaves to make beds.'

'Fronds,' Winston replies, and I can't help but smile as he proves me right.

'Whatevs, smart boy. Can you do it without talking?'

'Yup. You'd be surprised by how quiet I can be. Like when I'm reading a book, or gardening – I love to garden, it's one of –'

'You're still talking,' Raya says.

Winston blushes and gives her a salute before practically skipping towards the forest.

'What are we going to do?' I ask.

'We're gonna make sure Evie doesn't steal Zane.' She jerks her thumb over her shoulder. A girl stands close to Zane, staring up at him in admiration and chatting animatedly.

Raya scoops up a handful of fronds and mutters, 'Too bad she's not the one that choked.'

5

RAYA

I go straight for Zane and Evie, anger speeding me along like an out-of-control mine cart. When I saw her on the boat, I'd decided to pretend we'd never met in case it messed up the game somehow, but after that recording, I'm guessing the producers already know all about us.

At least mostly, 'cause it sounds like neither of us knew she killed two miners, not just one.

I clench my fists. The man in the video had a name: Enzo Casal. And a job. But I guess the producers couldn't be bothered with finding those things out. People with power rarely bother with the truth.

I glare at Evie. When the timing's right I'm going to tell everyone what she did and then take care of her.

I can't wait.

'Here are the lea– fronds.' I grip them tight so I don't slap Evie across the face with them. 'We should figure out where to sleep.'

'Then go figure it out – we're busy,' Evie says.

'Happy to. How'd you like to sleep next to the dead, Evie?'

Bex grabs my arm. 'We wanted to be respectful of Greyson, as well as everyone here, and we'd appreciate your thoughts on where we should sleep.'

Zane scans the area, and I do the same. If it weren't for the dead body, this place could've been taken straight out of a story, it's that perfect.

'Over there,' Zane points. 'Between where we landed and the table. Everyone should be OK with that.'

I roll my eyes. Zane speaks with the same kind of confidence Bex had at the transporter place, the kind that says he knows everyone'll do what he tells them to. Except his doesn't seem to come and go like hers.

Bex nods. 'Thanks. We'll start setting up.'

I trudge after Bex, pissed at Evie for being Evie, and at Zane for thinking he's in charge, and at Bex for doing everything she's told. And pissed at myself for following along because I need to win.

But me being mad is not the way to come in first. What was it Old George always said when I was upset? I picture him smiling that damn toothless smile of his and motioning me over, his face and clothes covered in dirt that never washed off.

His raspy voice rings in my memory. 'You have to learn to accept things the way they are, little Ray. Because being mad won't change a thing. Here, have a drink.' And he'd hand me a bottle full of fizzy red punch like that'd make everything better.

Because it did – until he died. And I grew up.

Whatever. I need to focus on winning. Taking a deep breath, I imagine me and Zircon in our new houses with super comfortable chairs and people in fancy outfits serving us fizzy red drinks.

That's how Zircon lived before me and him met. He's never complained about his new life with me, but I bet he'd love having a roof over his head again and steak every day.

Does paid-for steak taste better than stolen steak?

I wrinkle my nose. Probably not.

'. . . I'd rather put Evie next to Greyson, too, but didn't think we should say so.' Bex picks at her nail polish instead of looking at me. 'Do you think that was the right choice?'

I pretend I was listening. 'Yup. Zane even watched you walk away – I bet the guy likes you.'

'He doesn't. And even if he did, it wouldn't matter. He's promised to someone else.' She stops. 'This seems like a good place to set up.'

She drops her leaves, and I fling mine on top of hers. 'What the hell does that mean? How can you be promised to someone?'

'On Rikas, marriages are arranged. And permanent.' She frowns. 'Honestly, I've never thought much about it – no one does, really, unless something untoward happens. Matrimony's about making the right alliances, not love. Well, for us anyway. It's different for the common people.'

Rage surges through my veins – she's got to be kidding me. 'Common people?'

Bex slaps her hand over her mouth. 'Sorry. Wow, that was rude.' She drops to her knees and starts shuffling leaves around, all nervous and shit. 'I mean the civil workers, shopkeepers and servants.'

'Oh.' I bite back the sarcastic retort that's begging to come out. Between the dead kid, the game and a maybe killer, this isn't the time to lose alliances. I look back at Evie, who's still chatting up Zane.

I know it was her who killed Greyson. She's killed before, and she'd do it again because her mom went and taught her she can take what she wants by any means necessary.

'Raya?' Bex's peering at me. 'I really am sorry.'

I jerk my attention away from Evie. 'What? Oh, it don't matter.'

But it does. There's nothing I hate more than people thinking they're better than me. 'What do we do with the leaves?'

'I . . . have no idea.' She stops messing with them and stands, staring at the leaves as if she's never seen one before. 'Perhaps dig in the sand a little and lay the fronds out?'

'Is that what the book said?' Frustration leaks through my words, and I swallow hard. It's taking everything I've got not to lose it on her.

'I believe so, but I don't remember much. To be honest, I was hoping if I impressed Zane he might join our alliance.' She nudges a leaf with her foot. 'It was a stupid idea. You can't impress someone if you don't know what you're doing.'

Well, look at that, Rich Girl has a plan – even if it isn't much of one.

'Zane said you were making beds – need some help?' Oscar trots towards us like some prized racehorse, way too aware of his own importance. My skin crawls the closer he gets. There's something off about him.

68

Bex glances at the sun, which is starting to set and sending shades of rose quartz and fire opals flying across the sky. 'That'd be great, thanks.'

Oscar drops to his knees. 'I've made a ton of these. I used to spend my summers backpacking through the mountains of Mahast with my abuelo.'

Who you apparently killed for a few dollars. But who am I to judge – I killed a woman over a bag of food. I hadn't planned on doing it, but I guess the voice doesn't care about that either.

'I got more fronds,' Winston says from behind us. 'They can also be used to make a thatched roof or woven into baskets if someone knows how. It's something I've always wanted to learn but haven't yet. It may require a certain type of palm frond, though . . .' Winston studies the pile of leaves in his arms.

'Anyway, I did go into the trees to see if there were different species of palm, but it was getting dark, so I couldn't tell. But I don't think the forest is too deep, and the island seems small. I tried to only get the ones that were whole and green, but there might be a few that are broken in there. I guess we don't have to use them . . .'

I put my hands on my hips. 'Are you going to keep talking or help?'

'Oh, sorry. Help, of course. But I'm not the outdoorsy type. My parents were more into books and school and studying – anything that expanded one's knowledge, really. They wanted me to go to university, and not just any university but –' his eyes dart to Bex – 'Nessing College.'

'That's a really good school.' Bex doesn't look him in the eye.

Bet it's only for rich folks.

'Yeah,' Winston says. 'But it's expensive, which is why my parents were thrilled about me competing on *The Pinnacle*, especially with part of the prize being a scholarship.'

I almost laugh – that boy's not winning any games that don't involve talking.

'I hope you get in.' Bex points at the leaves. 'I can show you what we're doing with the fronds if you like.' Winston rushes to her side like a starving dog being offered a bone. He certainly has a thing for her. At least she's good for something.

'I think he always behaves that way,' Oscar says to me in a low voice as Bex and Winston shift leaves around.

'You know him?' I keep my face down so he can't see my surprise.

'Not exactly. I met him on the boat. We were the first to arrive and he kind of latched on to me. I couldn't shake him.'

I eye Bex and Winston – neither seem real sure of what they're doing. 'Makes sense he's guilty of giving his dad information – I don't think he has it in him to do something worse, except maybe talk someone to death.'

Shock crosses Oscar's face, but then he laughs fit to burst.

'Sorry,' he finally sputters. 'I needed that. With Carson ditching and then Greyson ...' His voice trails off like he doesn't know what to think about Greyson dying.

'Do you think the voice was telling the truth?' I make it sound as if I don't care what he thinks.

'No, of course not. It's all a bunch of crap – I'd never do anything to hurt my abuelo. I imagine Evie was right – it's part of the game.' He sits back on his heels, looking at the leafy bed instead of at me. 'That should do it for tonight.'

I glance at the sky. The sun's almost gone and dark's creeping over the island like a thief. Like me.

'Should we build a lean-to or some kind of overhead shelter?' Bex asks.

Winston's head jerks up, mouth already open to talk. Thank goodness Oscar beats him to it.

'I doubt there's enough time – it's practically dark. And without a knife or sharp blade, it'll be more difficult.'

My hand strays to my pocket – I'm real good with knives. I've made a ton of shelters out of nothing more than a few boxes and scraps of junk, but I don't say anything – they don't need to know I got a knife. Besides, it's not like I haven't spent plenty of nights under the stars before now.

'Maybe a fire?' Bex's eyes dart to me like she needs me to say OK. That girl cares way too much about what others think.

'Fire sounds good,' I say.

'Greyson had matches.' Winston's also eyeing the setting sun. 'Remember? He won them right before he . . . before he . . . anyway, he had the matches. Not that I want to get them, or think it's proper to steal from the dead, or anything like that.'

'I'll grab them,' I say. 'It's not like he's going to use them.'

Bex shoots me a warning look.

'I don't mean that disrespectively.' I add, turning so no one can see me roll my eyes. For goodness' sake, you'd think they actually knew the kid. But hey, if they want to pretend to be upset, I can pretend too.

Pulling off my shoes, I drag my feet through the super soft sand as I go over to Greyson. When I win, I'm going to buy this island. And then I'm going to bring Zircon here and teach him to swim and play fetch and all sorts of things. He's going to love this place.

But first, matches. I eye the lump under the blanket. I think Zane folded Greyson's hands across his chest, but I wasn't paying attention. I creep closer. Dead bodies are the worst. At least this one's wrapped neatly away like some sick package, instead of being left in the open, covered in blood. That stuff takes forever to get off.

'What are you doing?'

I spin around. Maria, Evie and Paloma stand in a half circle around me.

'Wishing it was you under there.'

Maria glares at me. 'You better watch what you say.'

I cross my arms and raise an eyebrow. 'You're choosing the wrong side, Maria. Join my team and I'll make sure you're in the final two.'

Maria sneers. 'Like that'd ever happen. There's no way you'd let me win.'

'Well, you should know Evie would choose Paloma over you. They're close. *Reeeeal* close. You know what I mean? So, who do you wanna lose to? Me? Or them?'

Maria's eyes flicker to Evie.

I laugh. 'You've got to be kidding me! Let me guess – Evie told you she'd betray Paloma for you, and you actually believed her? Never mind, I don't need that kind of stupid on my team.'

I'm lying like some old high-grader who swears the gold he found is his own. I don't know nothing about Evie and Paloma. But Maria doesn't either. The way she's shifting her feet back and forth tells me that much.

'Now, if you'll excuse me.' I crouch next to the tablecloth and move a couple of rocks. Lifting the edge, I catch a glimpse of Greyson's arm. At least he's not stinking yet.

'Looking for these?' Evie holds up the matches.

I fix her with my meanest glare. 'Robbing dead bodies, now? I thought that was beneath you. Or did you have one of your minions do your dirty work?'

Evie's always thought she was better than everyone else, especially us miners, because her mom owns several mines and we work them.

A smirk settles across Evie's face. 'What does it matter? We'll be warm, along with Zane and Oscar, and you and your two weaklings can huddle together in the dark.' She closes the gap between us, like she thinks she can intimidate me or something. 'Don't ever forget – I'm smarter than you.'

'You keep telling yourself that.' I pat her thin cheek before walking away.

Bex runs up to me as I head back towards the camp. 'What happened?'

I wait until we're closer to where Zane's standing to answer, speaking a bit louder than I need to. 'I went to fix the tablecloth and found Evie stealing the matches. I told her not to, but she wouldn't listen.' I glance at Zane. He's watching Evie, face twisted in disgust.

Good.

Bex opens her mouth, but I nudge her arm and tilt my head towards Zane.

Bex's eyes widen. 'We should tell the others,' she says all loud and slow. I have to keep myself from groaning. That girl couldn't be more obvious if she tried.

'Come on.' I drag her down the beach before she can say anything else.

Me and Bex are telling Oscar and Winston what happened when Evie calls out, 'Who wants to help me light a fire?'

Oscar's cassiterite eyes shift to where they're standing. 'No offence, but I don't care who got the matches.' He strides through the dark, calling out, 'I know how to do it. I'll help.'

'Well, I'm not going anywhere near that girl,' I say. 'She'll kill us all in our sleep.'

'Neither am I,' says Bex. 'Winston?'

'Me either. I can be cold for a night with my fellow explorers.'

You've got to be kidding me. I bet he talks in his sleep.

'Mind a little company?' Zane emerges from the shadows.

'No,' Bex says. 'But we don't have a fire.'

Zane shrugs. 'It's not too cold, and I'm sure we can do something to keep warm. Although there aren't many options, are there?'

'Nope,' I say. Even The Moons had heated places with screens and shows you could watch until closing time. Of course, fighting was involved if you wanted to choose the channel, but I'm a good fighter.

'We could watch the stars come out, if you want? I believe that one might be a planet.' Bex points near the horizon. 'See, it's red.'

I swallow a groan as Winston gets another case of word diarrhoea. 'Oh! I wonder which planet that is. I don't recognize any of the constellations, at least not yet, but if we look long enough I bet I can figure out where we are . . .'

I study the bright dots as Winston rambles on – I've never seen so many stars in one place. It's kind of amazing.

'. . . I wish I'd brought a telescope.' I scowl as Winston's squeaky voice ruins the view. 'I have three at home. One for close viewing, one for the planets, and one that can see things in different parts of the quadrant. In fact, I know most of the constellations in the quadrant. Well, only in the Asa and Vaurus sectors, not Inops or Amovi, but if we're . . .'

'Does he ever shut up?' Zane whispers as Winston goes on and on, gaze fixed on Bex like he's not sure how he got so lucky, and Bex listens like she's actually interested.

'Nope.'

'But he's smart?'

I shrug. 'School-smart.' There's no way he'd survive on the streets.

'Could be useful.' Zane peers at me out of the corner of his eye. 'What are your thoughts?'

'About Winston?'

'About you, me, Bex and Winston being a team.'

I narrow my eyes. 'What about Oscar and the rest?'

'Well, Evie seems like a real piece of work and the other two do whatever she says, so they're not what you'd call good allies. And I don't trust Oscar. He seems too . . .' Zane stares at the sky as though the answer's written for him somewhere up there. 'Charming.'

I snort. 'He's not charming.'

'Well, he's something. And I don't like it. So, teammates?' He holds out his hand all business-like.

'Sure,' I say, as if I hadn't planned it all along. 'Why the hell not?'

DAY TWO

6

BEX

A light drizzle wakes me the next morning, covering the island in a cool mist like the spring rain on Rikas – cold and grey but with the promise of new life hidden between the drops. I push wet strands of hair off my face and pull my knees to my chest – I love this.

'Rain,' Raya grumbles next to me. 'Perfect.'

I'm about to tell her it's not too bad, but my gaze drifts to the ocean where waves rise and fall and dark, towering clouds climb high over the water, lightning flickering in their depths.

On the beach, Maria sits alone, poking at the dead fire with a stick. There's no sign of the others.

'The film crew isn't going to make it.' Zane's studying the sky over the ocean as well. 'At least not until this afternoon. Maybe later.'

Maybe not until tomorrow. I rub my arms, glancing at the chequered tablecloth rippling in the wind. It seems wrong to leave Greyson's body lying there all day.

Raya swipes the rain off her face and glares at the sky before jumping to her feet. 'Guess we better find some food.'

'Do you think there's something edible in the forest?' Winston's voice is thick with sleep. 'I haven't figured out which system we're in yet, although I'll try charting the stars again tonight – see if there's a constellation I recognize.'

He sits and gazes at the sky, as though he can see the stars in the daytime. 'From there, I can figure out what we can and can't eat, since each system was terraformed a little differently. I mean, some things are the same, of course, but others are pretty specific to each planet, their climate and the indigenous plant life, and without knowing where we are . . .'

'There's some food left over from dinner,' Zane says. 'The crisps and water will be fine, and food might be a challenge reward, so hopefully we don't have to worry about foraging in the trees. At least not yet.'

Hopefully not ever.

Raya squints at the table. 'I think somebody already found breakfast.' She sprints off.

'No you don't!' Maria hurtles towards the table.

'Oh no.' Zane races after them.

I follow, my shoes sinking in the wet sand, slowing me down.

Raya lunges at a white bowl full of big, black, juicy berries, but Maria snags it first. 'They're mine!'

Raya dives for Maria. 'No they're not!'

Zane grabs Raya's arm. 'Maria found the berries so it's only fair –'

'I don't care who found them.' Raya twists out of his grip and charges Maria. 'Give them to me!'

'No!'

Raya snatches a large handful out of the bowl. 'Guess they're mine now.'

Maria knocks the berries out of Raya's grip with a snarl. Thunder booms and the rain intensifies.

'We should find cover,' I say, hoping to stop the fight. But either everyone ignores me or can't hear me over the growing storm.

'If I'm not eating them, you aren't either.' Raya stomps on the berries. They squish easily, their thick, purplish juice seeping out, mingling with the rain and darkening the sand.

My stomach growls, and my mouth waters. I haven't had anything to eat except a handful of crisps from last night.

As Raya grinds the fruit into the sand, an undamaged berry rolls over to me. Hunger surpasses my anxiety over the fight, and I grab it. Checking to make sure no one's watching, I raise the berry to my nose and inhale deeply.

It smells like summer.

'I'll eat what I want.' Maria stuffs a few berries into her mouth, jaw working furiously as though Raya's going to reach in there and grab them. Purple juice runs down her chin and spatters on her shirt.

I turn away and pop the berry into my mouth while scanning the ground for more.

'Maria?' Zane sounds concerned. 'Maria!'

I swivel as he dives at her. She's clawing at her throat, purple foam oozing out between her lips. She bends over, gagging.

'Spit them out!' Zane pounds her on the back. 'Spit. Them. Out!'

I stare at her in horror.

The berries!

I spit mine into my hand and keep on spitting, even though I didn't bite into it.

'What kind of fruit are those?' Winston wrings his hands as he stares at Maria. 'If we know what kind we can figure out an antidote. I'm sure I can figure out something . . .'

'Here.' I shove my berry at him. 'Do you recognize it?'

Winston holds it up, blinking the rain out of his eyes as he studies it. I stand still, waiting for him to say something, my heart racing like it's taking advantage of the few minutes it has left. I spit again, terror winding its way through my very core, squeezing tight.

I'm going to die because I was hungry.

'Well?' I can barely breathe through the chaos of my emotions.

His face falls. 'No.'

'No?' I grab my shirt and wipe my tongue. Spotting a bottle of water on the table, I grab it. Taking a swig, I swish the water around my mouth and spit it out. Still no foam, but my mouth tastes bitter.

Is poison bitter? I take another gulp of water, desperate to get rid of the taste.

'She's dead.' Zane's shocked voice slices through my panic.

'What?' I ask, not quite comprehending what I'm seeing. Raya's staring as well, mouth open and eyes wide.

'Are you sure she's dead?' Winston asks. 'Maybe she's just unconscious, or she fainted, or . . . something.'

'I'm sure.' Zane lowers Maria to the ground, defeat etched across his face. Dark, purple foam runs down Maria's chin and neck, and her eyes have rolled back so only the whites show. When Zane releases her, her head flops to the side.

I wipe my tongue again, the bitter taste finally gone, unable to keep my eyes off Maria.

Am I going to die?

I rub my mouth with the back of my hand, inhaling great gulps of air to convince myself I can still breathe.

Raya grabs one of the few berries that haven't been squished. 'Anyone know anything about these?'

I shake my head, as does Winston. Zane holds out his hand, a mask of grief obscuring his normal, easygoing expression. 'Let me see it.' He studies it for a moment before saying, 'This doesn't look like any berry I've ever seen.'

'Oscar or one of the others might know.' I glance around the empty beach, glad for the distraction. 'Where are they?'

'I don't know.' Zane's attention is fixed on Maria. 'I haven't seen them.'

'Do you think one of them . . .' I let the sentence trail off, the thought too horrible to bear.

'What'd you do to Maria?' Evie emerges from the trees and breaks into a run, Paloma and Oscar behind her.

'Nothing,' Raya shouts. 'What'd you do to her?'

'What are you talking about?' Evie slows to a jog. 'What's wrong with her?'

'She's dead.' Zane chokes on the last word. 'Who found these?' He holds up a berry.

'What do you mean, she's dead?' Evie pushes past Zane and gapes at Maria's still form.

'Just that. Dead. D-E-A-D – dead.' Raya draws out the words like Evie's a child. Wind whips across the beach, making the rain fall at a slant.

'You killed her! I knew you were dirt –' Evie's eyes sweep

over Raya's clothes – 'but I thought even poor scum like you had limits. Did that voice give you the idea? Kill off your opponents so you can win and buy something decent to wear?'

Raya raises her fists. 'Say it again. I dare you.'

Evie opens her mouth, but Zane steps between them. 'This is hardly helping.'

'The voice said she's a murderer!' Evie exclaims.

'It said we're all murderers, remember? So if Raya's guilty, you are too,' I retort, surprising myself.

'Like I'd take the time to kill some homeless man.'

Raya makes an odd noise but doesn't speak.

Evie glares at us. 'So which one of you killed her?'

'None of us did.' I cross my arms to hide my trembling hands. 'She ate some poisonous berries that were sitting on the table. Where'd they come from?'

'How the hell are we supposed to know?' Evie asks.

'Yeah!' Paloma echoes. 'How would we know?'

'We thought you found them,' Zane says. 'Maria said they were hers, so I just assumed . . .'

I jerk, horror washing over me – I'd assumed the same thing.

'Were they there when you woke up?' My voice trembles.

Oscar shakes his head, eyes focused on Maria. 'I didn't notice them, but, to be honest, I wasn't paying attention.'

'What were you doing in the forest?' Zane asks.

'Not getting wet,' Evie says sarcastically.

'We should've built a shelter like Maria suggested.' Paloma shoots me a triumphant look.

She's right. Clouds, black with anger, unleash their fury, the rain jabbing at my skin like a thousand tiny needles.

Thunder crashes and lightning flashes across the sky, briefly illuminating the island before plunging it back into a dark, threatening haze.

'Why'd you leave her behind?' Zane continues his questioning.

Evie starts to speak but Oscar interrupts her, almost yelling to be heard over the storm. 'She wasn't here when we woke up. We thought she'd gone into the forest to find food, so we went to find her.'

'Guess she found some,' Raya says.

I wipe my mouth again, still not able to shake the feeling I'm going to drop dead any second. I glance at Maria and shudder. I shouldn't have looked. The stains left by the dark foam on her chin, mouth and neck make her resemble a rotting corpse. A few berries lie scattered around her, and the white bowl rests on its side.

But there were no white bowls yesterday. Were there?

I step closer to the table and a flash of silver catches my eye. Secured under the edge of a blue bowl is a small piece of clear stationery with a silver border. I grab it.

'What's that?' Zane asks.

'I don't know.' I turn the thick, plastic-like paper over and gasp. My fingers go limp, and Raya snatches it from me.

'Holy crap,' she says.

'What?' Paloma asks.

'Please enjoy these berries for breakfast,' Raya reads. She flips the paper over. 'It's not signed.'

'Let me see that.' Evie tries to pluck the paper out of Raya's hand, but Raya whips it behind her back.

'Where'd you get the berries?' Raya demands.

'We. Didn't.' Evie says.

'Well, someone did.'

'Like you?' Evie fires back.

'I'm not stupid enough to leave a note. Or make a video,' Raya barbs with deadly calm, her body tense, like she's ready to strike at any provocation.

'Everyone calm down.' Zane turns to Raya. 'May I please have the note?' She gives it to him, and time seems to slow as he studies it. 'The message is printed not written – no one here could've done that.'

'He's right,' Winston says. 'And that's specialized paper designed to withstand ripping, tearing, spills . . . damage of any kind really. My dad's office uses it for really important documents. It's quite expensive and requires a specialized printing device that's rather large so it'd have to come from someone with the means to –'

'Evie's the richest person here,' Raya interrupts.

'Hardly.' Evie gives Raya a disparaging look. 'Don't tell me you didn't figure it out? Bexley Ryker. Rikas. Her family funded the terraforming and colonization of the planet and had it named after them. They make the rest of us look like paupers.'

I fiddle with my shirt, wringing water out of it even though it's useless in this downpour. I start to say something but don't. It's not as though I can deny the fact.

If Raya's surprised, she doesn't show it. 'Don't matter. She's not the only one with enough money to print that note.'

Evie's lip curls. 'How would vermin like you know that?'

'Evie Valentine, spawn of Alyssa Valentine. I know who you are.'

Evie stares at Raya for a moment, recognition dawning on

her face. 'You're that girl. The one who interfered when that miner died. You lost your finger for that.'

Raya plunges her hand into her pocket, gaze raking over Evie, face contorted with hatred.

'Raya . . .' I start, but trail off, unsure of what to say. What kind of punishment is cutting off a finger?

Zane lays his hand on Raya's shoulder. 'Not now. Maria's dead, and we need to figure out who gave her those berries.'

Raya jerks free of Zane's grasp but doesn't make any further movements towards Evie.

'It wasn't us.' Oscar tears his gaze away from Maria, his expression unreadable. 'I can vouch for these two, they were with me.'

'And the four of us were together. I woke up first, and the others soon after.' Zane studies the trees. 'There has to be someone else on the island.'

'Who also happens to be a serial killer?' Evie asks.

'If you haven't noticed, we've got a few dead bodies lying around,' Raya says.

'How could there be someone else?' Oscar asks.

'Maybe they were here before we were, or landed on the other side,' I say, thinking out loud. 'We'd never have seen them.'

'It could be Carson,' Oscar says.

We all stare at him.

'You mean that kid who said he couldn't swim?' Paloma's words tumble over each other with excitement. 'Oscar's right. Carson's the only one who didn't come to the island with us, but I bet he didn't stay aboard. He could've jumped off, swam to a different spot and hid in the forest.' She stops speaking, her expression smug.

'He didn't look like the killing type,' Raya says. 'Too weak and no gumption.'

'Weak and pitiful would be the perfect disguise,' Winston says. 'Just think –'

'One of us would've spotted him at some point,' Oscar interrupts. 'Either when Greyson died, or Maria . . . right?'

Zane gazes at Paloma with a new appreciation. 'Not necessarily. In all the chaos, he could've easily slipped away. I had assumed he didn't get off the yacht, but Paloma makes an excellent point.'

'So you think he's hiding on the island?' I ask Zane.

'It's possible. We don't know what's out there.'

'Not much, from what we saw earlier,' Oscar says.

'How far in did you go?' Zane asks.

'Not very.'

'Then we should break into teams and search the island.'

I turn towards the trees. The rain obscures their thick trunks and dense foliage, creating an air of foreboding. Maybe monsters are hiding in their depths, waiting for us to wander in too far.

'It could be ginormous. And there's no way I'm searching a whole island with *her*.' Raya glares at Evie.

'It's not too big,' Winston says. 'Of course I don't have the proper tools to measure it . . .' He steps closer to the table, running his hand along the edge like he's hoping he missed a ruler hiding amidst the bowls. 'But I went in there yesterday –'

'Like I'd go with you!' Evie shoots Raya a dirty look. 'You'd kill me the first chance you got and blame it on Carson.'

'What if it isn't Carson?' I ask. 'What if it's a stranger, someone who has nothing to do with the show?'

Raya crosses her arms. 'And they just happen to be on this island, picking us off one by one?'

I shrug. 'Maybe?'

The word hangs in the air, and we all gaze at each other warily. I shiver, as much from the rain as from fear. Lightning zags across the sky followed by a deafening clap of thunder. We all jump.

Oscar rubs his arms, eyeing the forest. 'We could wait here on the beach for the crew. Might be safer.'

'We don't know how long that'll be. Look, we'll stay in groups for added protection,' Zane says. 'Two groups of two and one group of three.'

'Not a chance,' Raya says.

'Yeah,' Paloma whines. 'What if I'm paired with the murderer?'

'What if you *are* the murderer?' Raya retorts.

Zane sighs. 'We'll cover more ground that way.'

'I think it'd be better if we split into a team of four and a team of three.' Everyone stares at me and I shift uncomfortably, waiting for them to shoot down my idea.

'She's right.' Oscar shocks me with his support. 'That's the safest plan.'

'Then that's what we'll do,' Zane says. 'If everyone agrees.'

'Yes,' Winston says. 'That's definitely the best plan. That way we can all protect each other and we're all witnesses so no one can sneak up on us.'

'Works for me,' Raya says. Evie and Paloma nod. I stare at my feet to hide the smile spreading across my face at their acceptance.

'How are we going to choose teams?' Oscar asks.

'We could draw straws,' Winston says.

Evie crosses her arms. 'What's that?'

'It's an old-fashioned way to choose teams. Or we could roll for it, but I doubt anyone has any dice.'

'How does it work?' I ask. 'Drawing straws?'

'We'll grab some stems from the fronds and break them into two different lengths. Whoever has the same length as you is on your team.'

'Sounds good,' Zane says. 'Everyone agree?'

Winston's thin face shines with happiness as we nod – he must be as desperate as I am for validation. What a sad pair we make.

'I'll be right back.' Winston takes off towards the pile of fronds we used for our beds, the sheets of rain obscuring him from sight.

'If that girl tries anything . . .' Raya says to me in a low voice.

'We'll be fine – I've got your back,' I tell her, my voice wavering. I give her hand a quick squeeze, as much for her comfort as for my own.

She startles and yanks her hand away. Embarrassed, I keep my eyes focused on the place where Winston disappeared. I have to stop assuming someone's my friend when they aren't. We're allies, not friends. She dragged me away from the men in the alley because that's what teammates do. My gaze drifts to Maria's body.

Am I allied with a murderer?

No. Absolutely not. Raya is not a murderer. I run a shaky hand through my hair – at least I don't think she is.

Winston returns, interrupting my internal debate, wet sand making muddy tracks on his skinny legs. My shirt hangs wet and sticky against my frame; we all look like we decided to take a swim with our clothes on.

'Here we go.' Winston snaps the fronds into two different sizes and places them in his fist. He turns around and, when he faces us again, the fronds are levelled so they appear to be the same size.

'Here goes nothing.' Raya draws one. It's short. Paloma draws next, and then Evie. They both draw long. When I step up, Winston ever so slightly pushes up one of the sticks. I arch an eyebrow.

He gives me an almost imperceptible nod. I draw it. It's short like Raya's.

'Thank you,' I mouth. He beams.

When we're done, we compare our sticks. I'm with Raya, Oscar and Winston. Zane, Paloma and Evie make up the other team. After we decide who's covering which side of the island, we trudge towards the trees, soaked, muddy and miserable. I glance at Zane, who's letting Paloma and Evie lead. I hope they come back alive.

I survey my team.

I hope I come back alive.

7

ZANE

'This is ridiculous,' Evie says as we enter the trees, the dense canopy protecting us from the worst of the rain. 'We all know Raya gave those berries to her.'

'Definitely,' Paloma echoes.

A tense silence follows Paloma's declaration, as though they're waiting for me to agree with them. But I refuse to be a part of their petty little schemes. I've spent far too much of my life forced to play someone else's games, and I'm done.

Keeping quiet, I stride through the forest, now in the lead, the lingering stench of decay made worse each time I lift my foot out of the muck. The lush foliage, dense underbrush and thick green vines crawling up the trunks create a wilderness that's eerie and pulsing with danger – nothing like the soft, quiet woods near my home.

My trousers snag on some brambles and I stumble, cursing as they rip and a thorn cuts into my skin. A bright red scratch trickles blood down my leg. Damn it.

I'm not normally clumsy, but Maria and Greyson's deaths have thrown me off my game. I take a deep breath and start counting, each number forcing my frustration back. By the time I get to ten, I'm calm.

I scan the ground and trees, but they're devoid of footprints or any sign of someone having been here. We're probably searching the wrong area, but the murderer has proved themselves cunning – maybe they've hidden their tracks. Or the rain, which has slowed to a drizzle, washed them away.

'My mom's going to be so mad when she hears about this. You know how she is,' Evie whispers to Paloma.

'It's not like she can blame you,' Paloma mutters, and I can feel their eyes burning into my back as though making sure I'm not listening. I squat and rustle the leaves of a blood-red bush, like I'm looking for berries.

'In theory,' Evie says. 'But ever since Dad's injury, everything's my fault.'

'It's not as bad as it used to be.'

I picture Evie shrugging as she says, 'I suppose, but it doesn't matter. I just need Raya out of the way and the game to continue. Mom wants that money. Things will be better once she has it.'

'And your dad?' Paloma's question comes out timid. 'Did that therapy –'

'No.'

'So then . . . that's it?'

'That's it,' Evie says with obvious bitterness and anger. 'There's nothing else we can do.'

I wait for more, but Evie's done talking, leaving me with a million questions and none that will solve our current problem. I refocus on my task, foreboding worming its way through me as I study the unmarred dirt. I have to find the advantage so I can take the murderer down before anyone else gets killed.

The preternatural quiet that permeates the jungle thickens the deeper we go; shadows slither along the ground as though following us. Overhead, the dense canopy ensnares the heat, causing everything to shimmer with an odd glow, like I'm in a dream.

Or a nightmare.

I keep walking but the thick, humid air presses down like a heavy hand determined to stop me. In an attempt to distract myself, I ask, 'Why do you believe it's Raya?'

'Because she's the most desperate for money, and she doesn't have the skills to win.' Evie marches forward with unnerving ease, not bothering to stop and look around. She's making herself an easy target.

I quicken my pace to keep up. 'But she'd be arrested the moment Hunter arrived and saw the bodies. There wouldn't be any chance of winning the money.'

Evie keeps moving. 'Not if the murders look like an accident.'

I stop. 'We need to search for signs that someone else has been here.'

They keep walking.

'Aren't you going to help?' I call after their retreating backs.

Evie swings around. 'This whole search is pointless.' She waves her arm in a frustrated arc that encompasses the forest. 'It's stopped raining so Hunter will arrive soon, and we'll get to play the game.'

'But the note. Raya couldn't have done that.'

Evie snorts. 'She's a thief, a liar and a miner who interferes where she shouldn't. It's not that hard to figure out she's the murderer. Come on.' Turning her back on me, Evie continues through the trees, Paloma an obedient little shadow on her heels.

Annoyed, I let them go. Who cares if the killer ambushes them?

Sigh. I do.

But I also don't plan on letting the others die because I didn't do my job properly.

With a mixture of guilt and determination propelling me forward, I start searching again, making a slow sweep of the area. None of the plants or trees, except for the palms, are familiar. I study different bushes, parting the leaves and pricking my fingers on thorns looking for the black berries Maria ate, but don't find any that match. I have to be missing something. But what?

I trudge on, sweat running down my face, chest and back in rivers, mouth parched with thirst. I shiver in spite of the heat, taking in the wide trunks and thick roots rising out of the ground like snakes waiting to strike. This place feels like a giant trap, but I refuse to let it get to me.

I'll never allow myself to be trapped again.

I wipe my face with my shirt. As a kid, I was convinced that if I ran fast enough I could escape anything. Especially my dad.

A scarlet flower catches my eye. When I was seven, I lost a race to a girl with hair that colour. I was focused on her instead of the street we were running down. One second I was on her heels and the next my foot caught on a crack, sending me sprawling to the ground, red-hot pain searing through my knees, elbows and ankle.

She asked me if I was OK and I nodded, afraid if I spoke I would cry. I limped to my house to grab some bandages, promising I'd be right back.

I can still feel the terror that galloped through me when Dad opened the door instead of Mom and I had to tell him what happened. In an even-keeled tone that was scarier than his drunk rantings, he told me I was never to lose again. I was a Wilder, and Wilders never lost.

Did I understand?

'Yes.' I meant to sound defiant, but my answer came out timid and scared.

'Never again,' he repeated as someone knocked on the door.

The red-headed girl stood there, holding out two cookies for me. My dad graciously thanked her, and she beamed in response. I picture my father flashing her his most charming smile, the one that always guaranteed him another supporter, another fan. People loved him.

When we were alone again, he stood towering over me like one of the Titans, ready to deliver his final blow. He said losers didn't get cookies.

And then he ate them.

A soft burble travels through the air, shattering the memory. Water! The one thing we forgot to bring with us.

I immediately switch directions and have to force myself to walk slow and quiet so I don't make myself an easy target.

Within a few minutes I stumble upon a gurgling stream in a small, airy clearing. Vivid green grass surrounds it and the flowers, whose scent makes the air sweet, resemble the wildflowers in the *All About Earth* book students read in the lower grades.

Too thirsty to worry about whether the water is safe, I dip my hands in, cup them together and drink handful after handful, pausing between each gulp to check my surroundings.

When I'm no longer thirsty, I splash some water on my head, welcoming the coldness dripping down my body and cooling me off, before stretching out on the soft grass for a quick moment. The soft roar of the ocean dances on the breeze. Relief sweeps through me – I must be close to the beach and the other side of the island.

Overhead, blue sky peeks out between grey clouds, marking the end of the storm. Hopefully Hunter and the crew will get here soon and this will all be over.

I jolt upright – Hunter! Why didn't I see it before? This could be a set-up and Hunter is the killer. Everything points to this being planned and, as the producer, Hunter has the most opportunity.

I swipe an angry arm across my forehead. Justice my ass. Dad's crimes were so much greater than mine.

I head towards the beach, still scanning the ground even as my hope wanes – we're not going to find anything. Unless . . . I halt abruptly, my mind racing.

What if Hunter's staying on the yacht?

He could've anchored it on the other side of the island so we can't see it and then used the small hover boat to sneak to our side during the night. That has to be it!

I race forward, crashing through the trees and bushes, honing in on the rhythm of my steps, struggling to ignore the fury building in me. But the steady beat does little to quell it.

Damn Hunter for setting me up and ruining my chances to get the money.

And screw Dad for stealing everything from Mom.

She'll be on the streets in a matter of weeks because of them. We both will.

I leap over a fallen log and keep running. I'll come up with another plan to make things right, once I catch Hunter. There's always a way to win, you just have to find it.

I dash out of the treeline and on to the beach, slowing so I can take it all in. But there's no yacht bobbing in the water. Nor any caves, or cliffs, or anything that would make a good hiding spot. Only endless sand and ocean, dimly lit by the sun breaking through the clouds.

I scan the beach again, desperate to find him, to find anything that'll lead me to him. A boat makes the most sense. Maybe Hunter –

A scream pierces the air, shattering the calm. Taking off down the beach, I race towards the sound, heart pounding.

Two forms appear in the distance, backing away from something on the sand.

One of them stumbles and falls. Paloma.

'What's . . . happened?' I yell between breaths, but no one answers. Paloma's on her knees, face buried in her hands. Evie's standing near her, so still she could be a statue.

'What is it?' I slow to a jog as I get within a metre of them.

Paloma gestures towards a strange shape in front of them, a strangled sound coming from her throat. Evie still doesn't move or even acknowledge my presence, her face frozen in an expression of shock.

The fear that running had kept at bay surges in me. Suddenly the sun is too bright, the air too still. Everything is wrong. I clench my hands as I approach the crumpled lump. Lumps.

This can't be happening.

8

RAYA

I wipe the sweat out of my eyes for the thousandth time. This damn heat! It's not like this on The Moons – it's cold and dead and grey. But here it's all emerald and sapphire and ruby and amethyst, with bushes thicker than mud and trees taller than mine shafts. It's more amazing than the transporter hub, and prettier than anything I've ever seen. It's perfect.

Except for the dead people.

I run my fingers over the rough, brown tree trunks as I walk, searching for anything living. I'd love to see the types of animals that live in these trees – Old George once told me small critters as colourful as gems live on islands – but I haven't spotted anything yet.

A noise cuts through the air and I freeze, fists ready; I know that sound.

'What was that?' Bex asks.

Oscar peers through the trees, inching forward. 'It sounded like a scream.'

'It might be a bird,' Winston says. 'Some birds sound like they're screaming.'

Bex wrings her hands while checking out the sky. 'But we haven't seen any birds.'

I say nothing as I try to make out any other sounds, but it's gone all quiet. The kind of heavy, dangerous quiet that sneaks over you right before you're caught doing something you're not supposed to. I study the shadows, searching for any signs of the killer, but there's nothing there.

Oscar scans the trees. 'Should we check it out?'

'We're supposed to be searching,' Bex says.

'We've been searching forever and we haven't found anything. I vote we head in the direction of the noise,' Oscar says. 'What about you guys?'

'There could be someone here,' Winston says, 'and even if they packed up their stuff there'll be a trail and we can find it.' He stares at the ground like footsteps are going to pop up out of nowhere. 'I mean, I haven't seen any evidence of a person being out here, not yet anyway, but it doesn't mean they aren't. We should keep searching.'

'Raya?' Bex asks.

'Check it out. Could have something to do with the killer.' I charge forward, not waiting to see if anyone follows. I swear, if someone else has gone and gotten themselves killed and ruined my chance to win that money . . .

Bex catches up to me. 'Are you OK?'

'Why?' I snap.

She flinches, and I'm almost sorry. But my feelings aren't none of her business.

'Because you look ... upset? And I ...' She looks at her feet before blurting out, 'And because you're my friend.'

I snort. 'We're hardly friends.'

'Well, maybe not *friend* friends, but, you know, acquaintance friends.' She looks all hopeful and shit as she rambles on. 'You're the first person who doesn't care about who I am, about my money, about the fact I killed those people.'

I jerk to a stop, shocked as all get out. 'You killed those people?'

Bex nods and peers over her shoulder. I glance back too. Winston's yammering on about something and Oscar looks like he's trying not to strangle him. I kinda wish he would, just to shut him up.

'Not on purpose, like the voice said. It was an accident.' Bex starts walking again, pulling her damp shirt away from her stomach. 'I was so excited to come here, where nobody knew me, where I wasn't the girl who killed someone. I even lied to my parents so I could compete. I told them I'm vacationing with friends.' Bex lets out a bitter laugh. 'Like I have friends.'

'Anyway,' she continues a second later, cheeks garnet-red. 'I'm sure you think I'm stupid. I don't even know why I'm telling you all of this. We'll be going home soon.'

She's picking at her nail polish again and staring at the ground like a lost puppy. I almost smile. She reminds me of Zircon – all fancy on the outside but with no survival skills on the inside. So I offer her a bone.

'We're not going home because two people accidentally died.' Except my gut tells me there was nothing accidental about it.

'I g-guess,' Bex says, shocked. 'But I doubt the Justice Seekers will let the game continue.'

'They will.'

'Maybe.'

Bex doesn't look too certain, but she has no idea how far I'm willing to go to make sure this game's not cancelled. I've already tossed Greyson's hamburger into the water and buried that damn note so there's no evidence. All that's left to do is to get everyone else on board with still competing and to convince the Justice Seekers that there's no need to overreact about a couple of sad accidents. Which won't be hard – I'm a good liar.

'But, if they don't . . .' Bex peeks over her shoulder again. Winston's still talking and Oscar still looks annoyed. 'I don't want to overstep any boundaries or anything, but, um, if you want, you can come home with me. You don't have to go back to The Moons. I have plenty of money to help you get on your feet. You could even live with me.'

I stare at her, fury raging through me. What does she think I am? Some poor, helpless girl who needs her charity? Does she think I can't take care of myself? I've been on my own since I was eight and I'm fine. No, not fine. The best.

Even Old George said so. 'Can't no one get away with stealing quite like you, Little Ray, you always outsmart them Justice Seekers.' And then he'd smile that stupid toothless smile of his and gum away on whatever candy I brought him. And he was right, too.

The Justice Seekers don't even know it was me who stabbed old Josephine Harris, even though that voice figured it out. How it knew is beyond me. Doesn't matter, though.

Old Josephine Harris should've let me keep the food. Her mistake, not mine.

Mostly, anyways.

I flex and clench my hands, not sure who I'm mad at, the ghost of my missing finger fuelling my anger. That mistake was all mine. But I got my revenge without the help of some snobby, spoiled girl who seems to think I need her handouts. Screw her.

'I don't need your help, Rich Girl.'

Bex stumbles, her eyes wide. 'Of course not. I'm sorry. I don't know what I was thinking.' Her voice catches at the end like she's about to cry.

Not wanting to be near her, I walk faster. In seconds I've put several metres between us, but an uncomfortable sense of regret steals over me. Which is stupid – she deserved it.

I crash through the jungle, the heat weighing me down, the air thick with humidity and the smell of rotting things. Even though it's not raining any more, I feel like I'm drowning.

'Are you sure you're going the right way?' Oscar calls.

Damn it. Bex's talking made me forget all about that scream. 'Yeah,' I lie. Except everything looks the exact same as it did when we first entered the forest, like someone went crazy making copies of trees. I was wrong, this place isn't beautiful. It's creepy.

'Shhh,' Winston says. He's a little behind me, head tilted to the side like a dog, eyes shut. 'I hear the ocean.' He points straight ahead.

Forget going in the right direction, I need to get out of this jungle before I suffocate.

I take off in a run and burst out of the trees. The air's still humid, but it's not so thick on the beach and I can finally catch my breath. Paloma and Evie are further on down towards the shore. Zane's squatting near them, staring at something.

I race towards Zane. 'Who screamed?' I demand.

Zane stands. 'We found Carson . . . and Hunter.'

'What?'

Zane indicates the large lump at his feet, his face a little green.

Bex jogs past me. 'Are they OK?' She stops a metre from Zane, stares, and then spins and throws up.

My stomach flips and twists. There's no way that thing is Carson or Hunter, it can't be, because if it is . . . oh shit. I creep towards the shape. It's definitely human. Or was.

Now it's bulging and grey and has too many arms and legs. Underneath one is a reddish ball of weeds. Except, it's not weeds. It's the chubby, scared, red-headed kid from the boat.

Swallowing hard, I lean over. A horrible, rank smell sweeps past me. I make myself look even though my stomach's threatening to send anything that might be in it back up. Breathing as little as possible, I search the pile of rotting skin until I spot Hunter's dark hair, no longer shiny.

I stumble back, all my plans petering out.

'Are they . . . dead?' Oscar asks from behind me.

I roll my eyes and force my voice not to shake. 'About as dead as they come.'

Zane glances at me and then Oscar. 'For a while, from the looks of it.'

'And the smell of it.' I glance at Bex, who's still bent over at the waist, hands on her knees, taking deep, heaving breaths. That's what she gets for what she said to me.

She gags some more and I look away, suddenly uncomfortable – again. She's just like Zircon – going and doing something stupid and then making me feel bad about being mad. Maybe she was just being nice, before; goodness knows Zircon never means to cause trouble. But people aren't nice for no reason – they always want something in return.

'How?' Oscar's wiping his palms on his pants like he's scared he's been infected with whatever killed Carson and Hunter, leaving smears of dirt behind. For once he doesn't look so put together.

'I think they drowned,' Winston says. He's standing over the bodies, studying them like they're some kind of science experiment. The smell doesn't seem to bother him.

Winston keeps talking. 'Carson told Oscar he couldn't swim. I bet Hunter didn't believe him and made him compete anyway. The storm probably washed him ashore, or we'd have never known he died.'

Bex wipes her mouth. 'What about Hunter? It doesn't make sense.'

'He was high on something,' I say. 'Maybe he fell out of his stupid hover boat and drowned.'

'High? Are you sure?' Zane asks.

'Yup. It was pretty obvious.'

'I thought so too,' Paloma says in such a low voice I almost miss it.

'But Hunter wasn't mentioned on the recording . . .' Bex's

eyes dart to the bodies and back to us. 'Why would he be dead?'

Zane shakes his head. 'Another accident?'

Evie takes a step back. 'It's because one of you is a crazy-ass psycho who didn't want him revealing that you're a murderer, determined to kill us all!'

I cross my arms and glare at her. 'I'm no psycho. And you're the only person here who's killed someone.'

'Stop lying!' Evie yells.

'You did . . .' Bex voice trails off and she studies at her feet.

Evie glares at her. 'I did what?'

'You're the one who . . . who suggested it was all part of the game.'

I stare at Bex – is she defending Evie? Or accusing her?

Zane steps forward. 'Evie, why do you believe it's one of us?' He's all calm and normal-sounding but his jaw's clenched tight.

Evie waves her hand around. 'Because there's no one else on the island.'

Zane doesn't back down. 'You didn't even look.'

'I don't have to – we all know it's her.' She points at me.

'You're the only one on the island I'd want to kill, and you're still alive.'

'See, she practically admitted it!' Evie gloats.

'Did you do it?' Oscar's staring at me like I'm some sort of monster.

I roll my eyes. It's typical they'd believe Evie and not me. Why did I think they'd give a damn about me . . . I know better.

'Well?' Oscar asks.

'No!'

'She did,' Evie insists. 'All because my mom chopped off her finger for breaking the law – she wants to get revenge on me.'

A shocked silence follows her declaration.

'Her mom . . . cut off your finger?' Bex looks all horrified and shit, like she's never heard of such barbarism before.

I keep my focus on Evie. 'I didn't break the law.'

Not that time.

'All you miners break the law. My dad was mugged by one of your kind. They cracked his skull, broke his nose and cut him with a knife. He'll never be the same.'

'You got no proof it was a miner!'

'We all need to calm down –' Zane interrupts before Evie can say anything else – 'and figure out what happened. We should start with Carson and Hunter because they probably died first. Agreed?'

There are nods and suspicious glances all around; our distrust is obvious. At least they're not staring at me any more.

Damn Evie, trying to blame me when we all know it was her. She's the only one here who's deluded enough to kill someone and think it's OK.

'OK, good,' Zane says. 'Who was the last one to make it to the beach? After we all jumped off the boat?' His eyes flick to me.

My muscles tense – he could've just said it was me. What's he playing at? 'Being a bad swimmer don't make me a killer, any more than getting my finger cut off does.'

'She's right,' Bex says, surprising me. She shoots me a nervous glance, like she's not sure if I'm going to jump her for sticking up for me. Guess it depends on what she says next.

Bex continues. 'Whoever did it could've easily caught up if they swam well.'

'Like you?' Evie asks and Paloma nods. Bex's face goes white.

'It wasn't Bex,' Zane says. 'I was behind her the whole time.'

'Unless it was you.' Evie's eyes narrow in Zane's direction.

'Shut up,' I say. 'You don't know anything.'

'What did you say to me, dirt digger?' Evie takes a step forward.

I raise my fists. One punch'll do it. Two at the most. Three if she keeps pissing me off.

Zane steps between us. 'Stop! Both of you. Please.'

'She started it.' Evie doesn't take her eyes off me.

'I didn't. But I sure as hell will end it.' I bounce a little, ready to strike.

'Someone's trying to kill us and you guys want to do it for them?' Oscar's backing away from us, stumbling in the sand. 'Or haven't you realized that we're stuck on this island and we're all going to die?'

Zane tosses Oscar a worried look but keeps his focus on us. 'Evie? Raya?'

'Fine.' I lower my fists, but it doesn't mean I'm letting Evie off. Choosing the wrong moment to fight guarantees all sorts of things'll go poorly, and I'm not letting that happen. Not this time.

Evie gives a triumphant snort, like I'm actually letting her off for making her crazy accusations. But I don't say anything – she can believe whatever makes her feel like she's still in control.

Zane turns to Oscar. 'We're not going to die. I'm sure we can figure this out.' He acts all confident, but his face says otherwise.

'We could establish alibis,' Winston says. 'That's what they do in murder cases. At least on TV. You know, the Justice Seekers try to figure out who was where and when.'

'That's a good idea,' Zane says, and Winston beams. 'Let's head back to our beach –'

'I'm not going anywhere with –' Evie starts to interrupt.

'As a group,' Zane bites off the words. 'And then we'll talk.' He glances at the lump that was Carson and Hunter. 'I don't know about you, but I'd rather not stay here.'

No one says anything, but we all start walking.

'Hey.' Zane falls into step with me. He glances around, as though making sure we're alone, and then says, in a low voice, 'Did you push Carson under the water?'

I stare at him. 'What are you talking about?'

'When we jumped off the boat. I saw you push someone under the water, and I can't shake the feeling it was Carson . . . that red hair. I didn't see what happened after that, but could you have . . . accidentally killed him?'

'Did I what?' Shit. I knew Evie hated me, but I thought me and Zane were on the same side.

Zane brushes sand off his pants, not looking me in the eye. I can't believe I'm defending myself to this guy. 'No,' I say through gritted teeth. 'I didn't kill anyone. I didn't know who it was – I was just trying to win.'

Zane studies me for a long moment before saying, 'OK.'

I eye him suspiciously. He gave in way too easy. 'OK, you believe me, or OK, I'm shutting up for now?'

'I believe you. It's not easy to drown someone.'

'And how do you know that?'

Zane's laugh is forced, as if he's not sure I'm playing around. 'I'm not telling.' He slows, scanning the beach and sky.

'Looking for something? Or someone? Because no one's coming to help us. Not now.'

'No. It's . . .' He glances around again. 'There's something off about this place.'

'How? It seems pretty normal to me.' Minus the dead bodies. And the heat.

'Ever been to the beach?'

'Nope.'

I swear a faint blush appears on his cheeks. 'I'm sorry.'

I almost laugh. 'I'm poor. Hell, I'm poorer than poor. It ain't like it's a secret.' I wave my hand to show off my ragged shirt and worn-out jeans. 'I'm not exactly high fashion over here.'

'Is that why you came? To win the money?'

'Isn't that why we all came?'

'I suppose.'

'It was great bait.'

'Yeah,' Zane says. 'When I asked my mom about coming she was nervous at first, but after a while she couldn't contain her excitement. Thought I had a real chance of winning. It didn't even occur to us to make sure it was legit, what with all the contracts and stuff they sent in protected files and the way they required our retina scans and signatures. It all seemed so real. What about you? What'd your parents think?'

It's such a ridiculous question, I think he's kidding at first. When he doesn't laugh or anything, I say, 'I've been on my own since I was eight. My mom chose her latest boyfriend over me.'

'Then how –'

'It's called forgery, Rich Boy.' I gaze at the azure ocean. 'It's not that hard to fool people.'

9

BEX

Winston, Zane and Raya carry Maria's body over to Greyson's while Paloma and Evie stand off to the side, whispering who knows what to each other. Oscar stands near the water's edge, a little further away from the others, staring into the distance. The whole scene gives me an eerie sense of deja vu. How often are we going to repeat it? My stomach flips.

Seven. Seven more times, if we can't figure this out.

No – six.

Whoever dies last won't get a burial – or what's passing for one here.

Winston stumbles and drops one of Maria's legs. He struggles to pick it up, and my chest constricts with shame. When we'd returned to camp, Zane said we should take care of Maria first and asked for volunteers, but once again I couldn't bring myself to do it. So now I'm standing here, useless.

But after seeing Carson and Hunter, or what was left of them . . . I shudder. I can't take another body.

I turn away from Zane and the others, my gaze landing on

the table. Striding over with some semblance of purpose, I gather what's left of the crisps and water. There's enough for each of us to have two bags and one bottle. It's only enough for a day. Two if we ration. My stomach grumbles in spite of everything that's happened. I glance at the hamburgers and hot dogs, which sit in sad, soggy piles in the centre of the table. But even if they were in pristine condition, I wouldn't risk it – I'd rather starve. Even the flies are avoiding them.

'Can I have a bag of crisps?' I jump at Oscar's voice.

'I'm sorry, I didn't mean to scare you.' His face is drawn and his clothes hang loosely on his frame, like he's been deflated.

I squeeze my hands together to stop them from shaking, but it doesn't help – fear's become a constant companion. 'You didn't. Do you have a preference?'

'No,' he says as the three pallbearers make their way back to us.

'We should bury them.' Zane's expression is somewhere between grief and resolve.

My gaze darts to the bodies – with Greyson covered and Maria lying out in the open, they look like some macabre art exhibit.

'Why?' Evie joins us, Paloma on her heels.

'Because they stink,' Raya says. 'Or maybe that's you.'

Evie's eyes narrow.

'They might attract predators,' Zane says before Evie can reply.

'But there aren't any.' I shift so I can't see the bodies. 'Hunter said –'

'That man's dead,' Raya says. 'And I don't think he knew anything.'

Heat crawls up my face. 'True,' I whisper.

'We didn't see any predators,' Oscar says. 'Or any signs of one.'

'We didn't either,' Paloma says.

'That's not so odd.' Winston indicates the trees behind him. 'It makes perfect sense the producers chose a deserted island. That way they don't have to worry about anyone being bitten or attacked or –'

'There's no competition.' Raya sweeps her arm in a wide arc. 'In case you haven't noticed yet – it's just us and a crazy person.' Winston flushes, and an uneasy silence falls over the group. An empty crisp bag blows across the sand and pauses at my feet before tumbling further along the beach, alone and forgotten.

'What's happening? Who's trying to kill us?' Paloma's voice shakes, her eyes widening with a look of horror as she takes us all in. Her entire body begins to tremble, and she shifts as though preparing to defend herself from one of us.

A loud rumble comes from Winston's direction, and he rests his hand on his stomach. His shirt's missing a button. 'I'm sorry,' he says. 'You can't stop natural biological functions, and I haven't eaten since last night. I know I shouldn't be hungry, but, well, my stomach's speaking louder than my brain.' He has the good grace to look embarrassed.

I'm also starving but don't want to admit it, not with the way everyone's staring at Winston. 'There's nothing but crisps,' I say.

'And whatever's in the other cryogel cooler.' Winston points under the table. I duck down to see a white container nestled neatly underneath. Blanketed in shadow, the cooler blends in perfectly with the sand.

'Was that there before?' I eye the cooler, not able to remember. 'Do you think whatever's in it is safe to eat?'

'We might not have much of a choice if we don't want to starve.' Zane bends down and drags the cooler out from underneath the table. He opens it and pulls out a small, silver package.

'What's that?' Evie asks.

Raya plucks the package from Zane's hand and squints at the small writing on the side. 'Protein squares infused with vegetable powder and vitamins.'

'They're emergency rations,' Oscar says. 'You find them on shuttles, military vessels, private ships and the like.' He stares at the cooler. 'I don't remember that being there.'

'Me either.' I take a step back as though it might explode at any moment.

'I think I saw it,' Paloma says.

'When?' Zane asks.

'This morning.'

'Are you sure?' Zane asks. 'Because I swear it wasn't there last night.'

'The tablecloth could've hidden it.' Oscar doesn't sound convinced.

'But you removed the tablecloth to ... to ...' Winston's staring in the direction of Greyson's body. 'Did you see it then?'

'No.'

'It doesn't matter, does it?' Raya rips open the package and pulls out a beige, gelatinous square flecked with green and brown. 'I'm not going to starve because I'm scared everything's poisoned.'

I might be imagining it, but I think she pauses before taking a bite, wrinkling her nose and swallowing. 'It's not too bad,' she says.

We all stare at her, waiting for her to choke, or gag, or fall to the ground, or something. She puts the rest of the square in her mouth. 'You can stop staring,' she says. 'I'm not dying.'

We watch her for another full minute, as though we're certain she's going to start foaming at the mouth any second now. But she doesn't.

I sigh in relief – fight or no fight, she and Zane are the closest things I have to friends. And Winston, I suppose, even if he's a little over-eager and annoying.

'There's plenty for everyone.' Zane breaks the nervous silence. He rifles through the cooler and pulls out a few. I take the proffered package, shuddering as I study its contents. I can't decide if I'm more worried about how it'll taste or whether it's filled with some sort of slow-acting poison.

Taking a deep breath, I bite off a corner. It's mushy, like too-ripe fruit, but doesn't really taste like much. I finish the square, feeling surprisingly full.

'We should build another fire before we do anything else,' Zane says. 'It'll be dark soon, and we want to make sure we have a good blaze and enough wood to get us through the night. We need to set up a watch as well, to keep us safe. Surely the murderer won't attack if we're awake.'

He eyes each of us for a moment, and I'm certain he's thinking the same thing I am – what if the murderer is one of us? I wrap my arms around my body in a futile effort to comfort myself.

'May I please have a match?' Zane asks Evie.

'What'll you give me for it?'

Zane's jaw drops. 'What?'

'I said, what'll you give me for it?'

'We're stuck on this island, dying one by one, and you're bartering for matches?' Zane asks through gritted teeth.

'Come on, Evie,' Oscar says cajolingly. 'This isn't a game, and the fire's for all of us. Zane's right, we need to be able to keep watch.'

'I want half the rations,' Evie says.

'You can't do that,' I say. 'We all need to eat.'

'Rations or no matches.'

'Here ya go.' Raya pulls something out of her pocket and tosses it to Zane.

He catches it, and a grin spreads across his face. 'Thanks.'

'What's that?' Evie demands.

'Matches,' Raya says. 'You should be more careful with your stuff.'

Evie's hands fly to her pockets. 'You little thief!' She lunges at Raya, but Raya deftly steps aside, sending Evie sprawling.

I suppress a giggle at Evie lying face down in the sand, a little ashamed of myself.

'Don't fight with the big girls if you can't handle it,' Raya taunts.

Evie scrambles to her feet, hands clenched. 'Afraid you can't beat me?'

'Oh, I'm not afraid.' Raya bends her knees like a cat about to pounce.

Zane and Oscar jump between them.

'Stop!' Zane commands. 'This isn't helping.'

'Well, what do you suggest we do?' Evie snarls, eyes locked on Raya.

'Calm down, make a fire and then figure out what the hell's going on.' Zane's gaze darts between Raya and Evie.

Neither backs down.

'Let's go, Evie,' Paloma says after several long seconds. 'We need to make a plan.' She glares at Raya. 'We can take care of her later.'

Raya raises her fists. 'Is that a threat?'

I start to defend Raya, but the words get lost in my throat. Does she want me defending her? She didn't seem to appreciate it before.

'No,' Evie says. 'But Paloma's right. And so is Zane. There's no reason we can't all get along.' Her mouth curves into something resembling a smile.

She's lying.

She's going to pay Raya back.

*

'There's not a lot to burn.' I grab another frond from the forest floor and add it to the small pile I'm cradling in my other arm. The smell of wet dirt wafts from the stack.

'Nope.' Neither Raya nor I have said a whole lot since we entered the forest to find more fuel for a fire, and the tension is as thick as the humidity. I want to talk, to make things better, but I don't know what to say, and Raya doesn't seem interested in mending things.

I shouldn't have stuck up for her earlier. I probably made things worse.

Stopping by a bush, I dig around the ground and find a few small sticks. At this rate, our fire will last all of an hour – if we're lucky. I glance upward. Pieces of blue sky streaked with pink and orange peek through the canopy as though trying to cheer us with its brilliant colours.

But there's nothing happy about this place. A shadow lives here, slithering in and out of the trees and creeping over the sand, shrouding everything in a dense, watchful silence.

I fiddle with the sticks in my hands, the small tapping noise easing my nerves. Should I keep trying to talk to Raya? Finally, I say, 'Does this place seem strange to you?'

'No.'

Keeping my gaze focused on the sticks, I force myself to continue. 'It's different from other islands I've visited.'

Raya doesn't say anything, and I quickly backtrack. 'Never mind, I'm being paranoid.'

Except I don't think I am. It might be the lack of animals, or the way everything seems the same, or the fact the island is strangely familiar even though I've never been here before. I shiver. The beauty of this place is nothing more than a facade to assuage us.

'What's that?' Raya drops her pile of firewood and disappears into the forest.

'Raya! Wait!' I rush after her, feet sinking into the soft ground and coming back up with a loud slurp.

Raya's standing in the middle of a small clearing. 'Well paint me yellow and call me gold.'

The branches tumble from my hands in shock.

A shuttle!

'What's that doing here?' I run my fingers over the sleek,

silver metal. It looks like a smaller version of a basic passenger shuttle with its slender, cylindrical shape, rear wings and double cargo doors that slide open – my eyes land on the keypad next to the doors – if you know the code.

'No idea.' Raya brushes a thin layer of dirt off the panel. 'Do you think it works?' She presses a button, but nothing happens.

'It's possible.'

'Can you hack it?'

'No.' I tap my nails, or what's left of them, against the hull. 'I can't even fly it, although it should have an autopilot feature. But I bet Winston could.'

Raya groans. 'No. There's no way we're telling him about this.'

'Why not?'

'Because he can't keep his mouth shut.'

'What about Zane?'

Raya tries to prise the doors open. It doesn't work. 'Nope.'

'Oscar?'

'Not him either.'

I take a deep breath, well aware I'm pushing the limits of her patience. 'What about the others?'

'We're not telling anyone unless we have to. I don't trust them.'

I stare at her. I suppose her attitude shouldn't surprise me, but this is going a bit far. 'We can't leave them behind.'

Raya crosses her arms. 'You wanna risk Evie finding out?'

My arguments fall away. She's right. If Evie saw this, she'd do everything she could to abandon us here. I can totally see her laughing and waving from the pilot's seat as the shuttle rises from the ground, Paloma at her side.

'No.'

'Good. Let's hide this thing for now.' She grabs a handful of mud and smears it on the shuttle's side. It doesn't help much – it's too big to hide. But we can try to make it less shiny, less noticeable.

I scoop up some mud, too. 'Who do you think left it here?'

'No idea. And I don't care.'

'But they might come back for it.' I press a leaf into the mud smeared on the side of the shuttle. It sticks for a moment before sliding slowly down. So much for that idea.

'Then we got to steal it first.'

Which we can't do if we don't tell Winston.

I brush a few stray strands of hair out of my eyes, keeping the sarcastic retort to myself. How do I convince her to tell the others? I try sticking another frond to the side, pondering. What if . . .

'Maybe it belongs to the killer!' I blurt out the idea without thinking it through.

Raya pauses mid-smear.

Encouraged by her seeming interest, I continue, 'What if they used the shuttle to sneak on to the island? They could be using it to hide in as well.' I pause, heart pounding as the possible truth of what I've said buries itself inside me and takes root. I swallow hard. 'What if they're in there right now? What if they kill us next because we know about it?' My voice becomes quieter with each trembling word.

'There's nothing we can do about it now.'

'Right.' I glance at the frond still slipping slowly down. 'But if there're more of us –'

'No.' She slaps another fistful of dirt on the shuttle. 'Me and you are taking it, killer or not. I just got to figure out a way to make it work.'

'But –'

'Stop worrying about it!' Raya snaps, scooping up the foliage I dropped. 'We'll figure out a plan tonight. Let's go.'

My gaze lingers on the shuttle – should we leave it behind? What if the killer isn't in there and this is our one chance to escape? Or what if the killer decides to abandon us here so we die of starvation? It could be gone by morning.

I bite my lip – I took a few programming classes in school, so I might be able to hack it. If I succeed, it should be easy to turn it on and engage the autopilot, assuming no one's in there. And, if I manage all of that, I can take whomever I want with me. I glance at Raya's retreating back before taking a step towards the shuttle.

'Coming?'

I jump. 'Yeah.'

Giving the shuttle one last look to make sure it isn't a figment of my imagination, I follow her.

The sun's sitting low in the sky when we join the others. Winston, Oscar and Zane are standing in a circle, an awkward silence hanging over them as they take turns stealing glances at Evie and Paloma further down the beach.

'What's going on with them?' I ask.

'Don't know. They started arguing and ended up over there,' Zane says. 'Did you find anything good?'

'Sure did.' Raya dumps the fronds and branches on the ground.

'It's not much,' I say apologetically.

'Don't worry about it. We found a lot.' Winston points to a pile of wood at his side. 'We chanced upon some old, dead bushes and dug them up. Well, Zane and Oscar dug while I organized. I made sure we only had dry wood so we don't have to worry about the fire smoking and –'

'Where'd you learn so much about fires?' I ask. People invented technology to replicate and replace fires long before I was born.

Winston's face glows with excitement, and he bobs a little on the balls of his feet. 'I love reading about Earth. I'd give anything to visit it one day and see if the people and cities are really like the articles I've read or completely different. I mean, our ancestors left three hundred years ago, and there aren't many opportunities to go back since it's like a five-year trip each way, so what if everything we've read about it is wrong?'

'Do you really think things have changed that much?' I ask.

'I don't know, but what if people don't even look like people even more? Or their technology is vastly different than ours? And it'd be amazing to see where we came from. I'd join one of their archaeological teams so I could dig through old cities or even abandoned garbage dumps. Can you imagine unearthing an old computer or one of the original smartphones? Or even a few history and science textbooks –'

'No one wants to touch a dirty old textbook.' Evie joins the group, Paloma a little behind her, eyes swollen and downcast.

'I'm glad he knows so much,' Zane says. 'Without him and Oscar, we wouldn't be able to start a fire.'

'I can help,' I say, hoping to avoid another argument. And because it's one way I can be useful and make up for not helping with the bodies. Hoisting a heavy log into my arms, I turn to Winston. 'If you show me what to do.'

Winston's a bit over-enthusiastic in his explanation, but, before long, I've started my first fire. I step back to admire the dancing flames, an unfamiliar sense of pride rising deep in my chest.

'Now we can try and figure out what's happening,' Zane says. 'We should start with where we were when each person died, like Winston suggested. Maybe we'll remember something important.'

Raya crosses her arms. 'Like people are going to tell the truth.'

Zane doesn't back down under her withering gaze. 'It's a start. Now, we were all at the picnic together when Greyson died.'

'He was sitting with Maria and Oscar,' Raya says.

'Who gave him the burger?' Zane asks.

'Me,' a small voice squeaks.

It takes me a moment to realize it belongs to Winston. 'No, you didn't,' I say. 'You were about to give him a hot dog when he reached over my head for the burger and . . .' My eyes land on Evie.

'And Evie gave it to him. See, I knew it was her,' Raya says with unbridled glee.

'Like I knew it was poisoned.' Evie's voice drips with disdain. 'Or even had a chance to poison it. This is stupid. No one saw anyone do anything.'

'What about the voice?' My body trembles as I force myself to make eye contact with everyone. 'What if some of us *are* murderers?'

Silence falls over the camp. The fire flickers and crackles, casting ominous dark shadows as the sun sinks beneath the horizon.

Evie breaks the silence. 'I didn't do anything wrong. I shouldn't be here with you imbeciles.'

Raya opens her mouth, but Oscar speaks first.

'Greyson did.' Oscar stares at his hands, his voice low.

'H-how do you know?' I ask in shock.

The firelight casts Oscar into shadow, making it hard to read his expression.

'We're both from Astos, in the Asa Sector,' he says, 'and what happened was all over the newsfeeds. Greyson went hiking with a group of kids from his school. They got lost and were missing for three days. And then Greyson appears at the trailhead, alone, saying he got separated from the others.'

'That doesn't mean he abandoned them to die,' Zane says.

I silently agree.

'No,' Oscar says. 'But when they found the bodies, there was no evidence of food or water, and they only had one thermal blanket between the three of them. Greyson had the other two, plus his own, along with several bottles of water and a few protein packs. He said the food and water were his and that the others gave him their blankets as an added precaution when he volunteered to search for help. But anyone who's ever been hiking knows you keep your thermal blanket with you at all times. They're designed to regulate your body heat no matter the outside temperature. It's your insurance against the elements. Against death. I don't believe his classmates would've given Greyson theirs. It doesn't make sense.'

'Why would he have taken the blankets?' I ask. 'Wouldn't his have been enough?'

'In case something happened to his? That's my guess, anyway.'

'What about Maria?' Zane asks. 'Does anyone know anything about her?'

Paloma surprises me by answering. 'Maria was the top-ranked athlete in the quadrant and competed throughout. The hundred-yard dash was her best event – and she was amazing. She was tapped for several athletic scholarships at some of the top universities.'

Oscar crosses his arms and eyes her. 'How do you know that?'

'I've been in track since I was little. Long jump, mostly, but I've seen her race. Anyway, London was an up-and-coming track and field star, rumoured to be better than Maria. We were at a meet together and –'

'You knew each other?' Oscar asks.

'No,' Paloma says. 'We were with our respective schools at the Quadrant Championship – Maria was from the Amovi Sector. It was cancelled when London died. We were later told she'd eaten something with nuts in it, which she was allergic to. They said the package was mislabelled.'

'Did Maria know her?' Zane asks.

'I don't know. They at least knew of each other. But if Maria perceived London as a threat ... I mean –' Paloma glances at each of us – 'she'd do anything to win. There were rumours she took drugs to help her run faster and ...' Paloma's voice trails off.

'And?' Zane prompts with kindness.

'I should've said something sooner, but I think Hunter was her dealer.'

Raya stares at her, fists clenched. 'What the hell do you mean by that?'

Evie sneers. 'Don't you know what a dealer is?'

Paloma's gaze jumps between the two of them, and she looks like she regrets saying anything.

Zane keeps his focus on Paloma. 'Why do you say that? Did you know Hunter before coming here?'

She shrugs. 'I mean, I've seen him hanging around meets before, talking with the girls, and there're always things said in the locker rooms . . .' Paloma brushes at a speck of dirt on her pants, not looking at us as she continues, 'And, um, there were a couple of girls who died of overdoses two seasons ago. The Justice Seekers never found out who supplied the drugs, but I've always thought it was Hunter. Most of us on the team do.'

'And you didn't think it was odd that he was on the boat?' Zane voices my question.

Why didn't she say something before?

Paloma tugs on her braid. 'I don't know. I thought maybe he got a new job on the show.'

'Who cares,' Raya says. 'That doesn't mean anything now. They're both dead.'

I think Zane secretly agrees with Raya because he changes the subject. 'What about Carson? Anyone know him?'

I shake my head along with everyone else.

'Who cares about the dead?' Evie says. 'We know they didn't do it. The real question is: which one of you did?'

10

ZANE

I start to say I didn't kill my dad or the others, but my eyes meet Bex's and the words die on my lips.

Should I confess?

Is she going to confess?

Is it worth the risk?

'You already said you didn't kill that homeless man,' I say, to buy a few extra seconds.

'I'm well aware of what I did and didn't do,' Evie says. 'What about you?'

I meet Evie's cold, calculating gaze – now is definitely *not* the time to admit anything, not if I want to regain control of the situation.

'Well?' she asks.

'No.' My words are smooth and full of conviction. I suppose being the son of a politician has taught me a few things. 'Is anyone else guilty of the voice's accusations?'

Bex shakes her head, her gaze darting to Raya, but Raya doesn't say anything.

Does she know?

My stomach clenches – did Bex tell her about me as well?

'I didn't kill my abuelo.' Oscar stares at the fire, a haunted expression flickering across his face. 'It's true he died, but it was of natural causes.' He throws a stick on the blaze. 'Heart attack.'

I wait for Raya to speak up, but she's too busy eyeing Evie. Maybe she doesn't know about Bex or me. I relax a bit.

'I never locked some kid in a closet, I would never do that.' Paloma looks at us with wide, pleading eyes.

'Yeah, you did,' Evie says.

'No, I didn't.'

'We attend the same school, and her boyfriend told me all about it,' Evie says. 'Dumped her after it happened. Paloma's dad paid him off to keep him quiet.'

'That's a lie!' Paloma's voice cracks and, in that moment, I have no doubt she's the one lying.

Perhaps we all are.

'It's about time the truth came out.' The false pity etched into Evie's features does nothing to hide her smirk.

'Is that what you think?' Paloma points a shaky finger in Evie's direction. 'She made the video about killing the homeless guy. I was there. I saw the whole thing.'

The smirk vanishes from Evie's lips. 'How dare you say that!'

Paloma flips her long, dark braid over her shoulder. 'She beat him to death. Her and her friends. They made me watch.'

'You don't have proof.'

'Neither do you.'

'You're worse of a liar than that one.' Raya jerks her thumb at Paloma, eyes boring into Evie with blatant disgust. 'We all know you're guilty. And that homeless man? His name was Enzo Casal. He was a miner, and not the first one you killed.'

Evie starts to respond, but I'm done with them acting like children when there's a killer on the loose. 'That's enough!' I say. 'This was a bad idea. I'm sorry.'

'It's not your fault, man.' Hands stuffed in his pockets, Oscar trudges towards the trees without another word.

'Where are you going?' I call after him, struggling to keep my tone neutral as the situation continues to spin out of control.

'I need to get away for a minute,' he shouts back.

I scramble to my feet as he disappears into the darkness – should I go with him even though he wants to be by himself? None of us should be alone. Maybe I should follow at a distance, to make sure he's safe? I rub the back of my neck, stuck between going and staying. When did I become this indecisive?

A yell slices through the air.

'Oh no,' Winston groans.

I take off in the direction Oscar went, stomach sinking. I shouldn't have hesitated. 'Oscar!'

A muffled 'Over here!' comes from a stand of trees.

He's still alive!

'Over where?' Raya's right behind me. 'Oscar, we can't see nothing!' She slows, searching the area. I join her.

'Here!' Oscar shouts.

Bex races past us. 'I see him!'

I peer in the direction Bex ran, Raya on her heels. There's a shape about four metres ahead of me, barely visible in the dim moonlight.

But something's not right.

Raya skitters to a stop next to Bex. 'Holy shit!'

I sprint to join them.

'Is that quicksand?' Bex asks.

Oscar's sunk to his waist in a dense, wet-looking pit.

'I didn't think that was a real thing,' Raya says.

Winston slows to a stop next to me, breathing hard. 'It's real, but it's not common. It happens when water in the sand can't escape –'

'Can you get me out of here?' Oscar wriggles and sinks a little further.

'Don't move,' Winston says. 'Quicksand's a non-Newtonian fluid so it liquifies whenever there's movement. If you don't move, you won't die.'

'We need a branch.' I'm already searching the area, heart hammering. 'Something long and sturdy.'

'Actually, you don't,' Winston says. 'Quicksand's similar to water, you can float and swim in it.'

'Um, guys . . .'

Oscar's disappearing fast.

'Stop moving!' I command. 'Stay perfectly still.'

Oscar's voice trembles. 'I am.'

The sand continues to engulf him – it's at his collar now.

'It's not supposed to do that.' Winston hops from one foot to another. 'Oscar, you need to lie on your back.'

'That's a stupid idea – I'll sink faster!' Panic laces Oscar's words.

'You won't! You can swim in it.'

Oscar doesn't move.

'Please, do as he says,' Bex pleads.

'How do I know he's not trying to kill me?'

The sand's halfway up his neck.

'Because you can't just make quicksand and hope someone wanders into it.' Bex shuts her eyes as a bit more of Oscar vanishes.

I swallow back my own panic. 'You don't have a choice. If you don't do anything, you're going under.'

'I'm not lying.' Winston clasps his hands together as though entreating Oscar to listen. 'A human body has a density of one thousand and ten kilograms per –'

'No one cares!' Raya shouts. 'Oscar, do what he says.'

'Lean back,' Winston begs. 'Trust me.'

I hold Oscar's gaze, willing myself to not show fear. 'Do it.'

'OK, OK,' Oscar agrees.

I can't tell if Oscar's moving, so much of him is submerged. Then his chest appears, his stomach, and finally his feet.

'I'm floating,' he gasps in surprise. 'What now?'

'Back stroke,' Bex says. 'Do you know how?'

'Yes.' Oscar's arm arcs through the air, followed by his other arm.

'You're almost there.' I squat so I can grab him, relief flooding every inch of me. 'Almost there.' I grasp Oscar under the arms, pulling him to safety.

'You OK?'

Oscar stands, slow and uncertain, muck dripping off him and landing with a wet slap at his feet. 'Yeah, I think so. Thanks.'

'It's not me you have to thank,' I say.

'I know. But if I thank him, we're going to end up getting a lecture on the properties of sand or something. Let's go.' Oscar plods towards camp, leaving a muddy path in his wake.

I trail behind him and the others, struggling to keep my composure. Oscar came so close to dying because I hesitated. I never hesitate. Thank goodness for Winston. If there had been a game, he'd have been a good ally. If . . .

Dread settles on me like a weighted vest – whoever the killer is, they're not going to stop until we're all dead.

And they have the home court advantage.

I glance over my shoulder. Could the murderer have made super-sinking quicksand before we arrived? Is that even possible? And, if it is, how could the murderer know Oscar would walk that way? Or were they simply hoping one of us would wander over there? It is close to camp . . .

My stomach drops. The whole island could be booby-trapped.

I take a deep, steadying breath. Get it together, Zane. You can't help anyone if you freak out. I focus on my steps and the length of my stride, refusing to let my mind wander.

'What happened to you?' Evie's asking Oscar as I reach the others, my heart rate almost back to normal.

'Quicksand,' Oscar says.

Paloma's hand flies to her mouth. 'Are you OK?'

'Yeah. I'm fine. I'm going down to the water to wash off.'

I join Bex, who's standing near the fire, absentmindedly rubbing a spot of dried mud off her arm. 'That was close,' she says.

I watch Oscar approach the water. 'Too close.'

'Do you think ...' Bex stares at the flames for a long moment before blurting out, 'Do you think it was an accident?'

'I don't think it could be anything else,' I say in an effort to calm her fears. 'Unless someone here knows how to make quicksand.'

Winston jumps into the conversation. 'You can't *just* make it. You need a lab and certain environmental factors and –'

'And a bunch of scientifical things no one's got,' Raya says.

'Right.' Winston falls silent, brow furrowed.

His words don't comfort me. How do you fight an invisible enemy?

Silence stretches over us, deep and unsettling as we shift around the fire, sneaking glances at each other, the distrust palpable.

'We should get some sleep,' I finally say. Anything to get this day over with. 'We can talk more tomorrow. See if we can figure out a way off the island.'

'I'm not sleeping with any of you nearby,' Evie says. 'For all I know, one of you did make the quicksand and lured Oscar over there.'

I'm so over her attitude. 'Then where, exactly, are you planning to sleep?'

'Far away from all of you.'

'Where someone can sneak up on you?' I ask. 'You're safer in a group.'

'Not with you guys, I'm not. Especially her.' Evie's eyes lock on Raya.

'We'll set up a watch,' I say quickly before another

argument breaks out between them. 'Two people at a time to make sure everyone's safe.'

Raya's eyes narrow. 'Which two?'

'Me and Winston, Bex and Raya, and Paloma and Evie,' I say, not sure Oscar's up to it right now.

'Not a chance,' Evie says as Paloma says, 'No.'

I clench my jaw, struggling to keep my anger at bay. 'Fine. Sleep wherever you want – the rest of us will take care of the watch.' At this point, I wouldn't mind if the murderer took one of them out next.

'What about Oscar?' Bex asks me.

'I'll talk to him in a bit. I'm sure he just needs a moment.' Or ten. If it was me, I'd need a good day or two to start feeling normal again – as though anyone could feel normal here.

'Do you think he'll be OK by himself?' Bex watches Oscar settle a good distance from the rest of us.

'He'll be fine.' I don't know if I'm trying to convince her or me. I look at Winston. 'I don't need you to stay up with me, I'm not that tired.'

'Are you positive?' He shifts his gaze from Bex – who he seems to have quite the crush on – and focuses on me. 'I think having two people on the watch is a great idea. That way there are witnesses, accountability, and we can all sleep a little better.'

'It's OK,' I say. 'I'll take the first watch, and the rest of you can sleep.' At that, everyone sits one by one, as though resignation is creeping through the camp and bending us to its will.

*

The fire crackles and pops as the night deepens. Stars cover the sky, undimmed by light pollution, and the red planet Bex noticed last night still sits on the horizon. A cool breeze dances around us, carrying the smell of sand and salt while the sea laps gently on the beach, the tide closing in on us.

I run my hand over my head, observing Oscar. He hasn't moved even though the water is now licking at his feet.

'Hey, man.' I settle next to him, the dampness from the sand seeping through my trousers. 'You doing OK?'

Oscar doesn't look at me. 'Are any of us?'

'No. I guess not.' I pull up my knees to keep my shoes dry, but Oscar doesn't seem to care that his are getting wetter by the second. 'You should come back to camp. It's safer there.'

'For how long?'

'We'll find whoever's doing this.'

'And then what?' Oscar finally meets my eyes. 'Even if we do find the killer, which I doubt we will, how do we leave the island? Do you know how to build a raft to support all of us? What about food and water? What if our entire campsite is surrounded by traps?'

Doubt ripples through me at Oscar's words. I shake it off. 'I'm sure the murderer has a way to get off this island. We'll make them tell us.'

'And what if they don't? What if they have a death wish and planned on dying here all along?' Oscar stares at the horizon. 'I never should've come.'

I grip his shoulder for a second, for his comfort as well as mine.

Oscar's silent for a long moment. When he finally speaks, his voice is distant, almost dreamy. 'Did I tell you my ancestors are from Colombia? It's a country on Earth, in South America. Legend has it that thousands and thousands of years ago my people were great warriors who conquered nations.' He runs his finger through the sand as though drawing a picture. 'I sure wish I knew how they did that; it might've given us a chance.'

He shifts his gaze to me long enough to say, 'I don't think we're going home.'

'We're going to make it,' I say with as much authority as I can command. 'And no one else is going to die.'

He doesn't respond. I sit with him a few more minutes in case he still wants to talk, but he doesn't move or say anything more. The tide is still coming in, and the wind sends chills down my arms. A few metres behind us the others sit near the fire, although as spread out as possible, with Bex and Raya making up one group, and Paloma and Evie another. Winston's lying on the sand between them, staring up at the stars.

I hope he figures out where we are.

I climb to my feet as the water continues to creep further up the beach. 'Don't spend all night over here alone. It's not a good idea.'

Oscar doesn't acknowledge me. Trudging through the sand I pass Bex and Raya, who stop talking when I get close, but I could swear they said the word 'flying'.

I'd love to know what flying has to do with anything.

I sit where I have a good view of the forest and the beach – at least from one angle. Perhaps I shouldn't have told Winston he could go to sleep, because now there's no one watching my back. Every rustle of the trees has me checking behind me, scanning the beach, staring at the jungle.

Where is the murderer hiding? When will they come out?

My heart skips a beat. *Is it one of us?*

I sift through the sand, searching for a rock, a stick, anything I can use as a weapon. My fingers close around a smooth stone about the size of a golf ball. It's not much, but it'll have to do.

Gripping the stone, I scan the area again, my gaze landing on Evie. After her argument with Paloma, I no longer have any doubt she killed that homeless guy – that miner. And the video . . . I wince. It was brutal. I can still see the poor man curled in a ball, covering his head and pleading for his life as homemade clubs struck him with vicious force, the crack of breaking bones audible over his cries of pain.

They never figured out who did it, either. The only thing the Justice Seekers ever concluded was that it was a group of girls and that's only because they were yelling and screaming while they killed him. According to the Chief Justice Seeker, the quality wasn't good enough for a proper voice analysis and their faces were obscured by masks.

I rub my thumb over the surface of the rock, studying the thick white line running across it. I get the feeling Evie's from a family that could pay off the law, and they're easy to bribe. My dad did it all the time.

I glance at Oscar, who's nothing more than a dark shadow. I need to make sure he moves closer to the group. I'll give him a bit longer before I ask him to sit watch with me. Make sure Evie doesn't take us all out. If it's her.

I doubt it's Paloma, she's too timid, too much of a follower. Same with Bex and Winston.

But Raya . . . Raya's a fighter. And someone who doesn't want, or even need, other people to tell her what to do. Still, that doesn't make her a murderer, and killing someone over a bag of food doesn't make sense to me.

Then again, if she was starving . . . I shake my head. Surely Raya wouldn't risk prison and the death sentence – she's too smart for that.

Yawning, emotionally and physically spent, I give up trying to figure out anything tonight. Things will be clearer in the morning. And we'll work out a way off this damn island so we can all go home.

*

'It'll be fine,' Mom says as I hand her a self-cooling ice pack.

'It's not fine.' My voice trembles with the effort to keep calm. Dad's passed out in his bedroom, and the last thing I want to do is wake him. Mom can't take another beating.

She rests her hand on my arm. 'It's my job to protect you, not the other way round.'

I can't meet her gaze. She's a slip of a woman, too small to take on Dad physically. He's at least twice her size, if not three times. Lithe and graceful, she'd been a dancer when she was younger. But when she married Dad, he made her stop. He made her stop doing a lot of things she loved.

'We could leave,' I say. 'Sneak out one night and grab a passenger shuttle.' I grip her slender hand. 'I'll make sure he doesn't find us. We'll hop shuttles, take a transporter, move around so much he can't trace us. If we make it to the Outer Planets, we can lie about who we are.'

'Zane.' Mom cups my face, framing it with her palms. 'We can't leave.'

'Why not?' I ask, too loud. I clamp my lips shut, heart pounding. Mom and I stay silent as the seconds tick by.

When there's no noise from upstairs, Mom says, 'There's no money.'

'What do you mean?' Mom comes from one of the wealthiest families on Rikas. It's the reason the Smythes signed the marriage contract between Beth and me.

'What your dad didn't gamble away he spent on alcohol and mistresses.' She's so matter-of-fact about it, I'm caught off-guard. We could be talking about my grades. 'There's nothing left.'

'But there has to be money.' My hands flop uselessly on to my legs.

Mom moves the ice pack off her arm, revealing a darkening bruise. 'There will be. When you marry Beth.'

'But her family think . . . the whole point . . .' The Smythes are good people, and when Beth finds out my fortune is gone . . . my stomach drops. I have no idea how Dad's been covering the truth for so long, but Beth deserves better than that. 'I don't want a marriage based on a lie.'

'I know. But we'll be homeless otherwise. There's no money to move to a cheaper sector, or to purchase new identities so we can hide from your dad. Your marriage is the only way to ensure we're OK.'

'But then there's nothing to stop Dad from gambling away Beth's money. You know he'll have paid off the right people so he has access to her fortune without her family knowing.'

Mom smiles. I stare at her. There's nothing happening now that warrants her reaction. 'Why are you smiling?'

'Because your grandfather, my father, was a lawyer for a bank.'

'So?'

'So, I know how financial contracts work for marriage. When I was about your age, which was a year or two before he died, your grandad taught me everything he knew, including the ways people change and manipulate contracts for their benefit and how to change them back. I'll take care of everything right before the wedding so your dad doesn't find out.' She clasps my hand between hers. 'I'm so sorry I didn't know what your dad was up to until it was too late to fix our own situation, but I'll make sure you and Beth are safe.'

My eyes bounce off the many bruises decorating her arms and chest, all in places that are easy to hide. 'But you won't be. Especially after Dad figures out what you did.'

Her mouth tilts in a half-smile, and she squeezes my hand. 'Don't worry about me. I'll be fine.'

I shake my head – there's no way she'll be anything close to fine. But it's pointless to argue. She won't even let me get between her and Dad, no matter how hard I try. 'We can't deceive the Smythes,' I say instead. 'It's not right.'

'What other choice do we have?'

'When I take his place on the council –'

'You're too young. Besides, he isn't retiring anytime soon.'

My heart sinks – there has to be some other way for me to make money before then.

'Asha?' Dad's slurred voice carries down from the bedroom. Mom glides to the stairs like a captive soul summoned by the devil. My chest tightens. I have to stop this.

'Asha!' Dad yells again. Mom straightens her back and squares her shoulders, ascending each step with measured calm, regal and beautiful.

'Mom!' I hiss. 'Don't.'

She doesn't look at me, or even respond, but her grip tightens on the banister. She's a prisoner sentenced to a lifetime of horror, and all I can do is watch.

*

'Guys!' Winston's panicked voice breaks into my dream. 'Guys!'

Jerking awake, I sit, wincing as pain shoots through my neck. Pink tinges the sky as the sun peeks over the edge of the horizon. Charred wood and ash sit where the fire once burned.

I rub my eyes, disoriented. When did I fall asleep?

'GUYS!' Winston's stumbling over the sand, trying to race to us, but falling more often than not.

'What?' Raya calls out.

'Stop yelling!' Evie's standing several metres away from the group, her clothes covered in sand and her hair sticking out at weird angles.

Winston stops a few feet away, bent over, breath rapid. 'It's ... it's ...' He doesn't get the words out. Instead, he raises a shaky hand and points towards the shore.

My eyes shift. Oscar's lying on the sand in a loose foetal position, the waves racing over him. My breath catches in my throat.

'What about him?' Bex asks, voice trembling, eyes fixed on Oscar.

'I went to get him up,' Winston says. 'The tide was coming in, and I thought he wouldn't want to be wet so I was going to wake him and . . . and . . .'

Winston gulps, struggling to speak.

'And he's dead,' I say.

DAY THREE

11

RAYA

The waves soak my shoes and socks. At my feet, Oscar's all curled up in a ball like he's sleeping.

In the water.

With a cracked skull.

A laugh bubbles unexpectedly in my throat, but I swallow it back. There's nothing funny about this.

'I thought you were the lookout,' Evie says to Zane, as if it's all his fault.

Zane stares at the sky, and I swear his eyes are teary. 'I fell asleep.'

Evie don't care and she obviously don't believe him. 'Really?'

'Yes.' Something in his expression makes me think he's not lying. 'I'm so sorry. I . . . I shouldn't have.'

'I should've stayed awake with you,' Winston says. 'It wasn't fair of me to expect you to be able to stay up with everything that's happening. Of course you fell asleep, it's the body's natural response when bad things overwhelm us.'

'But who killed him?' Bex asks.

'Who killed him?' I repeat. That has to be the stupidest question ever. 'One of us killed him, that's who. There's no one else here but us.'

The trembling starts somewhere deep inside me, growing and moving until my whole body's shaking like a shaft about to collapse. The others are talking, but it's like they're moving their mouths without saying a word.

There's no way this is happening.

It's a bad dream. Some awful, horrible nightmare that's never going to end. I giggle.

Heads swivel to stare at me.

They're going to die.

The giggle grows into a cackle.

We're all going to die.

I laugh fit to burst, gulping and snorting between guffaws as tears stream down my face. I spent years surviving and dodging the Justice Seekers and the body men, and it doesn't even matter now.

'Raya?' Bex says as I bend over, struggling to breathe. 'Are you OK?'

'OK?' The word comes out all choked and strangled as my laugh starts to die. 'None of us are OK.' I swipe my cheeks and straighten, ribs and stomach hurting from laughing so hard.

'It isn't funny,' Evie snaps.

Anger surges instead of laughter. 'You think I don't know that?'

Zane's watching me, all concerned like I've lost my mind. Maybe I have. Maybe we all have. But instead of also asking me if I'm all right like I'm expecting him to, he says, 'We should move him.'

'Why?' Evie asks.

'Do you want him to end up like Hunter and Carson?' Zane's voice cracks as if he might break apart any moment now, like glass dropped on rocks.

At least I'm not the only one.

Wiping my cheeks one last time, I move to Oscar's leg. I'm getting pretty good at moving dead folk around. Too bad that won't help me get a job when I get out of this place. I bet there's not a lot of folks looking for people skilled at moving corpses. Except for the body men on The Moons, and I don't intend on becoming one of them.

I grab a leg, but it doesn't move. 'He's stuck.' I tug hard, but Oscar stays all curled up.

'Let me help.' Bex's face is an interesting shade of green. It takes her a few, long seconds to actually grab Oscar's arm and pull. He doesn't budge. Bex drops his arm faster than I can pick a pocket.

'Rigor mortis,' Winston says.

'What?' I grunt, still trying to straighten Oscar's leg.

'It's what happens when someone's been dead awhile. When you die, the muscles in your body contract and, without oxygen, they can't –'

'Then what're we supposed to do? Leave him here?' I don't need a lesson on what happens when somebody dies – I've seen it often enough. I keep tugging on Oscar's leg, eyeing the sky. I haven't spotted any birds yet, but I know they aren't picky about what they eat. At least not on The Moons.

'Sounds good to me,' Evie says.

'Shut up!' I stop pulling and glare at Evie. 'You useless piece of –'

'Of what?' Evie closes the gap between us, hands on hips, expression smug as always.

I've seen her around The Moons load of times, her mom buying her anything and everything she wants. But it's her last trip to the mines that's most burned into my memory.

Her mom was doing her usual thing, pointing out everything wrong with the place and insisting we produce more even though the mine was running dry. Evie hung back, clearly not happy about being there. But neither of them gave me, or any of the other miners, a second glance. Except for Old George . . .

A pile of feelings I don't want to feel topples down on me.

Old George, the miner who taught us kids to read and fight and survive.

Old George, who was taking a short break because he was ancient, and who shared more of his food and water than he kept.

Old George, who Evie said leered at her even though he was just smiling his damn toothless smile like he always did.

Old George, who Evie's mom called 'a nasty old man' right before Evie knocked into him, sending him tumbling down a mine shaft leaving behind nothing but a heap of ragged clothes and broken bones and puddling blood.

Old George, who would still be alive if it wasn't for Evie. And who I promised I would get justice for. Whatever the cost.

I glare at Evie as my heart forms into a fiery orb of lava, pulsing with rage and hate.

Not just for Old George, but for the other miner, Enzo Casal, too.

Balling my hand into a fist, I punch the smug look right off her face.

*

'You shouldn't have done that.' Bex sits next to me, picking at the little bit of polish left on her nails, avoiding my gaze. 'But I'm glad you did.'

I stop watching Evie, who's off by herself down the beach with an eye turning black and blue, not to mention everywhere else I managed to hit her before Zane pulled me off, and turn to Bex, surprised. 'You are?'

'Yeah.' Bex scuffs her shoe in the sand, not looking at me. 'She deserved it.'

I tilt my head and narrow my eyes. 'Why're you being so nice to me?'

Bex flushes. 'I'm sorry. I forgot we aren't . . .' Her voice trails off, and she starts to leave. 'Sorry.'

I grab her arm. 'Stay.'

Bex sits like an obedient dog, and I bite back a smile. Someone trained her real good. 'Seriously,' I say. 'Why?'

'I . . . I don't know.' She rubs her arms, staring at her once-white tennis shoes with some fancy logo on the sides and their self-tying laces. Rich people really are lazy. 'I know you said you didn't want to be friends but, well, you haven't punched or killed me yet so I figured we were still kind of OK.'

Is she serious? No one's ever wanted to be my friend before, except Zircon. A weird sensation, almost like happiness, travels through me like a vein of gold. Two friends, now that'd be something.

I grin. 'You're just like a dog.'

Bex shoots to her feet. 'Um, OK. I'm going to go now.'

'What the hell? Why?'

'Because you think I'm a dog.'

'You are.' Why would that piss her off?

'So . . .' She's still staring at me. I stare back. 'Never mind,' she finally says. 'You obviously don't like me, and I –'

'Being a dog is a good thing,' I interrupt, still not understanding why she's so upset. 'Zircon's the best thing in the world, and you're just like him.'

She stares at me a moment and then bursts out laughing. 'Calling someone a dog is usually an insult.'

'Well, that's stupid. Dogs are the best.'

She sits back down, still smiling. 'You're right. And I'm happy to be your dog.' She pauses, brow furrowed. 'That didn't come out right. Anyway . . . thanks.'

'Sure,' I say as a troublesome, nagging feeling begins to gnaw at me. I take a deep breath.

Here goes nothing.

'I'm sorry about what I said in the trees. You were only trying to help.' I hope the words are right – I'm not used to apologizing.

'No, it was my fault. I shouldn't have made you feel as though I was offering you charity. I've . . .' Bex hesitates for a moment then plunges on as if she's scared she's not going to have the guts to say what she wants to say.

'I've never had a real friend before, not someone I could invite for a sleepover or to hang out with, and I thought it'd be fun if you . . .' She studies her hands, her smile gone. 'Anyway, I never meant to imply you needed my help. I'm just not used to people hanging out with me unless they want something in return. I'm sorry.'

Go figure, me and the rich girl have something in common. I nudge her with my elbow. 'Not everything's your fault, you know.'

'Tell that to my dad.'

'He blame you for everything?'

Bex rubs at some dirt on her leggings, not looking at me. 'Something like that.' She pauses a moment before asking, 'What happened to your finger? If you don't mind me asking, that is . . .' She stares at the ground.

For some reason, her question don't piss me off like it does when other people ask. So I lean back in the sand and stretch out my legs as if we're talking about unimportant things. 'Someone died in the mines – it happens all the time. You're supposed to wait until the end of your shift to take care of them, and I didn't.'

Bex's eyes widen. 'They chopped off your finger because you removed a dead body from the mines?'

And for insisting he be buried properly instead of being given to the body men to be thrown into the lake. But I don't want to go into all that. 'Evie's mom was using me to make a point about violating the rules of the mine.'

Bex still looks shocked. 'Seems a bit, I don't know, extreme, to cut off your finger for that. Why didn't you tell the authorities?'

'You're kidding, right?' When she shakes her head, I say, 'Nobody gives a shit about us, Rich Girl. Evie killed Enzo and streamed it without getting into trouble, that should tell you everything about the Gentry.'

'So she really killed two people and ... and no one cared?'

'Nobody cares whether a miner lives or dies. We're just fodder for their greed – a way to keep them rolling in gems. And we're a lot cheaper than machinery.'

Sadness creeps across Bex's face and, for some reason, that doesn't piss me off either. 'And the prize money would've meant you could leave – forever,' she says.

'Yup. That was the plan, before everyone started dying.'

'What would you have done with the money?'

I can't help but grin. 'I was going to leave The Moons and build a huge house for me somewhere. And one for Zircon, too. I didn't like him at first but turns out he's not half bad. I think he'd enjoy having his own place because he's used to nice things. Or he was before he became a street dog.'

I pause, shifting uncomfortably before blurting out, 'You know, I'd be OK with staying at your house for a bit if you were serious about that.'

Bex's face lights up. 'Really? Oh, that'd be wonderful! And Zircon can come, too. I really –'

'Sorry to interrupt.' Zane strides over to us. 'But we should search the island again in case we missed something or there really is someone else here.'

Poor boy seems desperate, and the rips in his clothes and scratches on his arms and face make him look as if he's already lost the fight. 'We already searched,' I say. 'No one's out there. And even if there's someone, we're not going to find them.'

'But they may have left clues behind,' Zane says. 'A food wrapper or a water bottle or something.' He glances over at Evie. 'Or we might find where they're hiding their stuff. Maybe on a boat. We could walk the coast. A boat or a cave would make a great hiding place.'

'Maybe. But I'm not going to tromp around this place with Evie.'

'We'll all stay together,' Zane says. 'That way we're safe.' He looks at Bex. 'You in?'

'I suppose. It's better than sitting here doing nothing, anyway.' She turns to me and raises an eyebrow. 'Raya?'

These people are damn fools, but Bex needs someone watching out for her – that girl's going to die if she's left alone. 'Why not? It's not the stupidest thing I've ever done.'

'I'll tell the others.' Zane strides over to Winston, who's eating a protein pack and eyeing Oscar's body as if he's not sure it's real. We haven't been able to move Oscar, so he's still lying in the sand like some creepy, sleeping baby. Winston says he'll loosen up soon, but I'm not so sure about that. I wrinkle my nose and look away.

'Should we tell the others about the shuttle?' Bex whispers. 'The killer could be hiding there.'

The shuttle. I was going to sneak out of camp tonight to see if I could break into it – it can't be that hard. And then I was going to fly to The Moons and grab Zircon before going to Astos in the Asa Sector. Old George once told me that even though it's where all the normal folks live – ones that aren't too rich or too poor – it's also a place where dreams come true. Where you can go as a nobody and, if you work hard and take risks, make a good living.

I check out Bex's dirt-streaked face, torn clothes and rumpled hair. She doesn't deserve to be here any more than me. Maybe even less so. 'Let's sneak away tonight. If the killer's there, I'll take them out first.'

'Are you sure you can do that?'

'Yeah, I'm sure. How many fights do you think I've lost?' A few, but I don't tell Bex that.

'What about the others? We can't leave them here to die.'

'At least we know we're not going to be killed or starve to death.'

'But we don't know how to hack the lock.'

'We'll figure it out. You're smart.'

Bex stares at me like I'm nuts. 'But Zane and Winston and . . .' Her eyes flicker to Paloma and Evie. 'We should at least take the guys with us.'

'Do you want to listen to Winston talking the whole way back? Because you know he won't shut up.'

'He's not that bad. And he's extremely smart. He'd be able to hack the keypad. And I bet he can figure out how to get us home.' She studies her lap for a moment. 'We shouldn't leave Paloma and Evie behind either.'

'Not taking them with us.'

'But –'

This girl's way too nice, and it's going to get us killed. 'No! I don't care what Zane says, I know Evie's the killer. Or at least helping the killer in some way. And Paloma's helping Evie. There's no way I'm trapping myself in a shuttle with them two.'

'They're barely even talking to each other,' Bex says. 'Not after what Evie said. We could at least bring Paloma.'

'Nope. That fight was all for show to throw us off track. Trust me, I've known Evie longer than you, and she deserves what's coming to her. It's just me and you tonight.'

Bex opens her mouth.

I start talking again before she can interrupt. 'And Zane and Winston. But no more. Got it?' There's no hiding my annoyance at giving in – this friendship thing is going to take some getting used to.

Bex nods even though she doesn't seem real certain about what I'm saying. 'OK.'

'Ready?' I call to Zane, who's arguing with Evie.

Throwing his hands up exasperatedly, Zane gives Evie a dirty look and walks over to us. 'Evie refuses to come with us. So does Paloma.'

I shrug. 'Then leave them.'

Zane shoots them a look that says he trusts them about as much as I do. 'I guess. But I don't like it.'

'Afraid they're going to poison the rest of the food?' We head down the beach.

'They wouldn't be able to,' Winston says from behind me. I sigh. I forgot he was coming. 'There doesn't seem to be anything they can use to do so. Or, at least, anything we know about. And I doubt they know a lot about poison. It's not as though they teach about that kind of thing in school.' He stops talking for a moment, eyes darting around the camp, before saying, 'Unless they took the berries. Are the berries still here?'

'I threw what was left into the ocean,' Zane says.

'What about the Justice Seekers?' Bex asks. 'They'll need to see them – they're evidence.'

Zane's shoulders slump. 'That didn't occur to me. I wanted to make sure no one else accidentally ate them.'

'Or used them to poison you?' I ask.

'Or that,' Zane admits.

'You planning on walking around the whole island?' I stare at the beach – it's as empty as ever.

Zane shrugs. 'If we have to.'

'How long is that going to take?' It's already hot as anything out here.

'It depends on how big the island is,' Winston says. 'From what we've seen so far, I don't think it'll take more than a couple of hours, maybe three. Of course, if I'm wrong, it could take longer –'

'I get it,' I snap to shut him up.

Zane marches forward so he's out in front. 'Watch out for booby traps,' he calls back.

*

'It's so quiet,' Bex says after we've been walking for who knows how long. Time disappears in this place, like it's not a real thing.

She's right, though. It's as unnatural as the silence in the deepest, darkest parts of the mine, the kind that makes you want to scream just to break it. And the trees have this weird shimmer to them, like they're warning us away. I swipe my arm across my eyes. Maybe the heat is starting to get to me.

We keep trudging forward, but it's pointless. There's nothing here. No people, no killers, no animals, no nothing. Not even the beach has changed – it's the same all around.

'Have you . . . have you thought about how Oscar died?' Bex's trembling voice breaks the silence.

'You mean how violent it was?' Zane asks.

'Yeah.' Bex rubs her arms, glancing around. 'Why do you think the killer did that?'

'Maybe they ran out of poison?' Winston says. 'Or thought we'd be suspicious of any food we didn't know where it came from . . . but the protein packs –'

A large crash interrupts him. I spin and go for my knife, hiding it in my palm.

'Who's there?' Zane calls out.

'Shh!' I hiss. Stupid rich boy. People who want to hurt you don't ever answer those questions.

Bex grips my hand without the knife, staring at the trees only a few metres away, eyes wide with fright. Winston's slowly backing up like he's preparing to skedaddle.

The noise heads straight for us. Adrenaline rushes through me, along with excitement.

Something's finally happening.

'Hello?' Zane hollers again.

Idiot's going to give us away. 'Shush.'

'Raya . . .' Bex whispers.

'Don't worry, I got this.' My knees bend and my muscles tense automatically. I need a good fight. I hope it's a wildcat. I could take one of those.

The noise thunders towards the beach. Zane raises his fists. Winston shrinks back even further, as if he's hoping whatever's coming won't see him. Bex don't move.

I press a button and the knife's blade swings out.

Evie breaks through the trees, out of breath, arms waving. 'I need you to come! Now!'

'What's wrong?' Zane asks. I keep my grip on the knife.

'Now!' She disappears back into the trees. Zane charges after her.

'Come on!' Winston follows them.

'Raya?' Bex says.

It's a trap, I know it's a trap – she never could've found us this quickly. But there's no way I'm staying behind.

'Might as well.' I take off after the group, Bex on my heels. But running through the trees is no joke. Branches scratch and claw at my skin and clothes and bushes keep getting in the way of my feet.

'Where are we going?' Zane yells from up ahead. There's no answer. Sweat drips down my entire body. My heart pounds, and I struggle to breathe in the thick air.

Damn this place and damn Evie.

I break through the suffocating trees and skid to a stop in a grassy clearing scattered with rocks. A couple of metres away, a cliff juts out into empty air.

I knew it. She's going to try and push us off. What a stupid plan.

Evie's standing next to a huge fallen tree that extends out beyond the cliff edge, breathing hard, barely able to talk. 'You've . . . got to . . . get her.'

'Who?' Zane asks.

'Paloma.'

12

BEX

'Evie?' Paloma's weak and tremulous voice comes from somewhere beyond the jagged cliff. I stop a metre or so from the precipice, terror coiling around me like a snake.

Zane rushes forward, sending rocks and dirt skittering off the edge. 'Paloma!' he yells. 'We're here!'

Raya pushes past me as she joins Zane. 'There's no way she's going to be able to hang on. Not for long.'

'Don't say that,' Evie shouts before focusing on Paloma. 'You can do it! It's like that time we climbed those huge boulders when we were kids. Just don't let go!'

'I can't,' Paloma whimpers. The branches rustle and sway, whispering terrible secrets into the wind.

'Yes, you can!' Evie calls back.

Gulping, I force myself to inch towards the cliff edge and peek over. Paloma's desperately clinging to a thick branch, the tips of her toes balancing on another branch beneath her. About fifteen metres below her a dark blue lake sparkles in the bright sun.

'I'm coming!' Zane yells. He steps back, eyeing the massive trunk of the fallen tree.

It'll hold his weight. It has to.

He puts his foot on the tree and pushes. It doesn't move. 'I'm coming,' he repeats as he scrambles on to it. My heart calms a little at the confidence in his voice. Zane's got this. Paloma won't fall.

He creeps along the trunk for a moment, as though testing it, before rushing forward. The tree shakes and wobbles under his feet. Paloma screams. I bite back my own startled cry.

Zane regains his balance. 'Sorry!' He glances back at Winston, muscles tense, his fear tangible. 'She still there?' Panic laces his voice, the calm reassurance gone.

Winston checks and nods, eyes wide, face white.

My stomach clenches and twists as Zane inches forward again, pausing between each step. His chest heaves and sweat pours down his face.

'I'm slipping!' Paloma cries. 'I can't hold on!'

'Don't let go!' Zane yells. 'I'm almost there.'

I wring my hands, trying in vain to hold my fear at bay. There's no way he can make it before she ... before she ...

'Almost there,' he says again, as though reassuring himself. He drops to his hands and knees as he reaches the section of the trunk that extends over the cliff.

'I can't.' Tears choke Paloma's words.

'Hurry up!' Evie stares over the side, blanching. 'She's going to fall!'

'You're not helping,' Raya snaps.

Evie whirls around, nearly losing her balance. 'Shut up!'

'Please!' Paloma's voice is desperate. 'Someone help me!'

'Stop scaring her,' Zane says, jaw clenched as he picks his way around the branches.

Evie turns back to Paloma. 'You can do this, Paloma. You always think you can't, but then you do better than any of us. It's going to be fine.'

I chance another look. Tears stream down Paloma's cheeks as she watches Zane. The lake looks deep enough for her to survive the fall. But if it's not . . .

'Give me your hand!' Zane's lying flat on the trunk, stretching his arm out. He's about half a metre short.

'I can't.' Paloma doesn't even try.

Zane scoots forward until he's only inches away. 'Can you swing yourself up?'

'No.'

'Try,' I whisper.

'Try!' Zane commands. 'You can do it.'

'You've got this!' Evie cries. 'Do it!'

Paloma shakes her head.

Zane edges closer. The branch trembles under his weight.

I bite my lip, eyes darting between Zane and Paloma, heart slamming against my ribs.

Zane reaches out again. He's so close.

'Grab my hand!' he shouts.

'You can do it!' I can't hide the desperation in my voice.

Paloma shuts her eyes and reaches one shaky hand up to Zane. Their fingers brush.

'She's got this,' Evie mutters, hands clenched, before calling to Paloma, 'You've got this!'

Silence descends as Paloma stretches her arm out. Suddenly

the branch she's hanging on to wavers and blinks, disappearing. Paloma plummets towards the water, screaming.

I cover my eyes.

'Paloma!' Evie and Zane yell.

There's a distant splash. Shaking, I peer through my fingers. Too many heartbeats later, her head appears above the surface. A breath of relief rushes from me.

What happened to the branch she was holding? I look at it. It's still there, completely solid. I rub my eyes – this island, the heat, everything is getting to me. Now I'm seeing things.

'She's not a great swimmer!' Evie's staring over the cliff in horror. 'We need to get down there!'

'I don't see a path.' Winston darts around the area. 'There has to be a path.'

'We don't need one.' Zane scrambles off the trunk and turns to me. 'Can you get to her?'

'W-what?' I peep over the side again. 'How am I supposed to do that?'

'The lake's maybe fifteen metres down,' Zane says. 'You can dive in and save her.'

I force myself even closer to the edge. Paloma's slowly making her way to a small beach, the lake sparkling innocently around her. But she's only using one arm, and her head keeps sinking under the water.

'Bex.' Zane's impatient now. 'Can you do it?'

I need to say yes. But what if I fail? What if she dies like Sam did when I hit that boat, and it's all my fault?

'Bex!' Zane fixes his brown eyes on mine. 'I've watched you dive. You're excellent. You can do this.'

'For goodness sake, do something!' Evie yells.

I shrink back.

'I've found a path!' Winston cries. 'Let's go!' Evie and Raya run after him.

Zane grips my shoulders instead of following the others. 'They'll never make it in time; you have to jump.'

I force the lie out. 'They might.'

'They won't. But you can save her. You're the strongest swimmer here.'

I squeeze my eyes shut for a moment and then meet Zane's gaze. 'Yeah?'

'Yes.'

I take a deep breath and, before I can talk myself out of it, say, 'OK.' I check on Paloma. For a moment I don't see her, but then her head pops above the surface before disappearing again.

I take one last look to measure the distance and back up. Zane nods at me, and I clutch at his confidence, struggling to make it my own.

Here goes nothing.

Breaking into a run, I leap off the edge. For a moment, I hang in the air, weightless and free, the island stretched out before me in one glorious snapshot.

Curving my body forward, I raise my arms over my head. The water zooms up to meet me. I slice through the surface and, for a moment, I'm home. It's only me and the water and the silence. I want stay here, to disappear forever in the cool depths. But I can't abandon Paloma.

I break the surface – she's nowhere to be seen. Where the heck is she?

I swim to where I think I last saw her. 'Paloma!' I call. 'Paloma!'

Each second of silence is an eternity.

A small cry and an anguished gasp. She's above the water for a brief moment before sinking under again. I strike forward, quickly closing the gap between us. But when I get there, she hasn't resurfaced.

Taking a deep breath, I dive under. The water's murky, cloaking everything in a dim, green-brown haze. I swim deeper, squinting, checking for any sign of her, but the water's cold and devoid of life.

I search the area, refusing to surface. But what if she's trying to make it to the shore? What if I screwed this whole thing up and she's already dead? What if . . .

'*You are so much more than your father says you are.*' Mom's voice interrupts my spiralling thoughts. I kick to the surface. It's blue and still. I swim in a circle, hunting for the smallest glimpse of her.

But she's not here.

I dive back under, dread enveloping me along with the water.

How long has it been? Two, maybe three minutes. Hopefully not longer. I kick towards the bottom. Please don't be there.

A distant voice echoes in my head.

'*We've found the woman,*' *the guy who heads the rescue team tells Dad. We're standing on the shore of the lake after the accident. My dad's boat has already been hauled in, the bow crumpled and bent. The other boat sunk minutes after I hit it.*

I don't want to look, but I can't stop staring. Two divers pull a woman towards their hover boat, her floral dress bright and cheery against her pallid skin; her limp, unmoving body. She looks nothing like I thought she would.

I shake my head, shutting out the memory.

The sunlight's faint at the bottom of the lake, darkness obscuring anything that's more than a foot or so in front of me. If Paloma's down here, there's no way she's still alive. No one can hold their breath that long. Not without proper training.

I slide along the sandy bottom. Please let me find her. Please. Seaweed brushes my face. I swipe it away and freeze. It's attached to a head.

'Paloma!' Her name bursts from my lips, along with valuable air. Wrapping my arm around her chest, I try to pull her to me, but she slips from my grasp. Weeds tangle around her legs and feet.

I rip and pull at them, but they have a life of their own, re-wrapping themselves around her as though they're an animal. I tear at them, prising the strands off, precious seconds ticking by.

I'm running out of breath. I yank hard, and the last weed finally gives way. I push hard off the bottom.

We rocket to the top. Sunlight and hot air hits my face. Kicking fast, I race to the shore, dragging Paloma behind me. When my feet hit the sand, I turn and drag her out of the water. Dropping to my knees, I check her pulse and look to see if she's breathing.

Her skin is ashy, her body limp, her chest still. I tilt her head back, plug her nose and blow into her mouth. 'Come on,' I mutter between breaths. 'Come on.'

She doesn't move. I blow harder and press on her chest, unsure I'm doing it right. 'Breathe,' I whisper. 'Please breathe.'

'Bex!' Raya's voice breaks through the haze of panic that surrounds me. Raya, Zane, Evie and Winston race over to me.

'Is she alive?' Evie flings herself to the ground.

No, my heart whispers. She was under too long, you know that. 'I don't know.'

Evie shoves me out of the way and begins artificial respiration.

'I don't think . . .' Zane's voice trails off.

'BREATHE!' Evie's pounding Paloma's chest. 'Damn it, Paloma! I didn't say you could die!'

'It's no use,' Winston says. 'She was under for a long time. No one can stay under that long. It had to be at least five or six minutes, if not more. The brain dies after six.' He peers at me. 'Are you OK? I didn't see you come up'

I ignore him, eyes fixed on Paloma, guilt turning into tears and dripping down my cheeks.

It's my fault she's dead. I shouldn't have hesitated – I should've jumped the second she fell.

'Evie,' Zane says. She doesn't seem to hear him. 'Evie!' he says louder. She doesn't stop. Zane pulls her off Paloma. 'She's gone.'

Evie swings at him, and he easily dodges. 'Let me go!' She strains against Zane's strong arms.

'Shhh.' He holds her tight, comforting her like a small child – like Mom comforts me when Dad's done yelling. 'Let her go.'

Let it go. Mom always said that, but I never could. I'm the only one in the family Dad hates, and I don't know why.

Evie struggles a moment more, but the fight quickly leaves her body. She slumps against Zane, tears streaming down her face as she sobs.

'She's faking it,' Raya whispers to me.

I jump. 'What?'

'Evie. It's all an act. She only cares about herself.'

I brush away my tears, not responding.

'You know I'm right,' Raya says.

I focus on Raya's intense black eyes, trying to understand what she's saying. 'Are you sure?'

'Yup. She's the reason Paloma died. And Maria. And she could've snuck up on Oscar when we were sleeping.'

'What about Greyson?'

'Doesn't matter how she did it – just that she did.'

'She's a good actress, then.' I'm not convinced Raya's right. As awful as Evie is, I don't believe she'd kill Paloma. Who murders their best friend?

Evie's sobs have quieted and her face is puffy, her eyes swollen. She pushes away from Zane and crawls over to Paloma. Kneeling next to her, she brushes Paloma's hair out of her face and whispers something in her ear before kissing her cheek and walking away. As a group, we follow, leaving Paloma alone on the shore, the sunlight dancing cheerfully on her face.

*

'Why the hell were you there?' We're halfway up the path that leads back to the top of the cliff when Raya lays into Evie.

'I don't answer to you,' Evie says.

'It doesn't look good,' Zane says apologetically. 'You refused to join us, and the next thing we know, Paloma's hanging off a cliff.'

Evie stiffens but doesn't say anything.

He's right. And Raya could be right too. Evie's already killed two miners, what's a few more murders to someone like her? But Paloma? Doubt gnaws at me.

'I told you,' Raya crows. 'I told you she did it.'

'I didn't do it!'

'Prove it.'

Evie glares at us, her swollen black eye doing nothing to dampen the hate burning in their golden depths. I pull my wet shirt away from my stomach and wring more water out of it so I don't have to see the accusation they hold. Raya may blame Evie, but I have no doubt Evie blames me. I brace myself for the coming tirade.

But to my shock, Evie's shoulders slump in defeat. 'Fine. After you left, we decided to do a little searching ourselves. We came across the cliff and that tree. There was fruit on it, and Paloma and I played Rock Paper Scissors to see who'd have to crawl out and get it. She lost.'

Raya snorts. 'Lost? More like you cheated.'

'I didn't cheat.' Her eyes rake over Raya. 'What would you know about it, anyway?'

'I know a lie when I see one. There was no fruit on that tree.'

'It's not a lie! There was fruit!' All semblance of control disappears as Evie lunges at Raya. Zane grabs her around the waist and pulls her back.

'Enough!' I can tell he's tired of having to keep Raya and Evie apart. Taking a deep breath, his face returns to its usual, measured calm. 'Fighting won't change anything.'

Winston takes a timid step forward. 'It's hard to tell how strong a tree is from far away. The branches could've been thinner or weaker than they thought. Or she lost her balance. What matters is that Evie ran to find us – she could've stayed until Paloma fell and then come after us.'

'Exactly,' Evie says.

'Unless you thought Paloma was going to fall while you were gone,' Raya says. 'We probably ran too fast, or Paloma hung on too long. And it doesn't change the fact there wasn't any fruit.' Raya holds up her hand and starts counting. 'Greyson, Maria, Carson, Hunter, Oscar and now Paloma. We all know the killer's right here.'

She doesn't say it, but we all know who she's implying.

I swallow hard. I didn't notice any fruit, either. I don't think any of us did, otherwise someone would've said something. So why did Paloma climb out there? How did Evie make her do it? It doesn't make sense. But the branch . . . is the heat causing some of us to hallucinate? Evie and Paloma wouldn't have seen the same thing, would they?

Zane rubs the back of his neck. 'Instead of wasting our time arguing over something that won't be solved, we should figure out a way to get off this island.'

'The producers will –' Winston begins, almost hopeful, as though he still believes this is all part of the competition.

'There are no producers!' Raya yells. 'This isn't a game. It's a trap, and we're all stuck.'

I glance at the cloudless sky, wiping off the sweat dripping down my face. Stuck. Like lobster in a tank waiting to be chosen.

'We should return to camp,' Zane says. 'We could all use some water and food. And then we can plan our next steps.'

'Sounds good.' Raya takes the lead.

I fall into step with her. 'We need to tell the others,' I whisper. 'About the, you know.'

'No.'

'But —'

'Shut up about it,' Raya hisses. 'We don't want anyone else to know.'

I glance back at Evie. She's walking next to Zane, talking in a low voice. Winston's between them and us, a small, ragged figure that seems ready to drop.

I bet he'll be next.

I jerk to a stop at the thought.

'What?' Raya asks.

'Nothing.'

But what kind of person looks at their friend and decides they're the easiest to kill? And worse, is kind of relieved by it? Someone like me, I guess. The longer I'm on this island, the more I'm convinced Dad was right. I'm nothing more than a coward, too weak and too timid to lead. The thought hangs over my head, dark and heavy.

Am I who he says I am? Or am I more than that? I did try to save Paloma, even if I hesitated.

I give Raya a sidelong glance. No more hesitating. I'm not leaving Evie behind. It's not right. Not when we don't know for sure if she's the killer.

I glance at Raya again, and my courage slips.

If I tell Evie about the shuttle, I'll lose the only friend I have.

13

ZANE

I lag behind the others, unable to stop glancing over my shoulder even though Paloma's body disappeared from view a while ago.

Where did I go wrong? Should I have jumped the moment she fell instead of waiting for Bex? I'm not as strong a swimmer, but would the added time have made up for that? Surely I could have saved her if I'd done something different?

A loud sniffle interrupts my thoughts – Evie's a few metres in front of me, looking small for the first time since we met. I jog over to her. 'You OK?' I don't like her, or trust her, but it's hard to see her so defeated.

'What do you care?' she asks.

I don't answer. I doubt she wants to hear I feel sorry for her.

Evie wipes the sweat, or maybe the remaining tears, off her face, flinching as she touches the bruise left by Raya's punch. Each step she takes is a little slower than the last until we're both meandering along the shore line, the others no longer in sight. At least they're not alone.

I rub the back of my neck as though it'll dispose of the trepidation that's clinging to me. Half of us have died. I have to get the rest of us out of here before someone else is killed.

'Paloma is . . . was . . . my best friend.' Evie's quiet voice breaks the uneasy silence that's been hanging over us for at least five minutes. 'I mean, I have a ton of friends, but you know what it's like. Do they like me for me, or because of who my parents are?'

I nod – I've often asked myself that question.

'But Paloma wasn't like that,' Evie continues. 'We've known each other since we were kids – we did everything together. And when we both received the invitation to *The Pinnacle*, I talked her into coming. She's never been a risk-taker, but we'd do anything for each other.' The ghost of a smile darts across her lips. 'I told her that as a team there was no way we could lose. It never occurred to me how odd it was that both of us were selected to be on the show.'

A sigh of regret escapes my lips. 'I think everyone missed the signs that something was off.' All because we wanted or needed the money or scholarship too much to ask questions. My heart sinks. Raya was right, the prize was the perfect bait.

'Why'd you come?' I ask.

Evie shifts her gaze to the ocean, the bright azure water a stark contrast against the darkness of Paloma's death. 'Why did you?'

Several reasons race through my mind, but there's no point lying any more. 'I needed the money.'

'But you're from Rikas . . .'

I give her a grim smile. 'My dad gambled away the family fortune. And I'm promised to someone who's marrying me for money I don't have.'

Evie's eyebrows shoot up. 'I'd heard marriages were arranged on Rikas, but I thought it was a joke.'

'It's not. And it's very practical when you think about it.' Unless you end up with someone like Dad.

'And you don't mind being told who to marry?'

'No.' At least I hadn't until recently. I swallow hard, but the lump lodged in my throat doesn't budge. If I don't go through with the wedding, Mom will be homeless and publicly humiliated. And if I do, I'm not sure I can live with myself. *The Pinnacle* was my way of fixing this mess, but now ... defeat slams into me, almost bringing me to my knees.

'My mom needs the money.' Evie's declaration pulls me back to the beach.

I stare at her in surprise. 'Why?'

'She wants to buy two more mines on The Moons so she has more voting power. She has big plans that'll change the way the mining industry works, and those extra votes would help ensure it happens. She's even figured out a way to not pay the miners.' Evie studies the ground, as though lost in thought, before muttering, 'Filthy, ungrateful scum.'

'What's so bad about the miners?' She's probably going to tell me something petty, like they smell bad or they're dirty.

She hesitates before replying, 'A miner kidnapped my little sister and held her for ransom when she was three and I was eight.' Evie's staring straight ahead now, her normal, defensive posture gone. 'Her favourite blanket was found with blood on it, a lot of blood, and we thought she was dead.' Evie pauses, blinking fast. When she continues, her voice is strained. 'The Justice Seekers tracked down the miner who did it the next day. He was part of a larger group planning a rebellion. They were all executed.'

'And your sister?' I'm not sure I want to hear the answer.

'She had a broken arm and a nasty gash on her leg, but she survived.' Evie shoves her hands in her pockets, still not looking at me. 'Then, about eight or nine months ago, a miner mugged my dad. They hit him so hard they cracked his skull, and the damage done to his brain . . .' She shakes her head. 'He'll never recover. And do you want to know what the worst part is?' She doesn't wait for me to answer. 'He actually advocated *for* miner's rights. My mom never agreed with him though, and after what they've done to my family, I'm with her. They're not worth the air they breathe.'

My chest constricts with compassion. 'I'm so sorry.' I wince at how trite the words sound.

She scoffs bitterly. 'It is what it is, you know. Your sister gets kidnapped, your dog runs away, your dad gets permanent brain damage – it's all just a part of life, right?' Sighing, she runs her hand through her hair and mutters, 'I really loved that dog.'

I rack my brain for something to say, something that might help, but there's nothing.

Evie straightens her shoulders and changes the topic, her words slashing through the awkwardness. 'I wanted to win the game. I was willing to do anything.'

Anything? Even kill? Her words from yesterday come back to me. Was it only yesterday? The days have started to bleed together into one continuous nightmare.

'Then why'd you rat out Paloma?'

Evie kicks the sand. 'I was mad. We had a stupid fight.'

I hesitate, weighing the question on my tongue before asking it. '*Was* she guilty of killing that girl?'

'Yeah. It was an accident – there was something wrong with the ventilation – but she's the one who put Rebecca in the closet.' Evie glances back, as though Paloma might be right behind us, and lowers her voice. 'She never got over it, not really. She used to be one of the most confident people I knew, everyone in school loved her, several universities were offering her track and field scholarships, and then Rebecca died and Paloma couldn't handle it. I told her accidents happen and that it shouldn't bother her so much, but ...' Evie shrugs.

Shouldn't bother her? Before I can say that of course it should have bothered her, Evie asks with startling frankness, 'Did you kill your dad?'

I start to deny it, but the words get caught in my throat. 'Yes.' I catch her eye and add, 'But not on purpose. I thought he was a robber.'

'I killed that man,' she says, as though we're discussing last night's football game. 'Except he wasn't homeless, he was a miner. I wasn't going to originally – I was just talking about how the miners deserve to be punished for what happened to my family, but one of my friends dared me to go through with it. Said he'd pay me if I did.' She shrugs. 'It was enough to buy the new Jack Penny shoes – the ones with the holo-chip that let you change how they look. You can even upgrade the chip so your shoes mimic designer brands. My mom wouldn't buy them for me – said she needed every last crian to cover the cost of purchasing the new mines. So I got my revenge *and* my shoes.'

I struggle to make sense of her story, her justification for killing a person. The pity and sympathy I'd been feeling for her vanishes as the truth sinks in.

My shock and disgust must be obvious because she adds, with disturbing casualness, 'It's not like his life was worth living. Who wants to be a miner?'

'He was a person.'

'They're not people.'

My mouth opens and closes a few times, but for the second time in a day, I'm speechless.

Her steady gaze meets mine. 'Don't act all upset like you have a monopoly on goodness. We're all murderers here. Or haven't you figured that out yet?'

Before I can reply, she says, 'See ya back at camp.' Striding ahead of me, she disappears down the beach.

*

A warm, salty breeze blows in from the ocean as the waves play at my bare feet. I've been wandering up and down the beach for at least an hour now, trying to figure out how we're going to get off this island. The only solution that's halfway reasonable is to build a raft, which I didn't even think to research before I came. I doubt I could construct one large enough to hold all of us or that could withstand a long voyage. Plus, I don't know where we're going, not to mention the issue of food and water. I kick the thick, wet sand, refusing to give in to the hopelessness of the situation. There has to be a way.

I eye Winston who's talking to Bex about something. That girl is a saint – it's no wonder he likes her. She always listens to him and somehow manages not to roll her eyes or walk away. But Winston's smart – the smartest one here. He might have some ideas on how to build a raft and what to do about turning seawater into something drinkable. And if he's figured out the constellations, he might know how to map them to get us home, too.

Bex says something else to Winston and then moves towards me.

'Hey.' She slips off her shoes and socks and joins me, allowing the water to run over her feet and splash at her ankles.

'Hey.' I bury my foot in the sand, waiting for her to say something. But, instead of speaking, she wanders down the beach. I follow.

'How're you doing?'

'I'm OK,' she says in a trembling voice that clearly says she's anything but. 'You?'

'The same.' We keep walking. But unlike the uneasy silences between Evie and me, this silence is peaceful and welcome. My mind stops racing and, for a moment, I enjoy the sensation of walking along a beach with a pretty girl. It's so normal.

'We found a shuttle.'

I stare at her, struggling to comprehend what she just said. 'I'm sorry, what was that?'

Bex keeps walking, shoes swinging by her side as though she's out for an evening stroll. 'Raya and I found a shuttle in the trees yesterday.'

Questions tumble chaotically in my head as excitement floods through me. Maybe we will get off this island before anyone else dies.

'We're leaving tonight and want you to come with us.' She doesn't look at me or give any indication that what she said is insane.

I grab her hand. 'Hold on, what are you talking about?'

Stopping, she tells me about her and Raya's plan. 'But,' she lowers her voice and glances behind me. 'Raya doesn't want to bring Evie.'

'That's –'

'Not OK,' Bex finishes, which is not what I was going to say. 'But I can't convince her otherwise – it took forever to persuade her to let me tell you.'

That's not a surprise. Raya's more stubborn than a dog with a bone. But I understand why she doesn't want Evie to come along. I don't want her to, either. Especially after what she told me. But I don't see how leaving her behind does any of us any good – it just makes us look guilty.

'I'll talk to Raya.' I turn back towards camp. Raya's sitting by herself and Winston's chatting with Evie who, instead of listening, keeps eyeing Raya. 'I can convince her.'

Bex touches my shoulder. 'No, don't. Please.'

I arch an eyebrow and wait for her to continue.

'We don't need any more fights.' She digs her toe in the sand. 'I thought you could tell Evie and have her arrive shortly after we get there.' Bex raises her blue eyes to mine, the brightness of their colour contrasting sharply with the dark circles beneath them. 'What do you think?'

'Raya won't let her board the shuttle. She'll try to block her.'

'You're stronger than her.'

I cross my arms. 'I'm not going to hit a girl. Or manhandle her.'

'I'm sure you'll figure something out.'

I'm a little annoyed by her response, but there are other far more pressing concerns that need to be addressed. 'What if the murderer's on the shuttle and waiting for us?' Bex had mentioned that as a possibility, and it was highly probable she's right. It would explain why we could never find them. And it gives them a place to store poisonous berries, laced meat, or anything else they might need.

'Raya has a plan for taking care of them.'

The corners of my mouth twitch. 'Beat them up?'

She laughs. 'Yes. But between her and you, I doubt the killer has much of a chance.'

Uncertainty cuts through the bit of joy Bex's laughter created. What if the murderer is armed? But I don't mention that. I don't want to worry Bex more than she already is. 'So Evie and I are leaving last?' I confirm.

'Yes. We'll start moving once the fire's burned low.'

'I assume you've told Winston about the shuttle?'

Bex nods. 'We need him to hack the keypad so we can actually get in.'

It's my turn to laugh, and it feels good. 'Is that how you convinced Raya to let him come?'

Guilt flashes across her face. 'He's the only one who can do it.'

'Yeah, you're right. It's not like they teach future councilmen the ins and outs of technology.' I scoop up a small conch and wash the sand off in the receding water. 'Do they teach it in the business classes?' Bex's dad owns the majority of the banks in the quadrant.

'No.' Bex chokes on the word. 'Not that it matters. Dad was only grooming me to be an acceptable wife.'

I rub my finger over the rough, pinkish-brown edge of the shell. 'I thought you were the oldest child?'

Bex's eyes shine with tears. 'I am. But after the accident . . .' She stops, pain and hurt contorting her features.

'What happened?' I keep my voice low, unable to imagine Bex's shame at being passed over. It's only happened a few times in the history of Rikas.

'We'd just lost a swim meet, because of me. If my time had been a little faster . . .' She hesitates, as though debating whether she should tell me more. 'I needed to get out of my house and away from my dad. So I snuck out to his yacht and took it for a sail. I love everything about the water.'

Her eyes brighten as she speaks. 'It's peaceful and yet uncontrollable. It hides an entire ecosystem and takes care of it. And, when you're swimming, especially when you're deep underwater, the world above melts away.'

Pink tinges her cheeks, like she thinks she's said too much. 'Anyway, I broke into my dad's onboard liquor cabinet and had too much to drink. It was the first time I had alcohol.' She gazes at the sky where the sun is beginning to dip beneath the horizon, turning the fluffy clouds cotton candy pink.

'There was another boat on the water, much smaller than mine, that I didn't notice in time.' She fiddles with the hem of her shirt. 'If I hadn't been drunk, my reflexes would've been faster, fast enough to avoid it.' Her voice goes so soft I have to strain to hear her. 'I rammed right into it and killed a mom and her little boy.' She pauses and swallows hard. 'He was three.'

A few tears escape and run down her cheeks. 'I stole him from his family, and I can't ever give him back.'

Before I can second guess what I'm doing I pull her into a hug, wanting to convey that it'll be OK even though I know it won't. She hesitates before wrapping her arms around me, gripping me tight. She seems so vulnerable, so young, nothing like the wild girl portrayed in the news. I still remember when the story hit the feeds, blaring Bex's name across the top in bold, black lettering.

PARTY GIRL BEXLEY RYKER KILLS MOTHER & SON IN BOATING ACCIDENT

ANONYMOUS SOURCE CLAIMS RYKER ACCIDENT NO ACCIDENT

DRUNK DAUGHTER OF ARTHUR RYKER KILLS TWO

The woman who had been killed left behind two older kids and was married to a judge. They'd been visiting Rikas on holiday when the accident happened. A few months later, her husband killed himself. The reports said he hadn't been able to deal with the loss.

Bex steps back, wiping the tears off her face. 'Sorry. I didn't mean to overshare.' She lets out an embarrassed laugh.

'It's OK.' I study her profile. 'Is that why you accepted the invitation to *The Pinnacle*? To get away from it all?'

'Yeah. After the accident, this seemed like the best option.' She scuffs her foot in the sand. 'You?'

'We need the money. My dad gambled all ours away.'

Bex's eyes widen. 'Councilman Wilder was a gambler?'

I almost laugh at her shock. 'Councilman Wilder put on a good act.'

'So does Mr Ryker.'

Now it's my turn to be shocked. 'Your dad?'

Bex doesn't look at me. 'He had an affair. With an outsider. He could've ruined our whole family if someone had found out.'

'But no one did?'

'No, thankfully. I'm the only one who knows about it. I wanted to confront him . . .' Her voice trails off, and she stares out across the water.

'But?' I ask gently when she doesn't say more.

'He wouldn't've listened. He hates me. Always tells me how he can't wait until I'm married and out of his house.' She says it like she doesn't care, but hurt curls around her words. 'He never thought I was good enough to bear the Ryker name. Thought I was too weak. Too timid. Not to mention my complete failure to perform well in school. So I came here. I thought I could buy my freedom with the prize money. Guess that wasn't such a great idea, either.'

'We'll get away,' I say. 'I bet Winston can hack that shuttle.'

'Probably.' She lifts her eyes to mine, her expression unreadable. 'But I suppose if I die, that won't be so bad. At least I can't disappoint my dad any more.'

'Bex . . .'

She interrupts before I can go on. 'We're leaving in shifts. Raya first, then Winston, and then me. Raya needs to believe

Evie's asleep.' She turns to leave but stops and glances back at me. 'I'm sorry you didn't get a chance to play. I would've enjoyed watching you compete.' Giving me a small wave, she walks away, shoulders hunched, head bowed.

I hold out my hand, ready to call her back, but don't. The water's past my ankles now, cold and cruel. I stare at the darkening horizon, Bex's words haunting me: *I wanted to confront him . . .* I never knew how to confront Dad without putting Mom in danger. So, a year ago, I sat in his office, waiting for him to come home from another night of carousing, a modified stunner gripped in my hands and the retinal security scanners attached to the front and back doors disabled so he'd have to climb in through the window.

It'd been so easy.

But everything's easier in the dark.

14

RAYA

It takes forever to go dark, especially because there's nothing to do but lie here, pretending to sleep. I stretch my arms over my head, stiff from not moving. I can't wait to get off this damn island and find me some nice mountain to live on. Or maybe a place that's completely flat so you can't go falling off edges and things. Somewhere there's no Evie.

I can't figure out why Bex wants her to come with us. It's too big of a risk. I've got to teach that girl she doesn't have to be nice to everyone.

I flop on to my side and study her – it doesn't matter that she's as dirty and rumpled as the rest of us, she's still the richest person in the whole damn quadrant. So why does she want to be my friend? I can't give her anything she doesn't already have.

But she doesn't actually seem to want anything, and that feels good in a way I didn't know was real. She even wants Zircon to live with us – talk about perfect. In exchange, I'll teach her dad a thing or two while I'm there.

Nobody messes with my friend.

'Raya?' Bex whispers.

I jump at her voice. 'Yeah?'

'I think it's time.'

Evie's eyes are shut, but I'm not convinced she's really sleeping. 'Let's give it five,' I whisper.

'OK.'

Shifting, I stare at the remains of the fire – it's all calm and peaceful and beautiful. That's been the only good thing about this whole crap game . . . trap . . . whatever the hell this is – getting to see all these new trees and bushes and the ocean and even a real live fire.

Zircon would love this place. I smile. Never thought I'd like a dog, especially one as fancy as Zircon, but he grows on you.

The first time I saw Zircon, Evie was swaggering down the street with him, smug as anything. She was wearing these crazy shoes that kept changing how they looked and clothes that cost enough to feed us miners for a month, but that was nothing compared to Zircon. She had dressed that poor dog in this black-and-white outfit complete with a bow tie and diamond-studded collar around his neck. It's a wonder he could hold his head up.

After that, every time I spotted Evie, Zircon was either in her arms or trotting behind her in another stupid outfit. Course Zircon wasn't his name yet – Evie'd given him some stupid, pompous name like Prince Bertrand Charles III. He's never said so, but he likes Zircon better.

The wood shifts, sending smoke and cinders into the air, the fire slowly dying. I bet me and Bex can take the shuttle straight to The Moons to get Zircon. We just got to avoid the Justice Seekers – they love punishing us miners. Evie'd help them if she was with us. And blame the murders on me.

Anger flows through me like melted ore. You'd think her dad being beat up would've made her rethink how she treats us. Says something when none of the miners turned in the guy who did it. The reward money was huge, but we all hated Evie's dad more. That man was a mean bastard, pretending he was for our cause when he was pocketing the little we made and letting us starve. And he did nothing when his wife killed Old George! So Evie's dad deserved a little justice, served up miner-style.

A smile creeps on to my face. I gave Evie a little justice of my own.

Every evening, when Zircon hung out in Evie's yard, I'd bring him a bone from the butcher's dumpster. The best bone I could find. And I'd pet him and talk all kinds of nice to him. Evie didn't do that for him – he was just a prop for her, something else to make her look special.

Guess that's why he had no problem coming with me. Evie was busy talking to who knows who outside a shop and ignoring her dog, who was staring at the shop window bored as anything. I clicked my tongue and held out a bone. We'd disappeared before Evie realized what'd happened.

I was going to leave him in some abandoned mine to make his own way, but he's on the small side, and super helpless thanks to Evie. Plus, once the missing posters went up an hour later, I had to make sure Evie didn't get him back. She took someone I cared about, so it's only right I did the same to her.

I roll over and stare at the sky. Zircon turned out to be pretty OK – even though he loves steak, and that takes some work getting. But he's worth it.

I used to break into the butcher's shop to get him the very best. Until the butcher hired a guard. After that, I checked out Old Josephine Harris's house. She was the meanest, stingiest, richest person on The Moons, even richer than Evie, and I knew she'd have food 'cause I'd seen her ordering meat often enough. I just didn't know how much.

She lived in this massive, salmon-pink house that stood taller and wider than any other dwelling on The Moons. And her kitchen – there's no words. Her pantry was bigger than some of the caverns in the mines and filled to the brim with food. On the back wall there were four freezers and three fridges, also stuffed full of anything and everything. Including the best kind of steaks.

I broke into her house a couple of times a week to get food for us. Not just steak, but ground beef and eggs and chicken and anything else I could fit into my sack. Zircon loved it all. I even brought him a cake once. It was yellow on the inside and the frosting was white and fluffy and sweet. It was the best thing I'd ever tasted. Same goes for Zircon too – I kept finding icing in his fur for a long time after that.

I rub my arms, suddenly cold. How'd that voice known what I'd done to Old Josephine? Even the Justice Seekers didn't figure it out.

Everything went wrong the day she decided to come home early and found me digging through her freezer. I guess she forgot something, not that it mattered. All that mattered was that she was in her kitchen, and so was I.

She started yelling and grappling for her digicell to call the Justice Seekers, demanding I give her the bag. But there was no way I was going to let Zircon starve. And I couldn't go to jail, or worse, the bottom of the lake – there'd be no one to take care of him.

So I grabbed my blade and told Old Josephine to let me go. She didn't move. I can hit a bullseye ten metres away and Old Josephine was maybe a metre in front of me, screaming her fool head off. I panicked and threw too hard. The knife got so buried in her neck it was hard to pull out.

And the blood.

Once that knife came out, blood went everywhere, including all over me. I grabbed the sack of food and ran, being super careful not to step in the red puddles pooling on the floor. I kept running 'til I got to the lake. I stuffed my clothes and gloves into my boots and weighted them down with rocks before throwing it all into the water. They were good boots, too.

I prop myself up on my elbow and check out the camp. Evie's curled on her side now, eyes closed, mouth open a little. Zane and Winston are watching me, eyes shiny in the dim light. We're leaving in shifts. First me, then Winston, then Bex, and then Zane.

Won't Evie be surprised when she wakes up? Wish I could leave her a note telling her it's payback for beating that miner to death. She deserves to be stuck here forever.

'Ready?' I whisper to Bex.

'Yeah,' she murmurs. Winston and Zane both nod.

'Let's do it.' I inch my way across the beach, staying low and trying to erase my footsteps as I go. There's no way I'm risking Evie waking up after all this.

It's silent and dark in the forest, but I'm used to being in places where there's very little light. A miner's life is all about slipping through the shadows.

I reach the shuttle, which shimmers a bit in the starlight, and excitement dances through me. Winston had better be able to make this thing fly.

'Wow!' he says from behind me, a minute later. 'How'd you find it? It looks as though it's been here for a while; I hope it works.' He runs his finger over the keypad. 'This is a basic security keypad. It probably uses a four-digit code. Which means there are 14,641 different possibilities, unless repeated numbers aren't allowed, then there are only 7,920 possibilities which is better, but not great.'

My heart sinks with each and every word. How the hell are we supposed to figure out the code with that many numbers involved?

'How's it going?' Bex jogs over to me, breathing hard, sweat trickling down the sides of her face.

'Not –'

'Great!' Winston's all happy and shit, like he's already figured out how to open the damn thing.

'Can you hack it?' Bex asks.

'Yes.'

'There's no way you can hack that,' I say. 'You said there's –'

Winston's still grinning, showing off all his teeth, and I clench my fists. I want to punch that damn smile right off his face.

'It doesn't matter if there're a million combinations. I only need a . . .' He drops to the ground and starts digging through the leaves, squinting in the dim glow of the stars.

'You need a what?' Bex asks.

'I need a stone or something with a thin edge.'

I slip my hand into my pocket – should I let them know I have a knife?

'Will this work?' Bex holds up what looks like a bit of shale.

Winston shakes his head. 'Close, but it's a little too thick.' They search again and a moment later Winston shows Bex a shard so perfectly formed it almost don't look real. 'This should do.'

He runs a finger along the edge of the keypad and puts the stone there. 'Excellent, it fits. Now, all I have to do is . . .' He stops talking as he jiggles the stone back and forth until the keypad comes loose. 'Perfect. Want to do the honours?' he asks Bex.

'Seriously?'

'Absolutely.' Winston steps back and gestures for Bex to take his place. With a grin, she grasps the keypad and pulls.

I tap my foot, keeping an eye out for anyone who's not supposed to be here, even though it's dark as all-get-out. Even the stars seem dimmer than they were. And where's Zane? Of all people, I didn't think he'd be the one to get lost.

'Got it!' Bex holds the cover over her head like a trophy.

Winston claps, and I roll my eyes – those two sure do feed off one another.

'Great job!' He lurches forward, like he was planning on giving her a hug or something weird like that, before jerking to a stop and turning to the control panel – probably to hide his embarrassment.

'You see this wiring?' he squeaks. 'If you know what you're looking at, you can easily rewire the whole thing.'

'It's that simple?' Bex leans in to watch like she's going to become a hacker herself.

'Yeah.' Winston reaches for the wires like he's done this a million times. 'You have to be careful so you don't electrocute yourself. And, if you don't connect things in the right order, the alarm will go off and the whole shuttle goes into emergency shutdown, which would be bad. So, what I'm going to do next . . .'

I stop listening. I can't take it. Maybe there'll be tape onboard and I can stick his mouth shut. Or I'll push him out of the shuttle once we're in the air. Wouldn't that be nice? Don't think Bex would be too happy, though.

'Got it!' Winston does a weird little dance, but the shuttle looks exactly the same as when we found it.

'Nothing's happening,' I say.

'Hold on,' Winston says.

A moment later, there's a soft hiss as the doors slide open.

15

BEX

I tense, convinced someone's going to crash down the gangplank yelling and screaming, ready to kill us all. But no one does. Instead, the lights flicker on and the shuttle sits there, as if welcoming us home. I don't know if I want to laugh or cry or cheer. We're finally leaving! Tears of relief prick my eyes. I didn't think I'd make it off the island alive. That any of us would.

Winston pauses at the top of the ramp and scans the trees behind me. 'Isn't Zane coming? I thought he was after me.'

'Not here.' Raya's halfway up the ramp. 'Is the shuttle empty?' she asks.

'Of course it's empty.' Winston's surprise at her question is evident – I didn't tell him about our killer-on-board theory. I swipe away the bead of sweat sliding down my face – what if the murderer's hiding out-of-sight?

'Then let's go.' Raya steps past him, hand in her pocket. When no one rushes her, my heart slows to something resembling normal. I step on to the platform – we're going home.

'Shouldn't we wait for Zane?' Winston asks. 'Maybe he's lost . . . and what about Evie?'

Raya swivels so she's facing us. 'Evie's not coming and it doesn't matter that Zane's not here. We're leaving now.'

I glance at the forest, my relief dissolving like salt in water – where are they?

'You're sure Evie's not coming?' Winston asks. 'And I don't think we should leave Zane behind. I mean . . .' His voice trails off as Raya's glare intensifies.

'I said we're leaving,' Raya snaps. 'Go see if you can fly this thing.'

Winston's gaze darts between the trees and me, his mouth moving as though he wants to say more, but then he just heads inside.

I turn to look at the forest, staying focused on the trees, determined not to miss a thing, but there's no movement or sound coming from them.

'Come on, Bex!' Raya calls from inside the shuttle. 'Winston's figured out how to turn it on.'

'Coming,' I call back, but I don't move. I won't leave them behind.

'BEX!'

I ignore her, my stomach sinking with dread. Did Evie kill Zane on the way here? Was Raya right all along? I wipe my palms on my leggings. What if I got Zane killed and we're next? Why do I always make the wrong choice –

'What do you think you're doing?'

I jump as Raya appears next to me. 'Watching for Zane and –' I stop abruptly.

She crosses her arms. 'And what?'

I turn away so she can't see my expression. 'And wondering where he is.' What will Raya do when she sees Evie? Or worse, when I tell her I'm the reason Zane's dead. 'Do you think something bad has happened?' I'm aiming for casual, but my voice ends on a high, squeaky note.

'I think I don't care. Winston's ready to power this thing up. Let's go.' She stalks back to the shuttle.

I start to follow, stop, and turn back towards the dark, looming forest.

I can't do it.

I can't leave them behind even if it means Raya leaves without me. Or Evie jumping me. At least I'm bigger than her. That has to count for something. 'Sorry,' I whisper, abandoning the shuttle.

'Bex!' Raya shouts.

I break into a jog.

Running footsteps follow me, and a small hand lands on my shoulder as I reach the jungle. 'You're not going in there.'

'I'm not leaving him behind.'

'Then you're not going in there alone – you'll end up dead.'

There's no chance I heard her right. 'You're coming?'

She pauses before saying, 'Someone's got to make sure you don't get yourself killed.'

A smile creeps across my face as hope flutters over my fear like a butterfly over a flower. For a moment, everything is OK.

Raya turns to the shuttle. 'Hey, Winston! We'll be back. Don't you dare leave without us!'

Her words scatter the bit of happiness lingering in my chest, and I cast a worried look at the shuttle. 'Would he do that?'

'No. He likes you too much. Besides, he'll be sorry if he does.'

Before I can ask her how she plans on making him sorry if he's in space and we're stuck here, Zane bursts through the trees, a new scratch on his forehead and twigs and leaves stuck in his hair.

'Sorry I'm late,' he says between breaths.

Raya eyes him. 'You're lucky you didn't miss your ride.'

Zane rubs the back of his neck, and a leaf falls from the collar of his shirt. 'I'm sorry, I took a wrong turn.' His eyes focus on something behind us.

Raya tracks his gaze, her face morphing into a mask of fury. 'Oh hell no!'

Winston's helping Evie into the shuttle, saying something I can't hear.

Evie smirks at Raya and makes a rude gesture before disappearing inside.

'You're not going anywhere!' Raya yells, running to the shuttle.

Zane and I race after her, casting worried glances at each other.

'Get out!' Raya's in the doorway, pointing at the forest. 'You're not welcome.'

Evie's lips curl into a sneer. 'You don't get a say.'

'I found the shuttle, I decide who comes, and I say you're not coming.'

'Raya,' I say. 'We can't –'

Raya turns on me, flying down the ramp, black eyes blazing. 'It was you!' She jabs me in the chest, and I stumble back. 'You told her about the shuttle behind my back. And you were –'

Zane interrupts. 'It was me. I'm the one who told her.' I stare at him, gratitude and surprise radiating off me. 'Thank you,' I mouth, the words nowhere near adequate.

'Well, she's not coming.' Raya tries to stare Zane down, and I'm pretty sure she's deciding if she can take him on. And then what? Do I leave him here after Raya's kicked his butt? Or stand by my decision and let Raya leave us all behind?

'I'm not getting off!' Evie calls out.

Raya whips around. 'I'll make you.'

Before she can charge back into the shuttle, Zane grabs her. 'You have to let her come, Raya. We can't leave her.'

'She's the killer!' Raya snarls. 'And you want her on the shuttle with us? I knew rich people were stupid, but you two give the word a whole new meaning.'

'I don't want her with us, not really,' I say.

'Could've fooled me the way you keep sticking up for her.'

'But we can turn her over to the authorities when we get home. Let them deal with her,' I say.

'Or we can deal with her here. Right now.'

'Please, Raya,' I beg. 'I don't want to be responsible for another death. Besides, what do you think the Justice Seekers will do to us if they figure out we left her here on purpose?'

'Bex makes a good point,' Zane says.

Raya looks between us. She's not going to back down.

I drop my gaze, uncertainty choking me. What will we do if Raya says no; if she's set on fighting Evie? Force her on board and tie her to a chair? That'll be one heck of a struggle.

'Fine,' she finally spits. 'But don't let her near me.'

'Agreed.' Zane releases her.

Raya marches up the ramp, shoulders straight, head high, hands clenched into fists.

'Thanks,' I whisper, still in shock Raya agreed. 'You didn't have to do that.'

'I did. I'm not completely sure I could win a fight against her.'

I fiddle with my shirt. 'I meant for taking the blame.'

He shrugs. 'It was nothing.'

It was so much more than nothing, but I don't know how to tell him that so I stare at the shuttle instead. I should head inside, but my feet won't obey. I'm still not convinced it's real – still not sure how it ended up here. But does it matter? Two days ago everyone was alive and ready to play a stupid game, and now ... now only five of us are left. Who cares how the shuttle got here as long as it gets us off this island?

Hoping for some sense of normality to wash over me, I ask Zane, 'What are you going to do when you get home?'

'I don't know. Convince my mom to let me get a job instead of get married? You?'

I shrug. 'I have no idea.'

A high-pitched whine turns into a smooth rumble as the shuttle powers up.

'We'd better go.' Zane's gazing at it with a look of incredulity I'm sure is mirrored on my face.

'You should board first.'

'Why?'

'Because Raya might leave you behind.'

He laughs, the sound rich and warm. 'You're that positive she won't leave you stuck on this island?'

'Yup.' I'm giddy with excitement at the prospect of Raya coming home with me. It'll be like having a sister. Another ally in a place where I'm so desperately alone. 'She likes me. But you . . . well, I wouldn't count on that helping you out.'

Zane laughs again, eyes bright, the smudge of dried mud on his cheek adding a charming touch. He'll do well when he's sworn in as a councilman – and maybe he'll make some changes on Rikas that will actually make a difference.

'She likes me, too,' he says as he strides up the ramp. 'At least more than Evie.'

I snort. 'That's not difficult.'

Zane tosses me a smile over his shoulder before disappearing inside.

I follow, and it's like I'm entering a dream even though it's only a sparse, functional little machine – nothing like the luxurious shuttles Dad owns or the public transport shuttle I took to El Nar. But I don't care. It could be filthy and smelly with no seats and I'd still take it – anything to escape this island.

Pairs of seats upholstered in grey fabric line each side and the pilot's seat, which just about swallows Winston whole, sits confidently in the front. A row of black, nylon loops hang from the ceiling so people who are standing have something to hold on to. The floor is carpeted in a thin, black material that does nothing to cushion the metal it's concealing.

But, despite its lack of amenities, the shuttle pulses with freedom and life like a heart resuscitated. I open a door on the side wall to find a small storage closet with thirteen light-brown pressure suits hanging in a straight row and a small, red cryogel cooler with protein packs and bottled water on the floor. The other door opens to reveal a toilet and sink.

I have to stop myself from jumping for joy. A toilet! No more squatting in a grove of trees hoping the leaf I'm using for toilet paper doesn't cause a rash or something worse, like death. I push the small button next to the faucet and water gushes out.

I could faint with happiness.

'Done sightseeing?' Raya asks as I wash my hands.

'Almost.' I shake my hands, the excess water dotting the sink and walls. 'Now I'm done.' I stare at my clean skin like it's one of the five wonders of the quadrant.

'I think I've figured out how the autopilot works,' Winston says. 'Sorry it took so long. I've never flown a shuttle before although I've read about it in books –'

'Can you do it?' Raya interrupts. She's positioned herself in the back, away from Evie and Winston. It's probably safer for all of us that way. I sit across from her.

The tips of Winston's ears turn pink. 'Of course, sorry. Everyone buckled?'

'Yes!' we say as one.

'Then we're off!' He turns around, and I hold back a cheer as he touches the small screen in front of him. Gripping the straps of my harness, chest heaving and stomach flipping, I close my eyes and let out a long, slow breath.

'We did it,' I say in disbelief. 'We survived.'

'Of course we did,' Raya says with a grin. 'Did you –'

The shuttle jolts and shudders. I bolt upright and am stopped short by the harness. 'What was that?'

'I forgot to turn off the locking mechanism, sorry about that. Such a simple thing, you'd think I would've thought of it . . . there.' The rumble of the engines increases as the shuttle lifts into the air.

'You said you could fly this thing!' Raya yells as the shuttle lurches and shakes again.

'It's the trees. I thought we were clear of them –' The roar of the engine slows and sputters.

I was wrong. We're going to die on take-off. It's another trap and we were all stupid enough to fall for it. I shut my eyes, heart pounding as I wait for the inevitable crash or explosion.

'Wait a moment . . .'

I peek through my eyelashes. Winston's bent over the screen as the shuttle wobbles in the air as though it's not sure it wants to stay there.

'There we go!' The engines roar back to life and the shuttle lifts with surprising speed. I don't stop holding my breath though – this thing could still explode.

'We're OK.' Winston flips a switch, and the large screen that lines the front of the shuttle flickers to life. 'Give me a minute to adjust the brightness.'

He changes the settings so it's as bright as daylight outside, making everything clear. I stare as the tops of the trees shrink and, as we rise, the entirety of the island comes into view. The breath I've been holding slips past my lips, slow and shaky.

We're going to be OK.

I lean in closer as the island shrinks below us, a memory gnawing at the corners of my brain. I swear I've seen this place before. But where?

'What the hell are you doing!' Raya shouts.

My eyes pop open. Evie's lunging at Winston and Raya's throwing herself at Evie.

'Let . . . me . . . go!' Evie elbows Raya in the chest before shoving in front of Winston, who does nothing but stare in shock.

'Stop!' I fumble with my own harness, panic making my fingers slow and clumsy.

'What are you doing?' Zane struggles to reach the pilot's chair as the shuttle bucks and jerks.

'Getting rid of her!' Evie yells.

'How?' Raya sneers. 'By –' Warning lights flash red as a siren blares.

A quick jolt throws Zane backwards. 'Winston, stop her!' he yells, but Evie's fist makes contact with Winston's face, and he slumps over in his seat.

'CARGO DOORS OPENING,' a cool robotic voice says.

Raya lunges for Evie. 'What'd you do?'

Evie ducks behind Winston, hugging the base of his seat as the shuttle tosses Raya to the floor. Zane grapples for a loop, barely stopping himself from falling.

'CARGO DOORS OPENING,' the voice repeats in the same dull, monotonous tone.

'Come on.' My harness refuses to unbuckle. I glance at the window – we're still climbing, but not fast enough to exit the atmosphere. My stomach plummets. We're going to crash.

A sudden drop in pressure yanks me against my seat. 'Do something!'

Zane stumbles back, still gripping the loop as Raya flies past him, scrambling to hold on to something.

'Raya!' Zane grabs for her with his free hand.

Her fingers brush his, but it's not enough. She tumbles closer to the gaping doors.

I finally slip out of the harness and am sucked towards the back. Terrified, I clamber for a loop, my shoulder wrenching when I grab it. I reach for Raya. She's grasping at a metal seat base, eyes wide with terror.

I will not lose her.

Adrenaline pumping through me, I let go of the loop and wrap my arm around the harness strap and reach.

I'm too late. Raya's fingers slip from the base.

I dive and grab her, my hand gripping her wrist. My triumph is short-lived as the shuttle tilts back. Raya's feet slip over the edge. Then her legs. Panicked, I swing my foot at a chair base and miss. Fear squeezes the air from my lungs as I try again and again, Raya sliding further out of the doors and bringing me along.

I'm jerked back as strong hands grab my ankles.

'Got you!' Zane yells.

He pulls again, dragging Raya and me up the aisle. We claw our way into a row of chairs, clutching loose harness straps and breathing hard.

'Winston!' Zane shouts. 'Close the damn doors!'

'Can't,' he grunts as Evie screams. She flies past me. I grab for her and miss.

'Get her!' I shout. For a second, Raya doesn't move. Then

she launches herself at Evie, grasping her fingers. I wrap my arms around Raya's waist and pull.

'Help me!' The words are scarcely out of Evie's mouth when she flies out the doors. I stare in horror at the empty sky as the back of the shuttle swings upward like a seesaw. I crash into the pilot's seat, Raya ramming into me a second later.

'Everyone!' Winston yells over the noise of the engines. 'Grab on to something!' I grip the base of the chair, shaking so hard I can barely hold on. Raya wraps trembling arms around me.

'CARGO DOORS CLOSING,' the robot voice says.

The shuttle lurches and stabilizes.

'Almost there,' Winston says. 'We should be –' A loud bang cuts him off, and the shuttle tilts forward.

We hang there for an eternity, suspended over the island.

The shuttle nosedives.

16

ZANE

I fly against the wall and bounce off, struggling to stay on my feet.

'Winston!' Bex cries out.

'Working on it!' He's hunched over the console, thankfully still strapped in. 'Evie must've done something. I'll find it. Give me a minute . . .'

The island's getting bigger every second – we don't have a minute. We'll be dead before Winston figures it out. I seize a loop to steady myself and aim for the next one. I stretch my arm out, but the shuttle jerks, and the loop sways sideways out of reach.

Frustrated, I grab at it and miss again.

We're running out of time. Taking a deep breath, I force my fear back. One . . . two . . . three. I launch myself forward – gravity propelling me at an alarming rate. My fingers close around the smooth material, and I jerk to a stop, wrenching my shoulder.

Ignoring the pain, I brace my feet so I don't go flying into the console, and reach for the last swaying loop dancing just out of range.

'Zane,' Bex gasps. 'Help!' Raya's on top of her as they struggle to get off the floor.

I glance at Winston and back at Bex, her eyes pleading with me to do something.

'Grab my hand!' I shout.

Raya swings and misses.

'Hold on.' Grunting, I shift and lean over as far as I can without letting go of the loop.

It's not enough.

Raya's face strains with effort as she stretches her hand out further.

I keep reaching . . . a few more inches . . . Bex pushes Raya, and Raya's slick palm meets mine. I yank her up, fighting against the downward pull of the shuttle, and shove her into a seat. 'Get buckled!'

I risk another glance at the screen. I can make out individual branches on the trees.

My heart leaps into my throat. This is it.

I reach for Bex, compelled to do anything that might help. She shakes her head. Pain shoots through my battered muscles as I struggle to get to her.

She doesn't even try to grab my hand. 'Save yourself!'

I almost laugh. There's no saving any of us from this. My eyes dart back to the screen, dread pummelling my senses. Any second now . . .

I reach for Bex again, desperate for human contact in these last seconds.

'Got it!' Winston shouts. The shuttle arcs up, and Bex tumbles into my legs, almost knocking me back. She rests against me, chest heaving. I don't move, my entire body tense and ready to spring back into action. Several long seconds later the shuttle's still stable, but I can't convince myself we're actually in the clear.

'Are we safe?' Bex asks Winston, as I help her to her feet, my hands shaking.

He's peering at the screen, his grin reflected in the glass. 'We're fine. I'm positive. When Evie overrode the controls so she could open the shuttle doors mid-flight she messed with –'

'Why would she do that?' Bex interrupts. 'She must've known it could kill her.'

Winston stares at his lap. 'After she triggered the doors to open . . .' He swallows hard and fiddles with his harness as though debating what to say. 'She went for the emergency tether.' He holds up a long, canvas strap with a latch on the end. 'It's for the pilot to use in case something happens to his harness or he needs to move around during an emergency.

'Anyway,' he takes a deep breath, 'she grabbed the tether, so I'm guessing she thought she could secure herself, but the latch is broken. See, it doesn't stay shut, so when she hooked it on her belt-loop she wasn't actually secure. Then she came at me again to stop me from closing the doors and . . . and . . .' Winston blinks rapidly, eyes fixed on the cargo doors. Long scratches run down his arms, and a bruise is beginning to appear on his jaw.

'It's not your fault,' I say. 'And you saved the rest of us.'

'Thank you.' Bex's voice is still shaky.

Raya brushes her curls out of her face, which is paler than normal. 'I don't care what happened, I just want to leave this place.'

'Me too,' Bex says.

'We all want to leave.' My heart refuses to stop racing. 'Winston, can you get us out of here?'

Winston bends over the control panel. 'That I can do. Buckle up, and I'll have us flying amongst the stars in no time.' He's trying to sound cheerful, but he's failing.

I squeeze his shoulder as though I believe we'll be fine, but doubt claws at me. What if something else goes wrong?

Winston interrupts my thoughts. 'OK, I think I've got it.'

'Great! Let's go home.' I limp to my seat, still not convinced we're going to make it off this planet. Not alive, anyway.

I flinch as I pull the harness over my shoulder, new aches making themselves known as adrenaline leaches out of my system. 'Are you OK?' I ask Raya and Bex as they finish buckling. They both look as haggard as I feel, and blood trickles from an angry gash on Bex's cheek. 'You might need a bandage for that,' I add.

Bex touches the cut and winces. 'If you're OK, then I'm sure I'm fine.'

'Do I look that bad?' I survey my own torn, dirty clothes and notice a few new bruises forming on my arms.

'Well, you're not going to win any beauty awards.' Raya's as beat up as Bex and me, and her arm's pressed against her chest as though it's injured.

'Is your arm all right?' I ask.

'Yup.' Raya tests the tightness of her straps, her face stiff as though she's struggling to hold an avalanche of emotions back. My own chest is heavy with the weight of everything that's happened, and although I manage to keep my expression calm, negative thoughts bombard me. What if the shuttle's another booby trap? What if we crash or explode mid-air? What if Mom never knows what happened to me? She'll be all alone, thinking I abandoned her. I blink back unexpected tears, shaking my head to dislodge the thoughts. This line of thinking never wins a game, and we're winning this one.

'Everyone ready?' Winston asks. 'Because, if you are, we can leave. I've set a course to the closest planet –'

Hope floods through me. 'You know where we are?'

Winston shakes his head. 'For some reason, there aren't any maps stored in the navigation system, or a log of our location. There is a listing of a few planets within flying distance, but they only have numbered designations. I even studied the star charts, but I don't recognize this sector.' He scratches his cheek. 'Which is odd, but I'll figure it out.'

'What about other cities or countries on this planet?' I ask.

Winston frowns. 'From what I can tell, the island is the only land mass here, which –'

'Makes it the perfect place to kill us,' I interject as the obviousness of it all crashes down on me.

'Damn,' Raya mutters.

Bex rubs her arms, eyes focused on the screen as though she doesn't want to think about what I said. 'Is the next planet habitable?'

Winston blinks and focuses on Bex. 'Don't know. There's very little information on the computer about ... well, anything to be honest. The data is noticeably lacking. There's

some system specs, general stuff, atmospheric controls . . .'
His brow furrows as he starts swiping through screens.

Bex leans forward, flinching as the harness presses into her. 'If the shuttle was put here by the killer –'

'Evie,' Raya interrupts.

'Evie,' Bex repeats. 'Then it makes sense she would've erased a lot of the information in case we found it.'

'True.' Winston's so engrossed in searching the files I'm not sure he's listening.

'What about communications?' I ask. 'That'd be a good place to start.'

Winston points to a red icon. 'They're down. Whoever messed with the shuttle –'

'Evie,' Raya says again.

'Knew what they were doing.'

I sigh, running a frustrated hand over my face. Why didn't I listen to Raya? She knew what Evie was, she had always known. And I should've been more suspicious after Evie told me why she killed that miner. Only a person with a complete disregard for life would murder someone to buy a pair of shoes, regardless of what happened to her dad and sister. Looking back, it's clear.

Evie gave Greyson the burger, she was the only one present when Paloma climbed on to that tree trunk, and she could've easily put the berries on the table for Maria to find, and killed Oscar while we slept. The truth was in front of my face and I ignored it.

Guilt wraps its cold, reproachful arms around me, squeezing tight. I could've prevented their deaths.

'I'm sorry, guys,' I say. 'For bringing Evie onboard.'

Bex studies a tear in her leggings, not meeting my eyes. 'It's OK.'

'Like hell.' Raya glares at me. 'If you'd listened to me instead of having to play hero –'

I raise my hands in surrender. 'I know, I know.'

Raya continues to scowl at me, and I brace for her next tirade of words. Instead, she slumps back in her seat and turns away. I want to say more, but I'm not going to risk Raya figuring out it was Bex's idea.

'Why do you think Evie did what she did?' Bex asks.

I shift so I can see her better. 'You mean try to kill us?'

'Yeah.'

'I don't know. I don't know why anyone would do that.'

'Because she was a bitch with a warped sense of what's owed her,' Raya says. 'And she enjoyed making people suffer. Trust me. I saw it a lot.'

'Still,' Bex says, 'this was a rather elaborate ruse. It took a lot of planning, and forethought, and –'

'Doesn't matter what it took,' Raya says. 'What matters is she's dead and we're leaving.'

I'm too tired to try to figure out why anyone would want to psychologically torture and kill people. 'How long until we reach the next planet?' I ask Winston instead.

Winston squints at the screen. 'Several hours at least. Hopefully not much more than that. But it gives us enough time to sleep. Since we have no idea what the next planet will be like, we need to make sure we have plenty of energy to find help and a way home.'

As he takes a breath Bex says, 'You should sleep too.'

Winston dismisses her concern with a wave. 'I'll be fine.

I'll eat a protein pack, and I'll be as good as new. Besides, I'm used to staying up late and not getting any sleep. It's what you have to do if you want to –'

'Good night,' Raya interrupts. She shifts so she's leaning against the wall, her legs stretched out on the seat next to her, and closes her eyes.

Bex manoeuvers around her seat until she's curled into a ball. 'Night. And thank you, all of you, for getting us off the island.' She brushes a stray tear off her cheek and rests her head on the arm of her chair.

'Are you sure you don't want me to stay awake with you?' I ask Winston, smothering a yawn.

'I'm sure. It's on autopilot, so even if I fall asleep it won't be a problem, although I'm not sure I can sleep after all that excitement. I know being tired is the body's normal reaction once the adrenaline's gone, but I guess I'm still too hyped up. And I want to make sure there aren't any more problems with the shuttle. I'm ready to go home.' He frowns and studies the floor. 'I can't believe it was Evie. I mean, she wasn't nice or anything, and she probably killed that homeless man, but still, to think someone planned all this . . .' He shudders and turns back to the screen.

*

The pull of the shuttle slowing jerks me out of a restless sleep.

'We're here,' Winston says. 'Wherever here is. There are a lot of mountains and forests so it took a while to find a safe place to set down, but now we've landed we can do a little exploring. Well, first we should put on the pressure suits.' He glances at the screen. 'For some reason the ship isn't giving me any information on whether or not this planet is terraformed or even suitable for humans, and we don't want to walk out and not be able to breathe and then we die and all this was for nothing.'

Raya rubs her eyes. 'We got it. Suits first, exploring second.'

Bex tugs her fingers through her hair, wincing as they catch in the tangles. 'Did you get the comms system working?'

'No.' Winston peers at the small screen. 'I tried, but still nothing. I wonder if the communications array is broken, or something like that.'

Bex's face falls – her disappointment matching my own. 'Oh. OK.'

Winston taps an icon. 'I'll keep working on it.'

'Turn on the large screen, would you?' I ask.

Winston's head pops up. 'Oh, yeah, sorry about that. I thought I had it up.' He touches the small screen in front of him again and the large screen flickers to life.

Raya leans forward, eyes huge as she surveys the landscape. 'Whoa.'

Whoa is right. We're sitting in the middle of a vast, empty plain rimmed with towering trees, their skeletal branches stretching heavenward like supplicants begging for mercy. In the distance, a large mountain range looms, wider than the view screen, the peaks disappearing into the clouds. Even the ground seems barren, its surface covered with a thin layer of frost.

I shudder as the despair looming over this place penetrates the shuttle and settles deep in my bones.

'Well, doesn't this look nice and homey?' Raya's staring at

the screen. 'It's worse than The Moons, and I never thought I'd see a place worse than The Moons.'

'Perhaps it's not as bad as it appears,' Bex says. 'We could always fly around and see what the rest of the planet looks like.'

Probably doesn't look like much, but I refuse to give up. 'That's a good idea,' I say. 'We might spot a settlement or something as well.'

Winston gazes at the screen. 'I didn't see anything in the initial flyover, but that doesn't mean anything, the mountains or trees could have shielded them from sight. But we should conserve fuel for now and search on foot. And, not to alarm or worry you, but the engines were acting up as we landed.'

My stomach sinks at his words. We have limited food and water and, if there's no oxygen on the planet, we only have a few days of air between the suits and the shuttle. 'What do you mean, acting up?'

'It's not a big deal.' Winston replaces the view of the outside with a schematic of the engines. 'If you look here, you'll see –'

'None of us can read that,' Raya says. 'Can't you explain it like a normal human being?'

Winston stares at her, blinking slowly, as though trying to figure out what she's asking. Finally he says, 'The engines made a grinding noise as we landed.'

Bex bites her lip and squints at the schematic. 'What does that mean, exactly?'

'Any number of things, really,' Winston says. He takes a deep breath, seemingly ready to plunge into another explanation, when his eyes drift to Raya. 'It means we should be fine but should also be prepared for trouble.'

Raya rolls her eyes. 'Well, isn't that the most helpful thing ever?'

A flash of anger crosses Winston's face – he's finally reached his limit with her. Before he can respond, I take charge. 'Why don't we put on the pressure suits and take a look outside? We could do a little exploring, wait for evening, and see if Winston recognizes any of the constellations. We can decide what to do from there.' It's not a fantastic plan, but it's better than sitting around waiting to die.

'Are you sure there isn't more information about where we are?' Bex glances at the cargo doors, brow furrowed. 'It seems like the computer should know, I don't know, something.'

Winston gives her an apologetic smile. 'I searched every file while you slept. I even managed to hack into a few areas Evie blocked off, but I didn't find anything important. We should do what Zane says. Who knows, we could find food or water. And, if not, at least we'll have a better idea of what's out there.' He pushes himself out of the pilot's chair and heads down the aisle with an authority he's never displayed before.

He opens the closet with the pressure suits. 'We should take notes too. For all we know, we're the first people to ever land here. We might even get naming rights. I've always wanted to name a planet. We could call it something cool, like Soldier Island.'

'That's a stupid name for a planet.' Raya reaches over Winston's shoulder and yanks a suit off its hanger.

Bex takes the suit Winston's holding out to her. 'Do you think we're so far out we're on an undiscovered planet?'

'I'm sure we're not that far,' I say. 'The transporter couldn't take us to an unknown place, not to mention that the shuttle isn't designed for deep space voyages. At most, we might be on one of the outer planets.' I pull the pressure suit on over my clothes, my muscles protesting the movement. 'Besides, Evie doesn't strike me as the type that'd want to take a long journey home.'

'I still don't understand . . .' Bex's voice trails off for a moment. 'Can we be sure it was her? Something seems off . . .'

'Of course it was her,' Raya says. 'And I'm glad she's dead.'

We all stare at her.

'What?' she says. 'Don't go pretending you all liked her or that you care that she died. She was trying to kill us – and nearly did, too.'

'We should eat before we leave,' I say before another argument breaks out. What's the point, anyway? I suspect we all secretly agree with Raya and don't want to admit it. 'I don't know about you guys, but I'm starving.'

Winston pulls out the cooler and gives us each a pack. 'There are four left after these.'

'Four,' Bex whispers. 'Like it was planned.'

I give her an encouraging smile. 'It's just a coincidence.' But now that she's said it, I can't get the thought out of my head.

'Zane's right,' Winston says. 'It's a coincidence.'

'Doesn't matter what it is at this point,' Raya says. 'Now eat, so we can leave.' She's already done with her pack. The rest of us eat ours as well. It doesn't take long.

Raya fits the helmet over her head, fiddling with it until it locks into place. 'At least we don't have to worry about watching our backs any more.' She marches to the doors.

My gaze drifts to the screen. While the planet appears lifeless, and rescue seems far away, worry seeps through my veins as I study the empty landscape.

What's lurking out there?

DAY FOUR

17

RAYA

Something's wrong with this place – it's too grey, too gloomy, too dead. And those trees are super creepy. Unnatural even. Wariness squeezes me, all tight and fierce, whispering in my ear:

Leave.

'Any readings?' Zane's voice crackles through the suit's comms.

'No. Nothing yet. But that doesn't mean it's not habitable.' Winston's holding his arm up to his face plate and studying the small screen built into the suit. It tells you all about the air and temperature and if your suit's OK or not. Apparently, it even tells you if you're about to die. Pretty useful if you ask me. Too bad none of ours are working.

Winston messes with the controls on the side of the screen. 'Since the internal comms are working, it means the entire system isn't broken. If you give me a minute, I'm sure I can figure out what's happening. Suits are harder to sabotage. You'd think it'd be the shuttle because then you wouldn't need the suits –'

I turn my comms off. It don't matter if we can breathe the air or if it's full of poison. We're not gonna be here long because there's no food or water. All we got to do is figure out where we are so I can get back to Zircon.

At least I no longer got to worry about Evie finding out her dog didn't run away. Last thing I needed was to go to jail because I took him. Or worse.

I tug on the sleeves of my suit – I hate this thing. Makes it impossible to go fast – especially since my body hurts every time I move, thanks to Evie trying to kill me. And this helmet. I run my finger along the rim, finding the latch, wanting to take it off. If I did, we'd know real quick if we could breathe or not. But what if my eyes pop out of my head or something? Old George once told me that things like that can happen if there's no air or atmosphere or whatever.

I jerk forward. Someone's trying to drag me along.

I yank out of their grip. 'What the –' They grab me again, pulling hard.

'Whatcha doing?' I struggle to get free. 'Let me go!' I dig my feet into the ground. The other two run ahead of us. Fast. Real fast. Like they seen a ghost.

I start to look behind me, but I'm hauled off again.

'What's going on?' I yell. They keep on running. Why is no one answering me?

My comms! I fumble with the switch.

'Why're we running?' I shout.

'Cat.' Bex's breath rasps against the speakers.

'Cat?' I twist until I see it. A huge white animal races after us. Its eyes are yellow apatite beams aimed straight at me, and I swear there's spit dangling off its fangs.

'Oh shit!' I jerk free. This time whoever's holding me doesn't resist. I keep running, and in seconds I've passed them all. The trees are only metres away. I risk a glance behind me. I got a good lead. And I only got to outrun one of them.

But I can't tell who's last. I know it's not Zane, and I don't care if it's Winston, but what if it's Bex? I go for my knife. Damn it, the suit!

The cat's closing in on ... someone. Who? My heart pounds so hard it echoes through my body. I'm not gonna let Bex die. But what if I die? My hand hovers over the zipper. To hell with it. I'm not afraid, and I'm not dying. Not today.

I unzip my suit and freeze for a second, waiting for my body to turn inside out or some shit like that.

Nothing happens.

I grab the knife. The cat's close, too close. Ready to pounce. Panicked, I throw the blade as the cat springs off its feet. The knife spins through the air, too low to hit where I need it to. I race towards the animal, ignoring the pain in my legs. I'll wrestle it to the ground if I have to.

The cat's mouth opens in a choked howl as it crumples to the dirt mid-jump. I leap, landing on its soft body. My knife's stuck in its belly. That's a nasty way to go – even for a cat as mean as this one. Long claws swipe at me. I dodge and yank the knife out with both hands, wincing as pain shoots through my arm. Blood spills on to the frost, turning it as red as rubies.

I thrust the knife up through the cat's ribcage, aiming for the heart. I don't know if the blade's long enough. I keep pushing. Please. Please be long enough. I don't want to die by cat.

I put all my weight behind the knife, shoving hard as I can. It slips in a little deeper.

There's a change. A shift in the air. I've seen it often enough to know I've won. The cat shudders and goes limp. The blade's buried to the hilt. I wait to make sure the cat's actually dead and not pretending. You always wait. But it doesn't move again. I let out a long, slow breath and zip up my suit again, in case I'm slowly dying and don't know it.

'Where'd you get that knife?' Zane asks.

I whirl around. All three of them are standing there, staring at me and the cat.

It's not worth explaining that only idiots walk around unarmed. 'It don't matter.' Standing, I wipe my hands on my jeans. It doesn't help – the blood smears all over me.

'T-t-thanks.' Winston's voice is shaking almost as bad as his body.

So it wasn't Bex who was in danger. What a waste of time. And now they all know I'm carrying.

'Do you want your knife?' Zane asks. He doesn't sound sure of himself, like maybe it's better if I don't have one.

'Sure.' I shrug as if it doesn't matter one way or the other and crouch in front of the cat. It takes several yanks before the blade slides out of the thing. I wipe it clean on the frost.

Winston's watching me. 'Where'd you learn to do that?'

I think of the guy Mom dated who taught me how to use a blade. He'd been a good one. The only good one in a long line of abusive bastards who used her and threw her away. But Mom had to go and cheat on him. She never could keep a good thing.

'The Moons. You got to eat somehow.'

'I don't recognize what kind of cat that is.' Bex is leaning forward like it'll help her see the animal better even though she's at least a metre away. Zane's not much closer, but Winston's hurrying over to the dead thing fast as anything, probably hoping to amaze Bex with more of his long-ass explanations.

While everyone's busy staring at the cat, I unzip my suit and slip the knife back into my pocket. Winston starts to speak and I fiddle with my comm switch, but I don't turn it off. I need to know if another cat decides we'd make a good snack.

'White fur, black spots . . .' Winston lifts the cat's lip. 'Large canines.' He picks up the cat's massive paw next and presses. Long claws slide out. 'It appears to be some variation of a snow leopard.'

'What's that?' Bex asks.

Winston steps back, his foot landing in a puddle of blood that's starting to freeze solid. I don't say nothing. If the animals on this planet enjoy the smell of blood, at least I won't be the only one covered in it.

'A snow leopard is a large cat from Earth. Similar to a tiger or a lion. Except snow leopards went extinct about six hundred years ago, so the settlers didn't bring any with them.' Winston leans over the animal again. 'But I don't think they were this big. And the canines seem off.'

Zane turns round and round, eyes darting this way and that. 'We need to get out of the open and make a plan.'

Winston nods. 'That's a good idea. We can figure out what to do when we're better hidden.'

'Do? There's nothing to do.' I wave my arm in a half circle to show how much nothing there is. But Zane either doesn't notice or doesn't care – he's already headed for the trees.

'There's nothing here but dead plants and killer cats. And probably other murderous things,' I call after him, but he doesn't respond. As much as I hate to do it, I ask Winston, 'Can't you fly us into space and take us somewhere else?'

He looks at me and then Zane, tugging on the sleeves of his suit. 'I don't know. There's only so much fuel left, and while we still have several hours' worth, if we don't know where we're going, and if we go in the wrong direction, we could be lost in space with no hope of anyone finding us. And we'd run out of food and oxygen so I think we should explore here first. I'm sorry.' Winston follows Zane, leaving bloody footsteps behind him.

'Hey,' Bex's voice whispers in my ear as we trudge after Zane and Winston. 'We need to talk.'

'We?' I glance at the guys. Winston's talking again from the looks of it, but I can't hear him. 'Something's gone wrong with my comms.' I reach for the button.

'Nothing's wrong,' Bex says. 'I'm talking to you on a private channel. I've muted the main one.'

'No way! You can do that?'

'Sure. It's simple. My brother and I used to do it so our parents couldn't hear us talking. He taught me how. He's super smart, like Winston.' She stops speaking for a moment, like maybe she's sad. I should put my hand on her arm, or pat her back, or something like that. I think that's what people do to make other people feel better. But before I can move, she's tugging me away from the other two like they can hear us.

'There's something I need to tell you about this planet. And the island.' She glances at Zane and Winston. Zane's finally stopped moving and he's standing with his arms crossed and head nodding as if he's actually considering what Winston's saying.

'What?' I ask.

She grips my hand. 'I figured it out on the shuttle, or at least I think I did, but then Evie died, and everything else happened, and I got distracted. But something Winston said reminded me.' She starts talking quieter. 'And if I'm right . . .' A loud gulping noise makes its way through the speakers. 'If I'm right, then we're in even bigger trouble than we thought. But I want to run it by you first because I might be going crazy.'

'What is it?' I'm having trouble holding my anger in – she's getting as bad as Winston.

'It's –' She glances at Zane, who's waving at us. 'Later,' she says as she fiddles with the controls on the side of the screen. A few seconds later, Zane's voice comes across the comm.

'. . . look around a little more.'

'What?' I ask.

'I said we're going to look around a little more before we head into the trees. See if there's anything we can eat or drink or use. Or if there's a settlement.' He sounds so hopeful. Like anyone would live in this cold, dead place.

I give him my meanest glare. 'That's the stupidest idea I've ever heard. You guys want to get eaten by another giant cat or something else then you go on ahead, but I'm not going to be some animal's lunch. We got to get back to the shuttle and hightail it out of here.'

'We should explore,' Bex says. I stare at her, shocked, but she doesn't seem to care. 'Zane's right. We may find something useful.'

'Seriously?' I shake my head. 'Y'all are crazy. And you sure don't know nothing about surviving. You've had things handed to you every damn day of your precious lives. I know you all think I'm stupid because I don't talk like you or act the same way, but –'

'I don't think you're stupid,' Zane interrupts. 'I've never thought that.'

'Me either,' Bex agrees. 'You're one of the cleverest people I know.'

'You're definitely not stupid,' Winston says. 'You have street smarts, you've survived The Moons, and I bet you know a ton about rocks and geology and how jewels are made and many other things.'

Surprise punches the words right out of my mouth.

Everyone's always assumed I was stupid because I was a miner – no one but Old George ever said I was clever, even though I am – you don't survive The Moons if you're not.

It takes me a moment to finish what I was saying. 'Just the same, I'm not hanging out here watching you fools tromp about wanting to get killed.'

'Raya,' Bex's voice cracks over the channel. 'Please come with us. We shouldn't separate.'

She sounds desperate. I'm about to tell her no, that I've been on my own my whole life and I don't need anyone's help, but the words don't come. I can't abandon her. She'll die out here without someone having her back.

I glance at Zane. He'd help her, but what if he's in trouble, too? It's not like Winston's going to step up and be the hero. I blow out my breath, annoyed. When did I start caring?

'Fine. Let's go get ourselves killed.'

*

After at least an hour of exploring we've only proved one thing: this place is as dead as it looks. At least we haven't been attacked by any more giant cats. Or anything else. Hell, there's nothing else here. No birds, no little ground animals, nothing that says anything other than that dead cat lives on this awful planet.

What a waste of time.

I cast a glance at Bex. She's staring at the ground as if she's expecting something to burst from it. Is that what she figured out? That there's some sorta underground monster that lives here? One that plans on eating us? I study the ground too, but none of the dirt's disturbed. What's she looking for?

I fiddle with my comms again, but I don't know how to make my own private channel and Bex hasn't said another word to me. That girl needs to learn to focus.

Zane stops and faces us. 'We should head back to the shuttle.'

'Finally,' I say.

'Oh!' Winston's surprised voice crackles over the speakers. 'It works!'

'What does?' Zane asks.

Winston holds up his arm. 'The suit. Told you I could figure it out if I had a little time. It wasn't that hard, actually. I doubt Evie knew what she was doing. If it'd been me I'd –'

'Can we take these stupid suits off?' I ask.

'Yes, absolutely. We can breathe the air. It's cold, though, so you should keep your suit on to stay warm, but if you want to lift your visor, that won't be a problem.'

Screw the visor. My fingers find the latch, and I unhook my helmet. It makes a small hissing noise before letting me take it off. The air smells good – cold, clean and crisp – not dead and rotten like I expected.

'Winston!' Bex cries out, her voice far away now my helmet's off.

I spin around. Winston's helmet is filling up with some sort of white smoke. He's saying something, but I can't hear him. I slam my helmet back into place.

Zane leaps forward, grabbing Winston's helmet and lifting. It don't budge.

I race over to them. Bex tries to help, too, but there's no room with me and Zane taking up all the space. She grabs his hand instead and starts telling him he'll be fine.

But Winston's eyes are wide with panic and fear like he knows it's a lie. He keeps trying to talk, but he can't stop coughing.

'Don't speak,' Bex says.

The helmet's stuck – we're not gonna get it off in time. I scan the area, spotting a large stick a few metres away. I sprint for it and scoop it up.

'We can break his visor!' I yell, waving the stick.

Winston's knees sag. Zane's still pulling on the helmet and Bex has taken my place, pulling too, but it doesn't seem to matter. Winston doesn't have long.

'You're not going to die!' I run faster. 'Don't be –'

The ground disappears beneath me.

18

BEX

Raya vanishes.

I stare at the empty spot, hands frozen on Winston's helmet, mind reeling. Where'd she go?

'Get her!' Zane's yell breaks me out of my stupor. 'I've got Winston!'

I race to where Raya stood seconds ago, skidding to a stop inches from a dark, gaping hole.

'Raya!'

'Down here!' she yells.

I lean over the edge, heart in my throat. Raya's gloved fingers grip a narrow ledge, her legs dangling over a bottomless pit.

I dive to the ground, on to my stomach. 'Grab my hand!'

Can I pull her up? What if she falls? I blink back tears.

What if she dies?

'I can't reach you,' Raya grunts. I creep further over the hole, the sharp edge pressing into my stomach, and try again.

There's at least a metre of space still between us.

Raya shakes her head. 'It's too far.' For the first time since we've met her voice trembles with fear.

'Don't give up!' I inch forward. 'I've got you.' I take a deep breath. I can't let her die.

Raya eyes my hand as though she's calculating the distance. I force my voice to be steady and strong. 'You can do it.' I try to reach further, make my arm longer – anything to get to her.

'OK.' Raya clenches her jaw and narrows her eyes. She swings towards me.

Our fingertips don't even brush.

Raya tries again. But she swings too hard and bangs against the side of the pit.

Her fingers slip.

'Raya!' I lunge to catch her, almost tumbling over the ledge.

I scramble back.

'Still here!' she shouts.

My breath comes in panicked gasps as I struggle to figure out how I'm going to save her. She's hanging on by one hand – her fingers grasping the dirt, her feet scrambling for purchase.

'Hold on!' I look around – there has to be a branch or something I can use to reach her. But there's nothing except Zane racing towards me.

'I can't reach her!' The words come out as a sob.

Zane peers over the edge. 'Don't let go!'

'Not planning on it.' Raya's voice is strained, but the sarcastic retort makes me laugh through my tears.

'I have an idea,' Zane says to me. 'But it puts you in danger.'

'I don't care. What do you need me to do?'

'Go over the edge.'

Uncertainty sweeps over me. 'What?'

'I'll hold your ankles. You grab her, and I'll pull you both up.' He gives me a wild look. 'Now. We don't have time.'

'Are you sure you can do this?'

'Absolutely,' he says with a confidence that leaves no room for doubt.

'You coming?' Raya yells.

'Yes!' I scoot towards the edge, ignoring the racing of my heart and the pit in my stomach.

I'd rather die with Raya than be the reason she dies.

Zane grips my ankles. 'I've got you.'

Raya watches me with wide eyes, face strained, fingers slipping as she struggles to maintain her grip.

I gulp as my hips slide past the edge. I'm almost upside down. Beneath me, there's nothing but a black, yawning hole and Raya's pale face illuminated in the glow of her helmet.

Zane inches me further down. 'Are you close?'

'Nearly there.' I focus on Raya so I don't freak out. 'A little more.' I grab her wrist in a tight grip. 'Ready?'

She nods. 'You better not drop me, Rich Girl.'

I give her the bravest smile I can muster. 'Never.'

She takes a deep breath and lets go.

'I've got her!' I yell. But for how long? Pain radiates up my arm and into my shoulder as I struggle to hold on. 'Pull us up!'

'Hang on!' Zane shouts. Dirt scrapes against my suit as I start to rise.

Raya's glove begins to slip.

'Zane! Hurry!'

He doesn't respond.

'Raya,' I whisper, near tears as the glove slips further off her hand.

'You're not going to drop me.' Her black eyes fix on to mine. 'You hear me? You're not going to drop me.'

'I'm not going to drop you,' I repeat.

'Promise.'

'I promise.' I choke on the words. The ground scratches against my hips . . . my stomach. I'm almost there.

She slips a little more. I grasp her fingers, struggling to grab her wrist with my other hand. 'Zane . . .' I plead, tears welling up. My weight is finally back on the ground. Only my arms still dangle over the pit.

Zane releases my ankles and is by my side in seconds.

Raya's fingers slip out of my hand.

'Raya!' I scream.

Zane lunges.

I force my eyes open, tears streaming down my cheeks. 'Raya?'

'Still alive,' she says as Zane hauls her over the edge.

I tackle her, wrapping my arms around her small frame, our helmets knocking together. 'I thought I lost you.'

She lets out a shaky laugh. 'It's not that easy to get rid of me.' Her arms wrap tentatively around me. 'Thanks,' she whispers like the word is unfamiliar.

'Any time.' I release her and sit back. 'Are you OK?'

'Arm's a little sore, but it's not bad.'

'Zane?' I ask. He's kneeling on the ground, palms resting on his thighs, taking deep, steadying breaths.

'I'm fine.'

I let out a sigh. We won this round. Now I need to find a way to tell them the truth about the island and this planet. 'Where's Winston?' I ask.

Zane's shoulders slump. He shakes his head.

'He's . . . ?' I don't want to say the word.

'I couldn't get his helmet off. I tried. I promise I tried.' He sits back, head hanging in defeat.

'It's OK,' I say. 'We know you did.'

'It wasn't enough. It's never enough.' He sits still for a moment and then raises his fist, slamming it into the ground in one, swift motion. 'Damn it!'

I glance over my shoulder. A little way off, Winston lies sprawled on the ground, a small, shiny brown mass on the frost. Grief and despair flow through me – this can't be happening. I close my eyes for a moment to gather myself before saying, 'We should see if there's anyone else here. A settlement, like you said.'

I have to get them away from here. Somewhere we'll be harder to see. And harder to hear.

'Seriously?' Raya asks.

'And Winston said the air's breathable, so we should save our oxygen,' I add. I don't care about the oxygen, I just need to talk to them without being overheard. I should've thought of that before I spoke to Raya on the private channel.

Zane runs his finger over the latch connecting his helmet to his suit. 'Winston was fine until he tried to take his off.'

'Mine's OK.' Raya lifts her helmet off her head.

'Maybe it was only Winston's suit and we'll be OK.' I sound about as sure as I feel.

Zane bites his lip, staring at Winston. 'I suppose we either take them off and possibly die or we eventually run out of oxygen and definitely die.' He places his finger back on the latch. He looks at us and flashes a humourless smile. 'I feel like a rat in a cage.' He presses the button.

I tense, waiting for gas to fill his helmet.

Zane slowly pulls it off, releasing a long breath when his head is clear. Relief floods his expression. 'OK. Now you.'

Squeezing my eyes shut as though that'll save me, I press the button, lifting the helmet off my head in slow, measured movements. Cold air hits my face and I laugh, holding my arms out wide.

'You're alive!' Relief fills Zane's voice. 'We're still alive.' He tucks his helmet under his arm. 'Let's return to the shuttle and find our way home.'

I shake my head, the air icy on my cheeks. 'We need to explore first.' I'm worse than a broken cleaning bot.

Raya cocks an eyebrow. 'You were serious about that? Are you nuts?'

'I have to agree with Raya,' Zane says apologetically. 'We need to figure out how to pilot the shuttle and get off this planet.' He pauses. 'Unless you suspect Evie sabotaged it?'

I grasp on to the idea like a drowning man clinging to a life raft. 'I do. Remember what Winston said about the shuttle making a weird noise? What if we can't lift off? Or the whole shuttle fills with gas? Or it explodes?' I try not to sound too eager. I lower my eyes and rub my arm to soothe the dull ache from holding on to Raya.

'I suppose it's worth looking around and seeing if we can build a shelter or find food before we mess with the shuttle,'

Zane says. 'That way we're prepared when night falls, whatever happens. If you're good with that, Raya?'

Raya's silent for a moment. I clench my fists. Say yes. Please say yes.

'Raya?' I prod. 'We can always go back to the shuttle later.'

'Why not?' she says. 'I'm feeling lucky.'

I have to stop myself from sighing in relief.

'Let's go.' Zane heads away from Winston.

'Wait,' I say. I study the horizon until I find what I'm searching for. 'We should go that way.' I point in the direction of Winston's body.

Zane furrows his brow. 'Why?'

'A gut feeling.' My voice squeaks at the end, giving away the lie.

Zane shoots me a critical look, as though he's going to argue with me, but something in my expression must convince him. 'Sure.'

I want to hug him for agreeing.

'Then let's go,' Raya says. 'There's no point hanging around here.'

'Should we move him?' I ask as we pass Winston.

'Why?' Raya asks.

'Because he's lying here, in the middle of nowhere – anything could happen,' I say.

'He's dead,' she says. 'He doesn't care.'

'But his family . . . I don't know . . . it doesn't seem right.'

'We could put him in the shuttle,' Zane says.

Raya plants her hands on her hips. 'You all were just talking about how it could explode and now you want to go and open it up?'

'I only meant if we turned it on,' I say.

'That's going to be one long walk,' Raya says. But she positions herself next to me, ready to help.

'Thanks.' I grab a leg. It doesn't bother me as much as it used to, which is disturbing in and of itself. I don't want to consider the bigger ramifications of what that means.

Raya grabs the other leg. 'I'm not staying around if something comes at us. He's not worth dying for.'

'Don't worry, if we get attacked we can throw Winston at whatever animal it is and run for it,' Zane says.

Raya and I stare at him and then burst out laughing. I laugh so hard I drop Winston's leg and bend over at the waist, gasping. Raya and Zane's laughter joins mine, ringing through the air, a bit hysterical.

Somewhere along the way, my howls of laughter turn into sobs. Deep, gut-wrenching sobs for everyone who's died; and for us, for the fact there's a good chance we're going to die, too. I sink to the ground. 'This is so messed up,' I say through my hiccups.

Arms wrap around me. 'It'll be OK,' Zane whispers. I can hear the tears in his voice.

'We're not giving up,' Raya says, fierce and determined like always. Her small arms slip around me as well, and I relax a little, giving in to my heartache. We sit there, crouched and holding on to one another, not moving, until our tears run dry.

'We need to go.' Zane wipes his cheeks and stands. He offers his hand to me and then to Raya. 'We don't know how long the daylight lasts here.'

I stand too, a strange sense of calm washing over me. 'What about Winston?'

'We can leave him here,' Zane says. 'He'll be OK.'

'All right.' I bend over and whisper to Winston, 'I'm so sorry. You didn't deserve to die.' Straightening, I head across the frost plain towards a dense grove of trees and don't look back.

*

'How much further are we going to go?' Raya asks as we wind our way around thick, dead underbrush, the branches snagging on our clothes and slapping our legs. Overhead, lifeless tree branches create a bone-like canopy, filtering the light into oddly shaped shadows that leap and shudder as we move.

I stop. 'This is good.' My nose and cheeks are numb from the cold air, and my breath comes out in little white puffs. I shouldn't have left my helmet behind.

'Here?' Zane studies the desolate landscape.

I glance at the trees that hopefully provide enough cover. 'Yes, here.' Grabbing a long stick from the forest floor, I start breaking it into little pieces. The sharp snaps echo around us.

'Whatcha doing?' Raya's staring at me as though I've lost my mind.

'Firewood,' I say.

'Wouldn't it be easier –' Zane starts.

'No,' I interrupt, pleading with my eyes for him to be quiet – it's imperative that we look and act normally. He raises his eyebrows but doesn't say anything.

'You should help me.' My voice isn't natural, and I grimace. Lying on the spot is a skill I've never fully mastered.

Zane gives me an odd look, but nods. 'Come on, Raya,' he says as he grabs a stick. For once, she doesn't argue.

I step closer to them and say in a low voice. 'The killer isn't dead.'

'I knew it!' Raya lunges for Zane.

Zane grabs her arms, struggling to hold her back. Raya jerks free and lands a swift kick to his stomach. He doubles over with a pain-filled grunt. Her fist flies towards his face.

'Raya!' I yank her back before her punch lands. 'It's not him!'

She rounds on me, fists up, practically snarling. 'You?'

'No!'

Her eyes narrow as she scans the trees, knees and elbows bent, always ready to fight. 'Then who?'

'Nobody.' I let out a forced laugh. 'You misheard me. More firewood?' I'm aiming for unconcerned, but I sound unhinged. I wipe the sweat off my forehead, trying to be inconspicuous. I should've known Raya would react like that—hopefully no one noticed.

'Sure . . .' Zane eyes me, hand on his stomach, face a little green.

Raya opens her mouth and I glare at her, giving the briefest shake of my head. She ignores me. 'Don't you –'

'Firewood!' I say through gritted teeth.

Shock and anger flit across Raya's face, but, to my surprise, she picks up another branch.

'Did you notice anything odd about the island?' I break a twig into pieces too tiny to use.

'No,' Raya says as Zane says, 'Yes.'

'No, there wasn't.' Raya grips a small branch and tries to snap it in two. 'It was perfect, like something out of a story.'

'That's because it was out of a story,' I say.

Raya raises the branch above her bent leg. 'What do you mean?' She whips it down, breaking it across her thigh.

'It's the same island as the one in a children's book about Earth. Every kid reads it in school.'

Raya snorts. 'Well, it's not like I went to school.'

Zane's mouth falls open, a half-broken stick dangling from his fingers. 'I remember that book. I read it in second grade. I even remember the island with the trees and beaches and . . .' His eyes widen. 'A cliff that rose above a dark blue lake. You're right. The island was an exact replica of the one from that book, wasn't it?'

'Yes.' I lean in closer, lowering my voice. 'And the red planet we saw on the horizon?'

'The one Winston was trying to figure out?' Zane asks.

'Yes. I think it's the emergency shut-off switch.'

'What the hell do you mean? How do you turn off a planet?' Raya asks.

'We're not on a planet,' I say. 'We never were.'

'Then where are we?' Raya says slowly and deliberately, anger simmering beneath each word.

'We're in a holo-theatre.'

19

ZANE

'You're joking,' Raya says in disbelief.

'I'm not,' Bex says.

While she explains her logic to Raya, I pace back and forth, counting to ten to ease the outrage and confusion tearing through me. How did I not see it? The strange quicksand, the absence of any living thing on the island, that odd giant cat that looked like a snow leopard – it all makes sense now. A holo-theatre with safe mode turned off – it's brilliant.

And terrifying.

If only I'd figured it out earlier. Determination sprints across my regret – I can do something about it now. 'Who do you believe is controlling it?' I fight the desire to look for the control room, even though it would be hidden in the program.

Bex glances around like she might be heard. Of course, there would be microphones everywhere, and cameras. She came into the forest because it was our best chance of not being seen.

'This may sound crazy,' Bex whispers, 'but what if it's Evie?'

'She's dead,' Raya says. 'She's not controlling anything.'

'I know, but . . .' Bex bites her lip. 'What if falling out of the shuttle didn't kill her because she didn't actually fall that far? What if it was a ruse designed to make us think she was dead?'

Raya and I stare at her. Is it possible? A holo-theatre tricks the mind into believing all sorts of things, including falling long distances. There are numerous studies showing that death is possible if the brain is properly manipulated. 'I don't know . . .' I picture Evie flying out of the back of the shuttle and shudder. 'Her fear seemed real. And even if the fall didn't kill her, the murderer could've easily done so when she landed.'

'You're right,' Bex backtracks. 'Like I said, it was a crazy idea. But if whoever is running this realizes we've figured it out . . .' Bex rubs her arms, fear flickering across her features. 'Well, we'll be in real trouble.'

Raya stares at her feet as though she expects the ground to disappear beneath them again. 'So they can kill us whenever they want? Make another hole open up, or have a tree fall on us, or a huge cat eat us, or whatever?'

Words a holo-theatre tech said to me years ago float through my memory. 'Kind of. There's a pre-compiled program that can't be changed mid-process. So you either stepped on a trigger or whoever's in the control room saw that you were in the right vicinity for them to activate the hole.'

Bex's eyes widen. 'The branch!'

'What branch?' Raya asks.

'The branch Paloma was holding on to before she fell disappeared for a second – I thought I was seeing things, but it was probably designed to do that. And the fruit!' Bex bounces on the balls of her feet. 'Remember Evie said there was fruit on the tree? What if it was put there to lure one of us out over the lake?'

Shock reverberates through me.

She's right.

'So you're saying this whole damn place is one giant, digitized booby trap?' Raya shifts her gaze to the trees surrounding us, bleak and grey and ever repeating.

Foreboding creeps through the shadows and pricks at my skin. 'Maybe,' I say, even though the answer is probably a firm yes. 'It's impossible to know for sure.'

Raya throws her hands up in the air. 'Isn't that great. And what about the cat? Was that another booby trap?'

'Not a booby trap, per se, but I think it can still kill us.' Bex's voice trembles on the last word, as though she's fighting to stay in control.

'How can a fake cat kill us?' Raya's gaze darts between Bex and me, like she can't decide if we're lying.

'Holo-theatres use force fields for interaction,' I say. 'Each building, animal or whatever is programmed with a certain amount of force around it so we don't fall through it when we interact with the holographic world. If that cat was programmed with a high enough level of force, it could have crushed us with its paws, its body, or even its jaws.'

Raya glances around the forest. 'But not eat us?'

'Not that I'm aware of.' I look at Bex who shrugs, no more sure than I am.

Raya grabs another stick and whacks it against a tree like she's testing my theory. 'Then how'd Paloma die?'

'You can turn off the oxygen in holographic bodies of water,' Bex says. 'Professional swimmers train in holo-theatres all the time, and being able to turn off the oxygen simulates a real pool.'

'What about falling? What if Bex is right and it's Evie?' Raya asks. And, before I can answer, adds, 'And how the hell did I kill that cat if it's not real?'

'Holo-programming manipulates the mind into believing certain things are happening, like falling or walking long distances. As for the cat . . .' My eyes dart to Bex, but she seems as perplexed as me. 'I'm not completely sure. Perhaps it's programmed to "die" if certain conditions are met, like in VR games, or maybe whoever's orchestrating all this still believes they have us fooled so they allowed the cat to die? But if they realize we know the truth then there'll be no reason for them to turn the next animal off . . .'

'And so it crushes us or whatever,' Raya finishes for me.

'That's not going to happen,' I say with a confidence I no longer feel.

'Then what's your plan, Rich Boy?' Raya asks. 'Because I'm not becoming some fake cat's fake meal.'

A cold breeze rushes through the trees, its icy fingers heightening the dread settling over me, making it impossible to think.

'We can still escape,' Bex whispers.

'How?' Raya demands.

Bex starts to look over her shoulder then stops. 'We need to get to the emergency shut-off switch, which you can just see through the trees behind me. If we can turn off the program, we'll be able to find the exit.'

'But whoever's watching is going to kill us before we get to it,' Raya says before I can respond to Bex's brilliance. 'Unless we kill them first.'

'No,' Bex says. 'They won't be able to. When my family went on holo-adventures, the attendants always showed us where the switch was and said we could turn off the program in an emergency or for any other reason. It automatically alerts the front desk if there's a problem, and they'll send help.'

'I'm not so sure that's the case,' I say as the problem unfolds in my mind.

Bex stares at me. 'Why not?'

'Let's keep walking,' I whisper, 'so we don't seem suspicious.' Once we've gone several metres, I continue, 'We've been in here for days. Someone had to rent out the theatre to ensure no one would find us. What if they also paid to staff it with their own people?'

'You think there's more than one person doing this?' Bex slows. 'Why?'

'Because this would be incredibly difficult for one person to pull off. The holo-theatre has to be manned at all times. Or it should be. What if something glitched while the murderer was in here killing Oscar or setting up the berries? They'd have to have a backup.'

'Great,' Raya says. 'So we're dealing with a whole bunch of crazies?'

'Probably only two or three,' I say, like that's a better alternative.

Bex buries her face in her palms. 'Why are they doing this?'

I sigh in defeat. There's no point hiding the truth any more. I'm not sure why I ever believed I could.

'Because someone has a strange sense of justice.' I study my boots, not wanting to see the look on their faces at my confession. 'I killed my dad. On purpose.'

'What?' Raya exclaims.

Bex drops her hands. 'Why?'

I make myself look them in the eye. 'He was a bastard. Used my mom as a punching bag, gambled away all of our money, drank a ton, stuff like that. So one night I disabled the retina scanners on our doors and waited for him to break in through a window. And then I shot him and told everyone I thought he was a robber and that I didn't know the stun gun had been modified.' I pause to regain control of my voice. 'I was trying to save my mom. She did everything she could to give me a great life despite my dad, and I wanted to give her that in return.'

I clench my jaw, ready to defend myself further, but no one says anything as we trudge deeper into the forest, the silence engulfing us in its malignant arms.

'I killed that old lady.' Raya's voice shatters the quiet.

'You did?' Bex says. 'On purpose?'

'It's not like I planned it or nothing. I'd broken into her house before, to get food for me and Zircon. She had a ton, more than any one person could eat – there's no way she'd miss it.' Raya swipes some branches out of her way, and I leap to the side to dodge them.

'And I was right – she had no idea. But then she decided to come home early one day and found me in her kitchen.'

'What happened?' I ask.

Raya shrugs. 'She started yelling and screaming and threatening to have the Justice Seekers make sure I never even made it to jail. She was rich enough to do it, too. Plenty of miners have disappeared that way, and no one says anything about it. There was no way I was letting them throw me into some lake to disappear like all the rest. So I stopped her.'

I cast a sidelong glance at Raya, appalled by her justification. The Justice Seekers wouldn't have killed her. But uncertainty threads through my thoughts.

If they can be bribed for political favours, why not murder?

I rub the back of my neck, suddenly uncomfortable. Before I came here, I never wondered where my next meal was coming from, or where I would sleep, or if I'd have a roof over my head. But I do know what it's like to be stuck.

In the end, we made the same choice.

'I would've killed her, too,' Bex says. She doesn't sound very convincing, but Raya flashes her a grateful smile anyway.

'What about you?' Raya asks Bex.

Bex wrings her hands together, her gloves almost coming off with the force of the movement. 'It's like I told you. I had too much to drink and ran into that motorboat, killing that mom and her three-year-old son.' She hangs her head. 'It was an accident. A horrible, awful accident.'

Raya puts her arm around Bex's shoulders, the movement stiff and awkward as though she's not sure she's doing it right. 'But that's not your fault.'

Bex gives her a shaky smile. 'Perhaps. But it seems like whoever planned this whole ruse believes it was. And that all of us deserve to be punished.'

'Maybe we do,' I say.

'No, we don't,' Raya retorts.

'Why?'

'Because me and you was protecting others, and Bex didn't do it on purpose. I don't care what you think – no one has any right to judge us.'

Silence falls over us again as we continue our trek towards the red light. I try to convince myself Raya's right, but it doesn't matter.

Somebody obviously disagrees.

*

'How far away is that damn switch?' Raya asks.

I glance at the overcast sky, which offers no warmth and little light. We've been walking for what feels like hours and have long since left the protection of the forest. The vast plain we're plodding through is virtually identical to the last one. In the distance, more dead trees rise to greet us. It has to be a repeating pattern designed to create despair.

It's working.

'I have no idea.' Bex's forehead creases as she studies the land around us. 'Depends on how big the world is.'

'How big could they make it?' I ask, more to myself.

'I don't know,' Bex snaps. 'I'm not exactly an expert on holo-programming.' She runs her fingers through her hair. 'Sorry. I'm hungry and tired.'

'It's OK, we all are.' We should've grabbed the rest of the protein packs, but I doubt we'll find our way back to the shuttle now. Assuming it was real and not part of the programming.

I squash the hopelessness pressing against my chest. 'When we get to the trees, we can camp for the night.'

'It's not safe to sleep,' Raya says. 'Just because we haven't run into another booby trap doesn't mean we won't.'

'She's right,' Bex says. 'We don't know what this person has planned.'

'We need to rest,' I say. 'Otherwise, we'll make mistakes. We can set up a watch to protect us.'

'There's no protecting us,' Raya scoffs. 'They can send a million giant cats to kill us, or wait until we starve to death, or open another bottomless hole. It doesn't matter what we do, they'll have made it so we never get close to that switch.'

Even though I don't want to admit it, she's right. But it doesn't mean we have to give up. 'I'd rather go down fighting,' I say. 'We'll make a plan tonight.'

Raya grins. 'Hell yeah! We'll show those bastards a thing or two.'

'I don't think that's a good idea,' Bex says. 'We'd be much safer –'

A howl skitters across the frozen plain, and my heart skips a beat.

'What was that?' Raya turns in a slow circle, fists clenched at her sides.

Bex glances behind her. 'I-I don't know.'

Another howl chases her words.

'Wolves, I think.' The words come out steady even though I'm battling to reign in my fear. What kind of horror is headed our way?

Raya unzips her suit. 'What are those?'

'They're similar to dogs.' I keep my gaze fixed on the horizon, searching for the source of the noise. 'They're animals that live on Earth.'

'Then how do you know what they are?' Raya asks in a slow, even voice.

'The leopard,' I say. 'Winston said it looked like an animal from Earth. The island was shaped like an island from a book about Earth. I've read about Earth predators, and I've even heard a recording of wolves. I'm positive that's what it is.'

I search the area again. Nothing.

'We should head for the trees,' Bex says.

Barks and growls rip through the air. My heart leaps into my throat. 'They can outrun us.'

Raya holds out her knife, a slight tremor in her hand as though it's a bit too heavy. 'I'm done running.'

My mind races, struggling to come up with a plan that'll work. 'We can't win. They travel in packs – there'll be too many to fight without Bex and me being armed.'

Unconsciously, we've backed into a circle, all of us facing outward, watching every direction.

'Then what do you suggest?' Raya asks in a low, dangerous voice. 'That we wait here so they can crush us to death?'

She has a point. 'Let's make a run for the woods,' I say. 'I don't think they can climb trees.'

'Neither can I,' says Bex.

'I'll help you. On the count of three, run. One –'

'There they are!' Bex shouts. A pack of massive beasts with grey fur appears on the horizon. Even from this distance they look too large to be real.

'Go!' I yell.

We break for the trees, Raya in front. I'm not far behind.

'Bex!' I shout.

'Coming!'

Raya whirls around and sprints in the opposite direction.

'What're you –'

She passes me.

I spin around as she grabs Bex's wrist. Pulling her along, Raya races back towards the trees. Behind them, the wolves are closing in. If they're actually wolves. They're so big. So fast.

'Move your feet!' Raya charges past me with Bex in tow. I follow, sheer terror propelling me forward. Frost crunches beneath me and cold air whips my face.

The baying intensifies. I force my eyes forward.

Raya paces herself with Bex. I stay half a metre behind.

A growl almost brings me to a stop. I risk a glance behind me. The beasts are some kind of aberration of a dog – massive and hairy with yellow eyes and long snouts. Their mouths hang wide open, fangs glinting in the weak light. They move with unnatural speed.

'Faster!' I hurl myself forward. Bex throws a look over her shoulder and stumbles.

Raya jerks her up.

The wolves' panting vibrates through the air, their massive paws pounding across the frost. Raya and Bex pull further ahead, but the trees are too far away.

They're not going to make it.

With one last glance at Raya and Bex, I veer to the side, whooping and hollering.

Like a giant grey wave, the wolves turn towards me. I run faster, risking one last glance at the girls. They're still running straight ahead. Good. I pump my arms, speeding away and bringing the wolves with me.

Trees appear in the distance. Hope skirts around my fear, teasing me with life. There's a chance I might make it. Refusing to glance back, I keep running. This is nothing but a race.

One I will win.

Pain shoots through my side, but I ignore it. I won't be crushed to death by some computer creation because of a cramp. The forest is so close. I force my feet to move faster. I'm metres away.

My boot dips into a small hole, and I go flying.

Scrambling to my feet, I fall right back down. My ankle won't support me.

'Shit!'

I try again. And again. Why haven't they attacked? I look behind me.

They're gone.

My breath catches in my throat. Raya and Bex! The pack went after them instead!

I push myself up, careful to stay off my foot, and hop forward, searching for them, frantic. But there's nothing there. No wolves. No Bex or Raya. Only an endless plain of frost in front of me and trees to my back.

Where did the wolves go? Are they still here or have they been turned off? Sweat drips into my eyes, blurring the landscape as I scan the area again. It's as if the beasts never existed.

Wary, I hop towards the trees, wincing as pain slices through me. I need to get this boot off before my ankle swells too much. Then I'll find the girls.

Leaning against a rough, brown trunk on the edge of the forest, I slide to the ground and unlace my boot with fumbling fingers. My ankle throbs. Gripping the tough, synthetic leather, I pull. The boot doesn't budge. Groaning, I yank again. Pain shoots up my leg.

'Come on.' My panic increases with each passing second. I'm wasting time. Bex and Raya might be hurt. Or dead.

With one final tug, the boot comes off. I bite back a yell of pain. Rolling down my sock, I study my swollen ankle. It's either broken or a bad sprain. I graze my fingers over the skin and air hisses through my teeth.

This is bad. Very bad.

Struggling to scoop up a bit of frost, I dribble freezing water on my ankle, but it does nothing to numb it. I glance again in the direction Bex and Raya ran, an image of two crushed, bloody bodies rising in my mind. I push it away. Raya's a survivor, and she'll help Bex. They'll be fine.

Clenching my jaw, I stagger to my feet and hop along the edge of the forest, using the tree trunks for support. I should call out for them, but those wolves ... I shudder. What if they're voice-activated? Is that a thing? I don't remember what the tech said.

Screw it. 'Bex!' My voice echoes in the air. 'Raya!' I pause, holding my breath, listening for a response.

Silence.

'Bex! Raya!'

Still no answer.

Above, the sun is sinking in the grey sky. It'll be night soon, and then what? I don't have my helmet to seal my suit, so there's a good chance I'll freeze to death before I find the girls.

A short, harsh bark echoes through the air. I halt, gripping a trunk in trepidation, muscles tense, ready to run even though I can't, but there's only silence. Anger engulfs me, swift and hot. Enough of this! I'm turning off the switch and getting us out of here. Alive.

A crack reverberates behind me.

Using the trunk, I turn myself so I'm facing the trees. 'Bex?'

A crunch and another crack.

'Raya?'

Silence.

Fear crawls up my spine, fierce and gripping. 'Hello?'

'Zane.'

I peer into the trees. Did I imagine that?

A figure emerges from the shadows.

No.

I take a step back, forgetting about my bad ankle. It buckles, and I fall.

'What are you doing?' I stare at the gun pointed at me.

'What do you think?'

I gulp, heart racing, hands scrambling to find a weapon – something, anything, to defend myself.

'It's too late for that.' So cold and unexpected. Is this how my dad felt when he saw me? He looked so surprised to see the gun. I thought it was because he was drunk.

But it was because he'd been betrayed.

'Goodbye, Zane.'

20

BEX

The howls fade away as we race to the trees. I slow, lungs burning, chest heaving, legs about to give way.

'Don't stop!' Raya pushes me forward, but my body's shutting down. I can't do this.

Another shove. I stumble but keep moving. I won't let Raya down. Or Zane. We're all going to survive.

I stagger into the trees. They shudder, blink, and solidify. 'We . . . made . . . it . . .' I wheeze. I lean against a trunk, the bark scraping against my palm as I struggle to get air into my lungs, my heart racing so fast I'm pretty sure it's going to fly right out of my chest. 'Raya,' I say in disbelief, 'we did it.'

She doesn't respond.

'Raya?'

I turn around. Nothing but trees and bushes.

'Raya!' I reel forward, fear surging through me. 'Zane!'

I lurch out of the trees. The expansive plain greets me, silent and empty. Even our footprints have disappeared. Or did we leave any?

'Raya . . . ?' Her name is a whisper on my lips. Where'd she go? Where's Zane? What happened to the wolves? I squeeze my eyes shut and open them again, waiting for them to reappear, sure it's a trick of the light. But nothing changes.

I retreat into the trees, branches scraping and tugging at my suit. What happened to them? Did Raya run past me? Did Zane? How would I have missed that? What is happening?

'Raya! Zane!' I scream, terror driving my desperation. 'Raya!' Her name comes out choked with tears. I sink to my knees, the ground cold and hard.

What kind of trick is this? Can someone just disappear? A soft rustle of branches is the only response. A sob rises in my throat, and I swallow hard to dislodge it. Crying will not help. I force myself to my feet, trembling. For once, fear's not going to win. Raya and Zane didn't vanish into nothingness. I will find them.

I squint in the dim light, trying to see further, to spot them. But there's only trees. And since we're in a holo-theatre, anything could've happened. They could've fallen down a hole, been killed by wolves –

I shake my head, hard. I'm not going there. I peer through the forest again. I'm certain no one passed me, which means . . . I straighten my shoulders with a new confidence. The landscape changed. Because real trees don't blink and disappear.

I have to go back into the open to find them. My stomach plunges with apprehension. At least the trees offer the illusion of safety. But out there, by myself? I take a step back, bumping into a trunk.

Terror and doubt make it impossible to move. What if I screw this up? What if they're already dead because they helped me? What if . . .

Mom's voice echoes in my ear. '*You are so much more than your father says you are.*'

She never stopped believing in me.

I stare at the plains peeking through the trees. I lied to Raya. I told Mom where I was going. Told her I was going to win enough money for us both to leave, even though I knew she wouldn't. I'd do anything for her.

'*Are you sure this is what you want?*' Mom asks.

'*Yes. I can't stay here. You know that. Especially with . . .*' *I can't say it. Between the accident, my father and being passed over in favour of my brother, I no longer have a place on Rikas. Like I ever did.*

'*I know.*' *She tucks a stray hair behind my ear and cups my face.* '*Go show the world what you're made of.*'

What am I made of? I am not this shivering, frightened girl.

I am Bexley Anne Ryker.

I am brave and smart and capable, and I will show this place what I'm made of.

I step out of the trees.

The frozen plain greets me, cold and unchanged. I stare at it – what did I expect, exactly? Raya and Zane standing right in front of me?

I breathe in the cold air, gathering my courage, and take a step forward, then another, the crunch of the frost strangely reassuring.

Another blink and the plains flicker and disappear. I'm back in the forest.

I turn in a slow circle. Trees tower above me, hiding the feeble light from above. The air's harder to breathe. Panic grips my heart – whoever's running this thing must've figured out we know the truth, and now they're playing with us. What if I'm stuck between plains and forests until I starve to death? Or freeze?

No.

For once, I'm going to win. I won't stop searching for my friends even if the landscape changes a million times. I'm more than anyone thinks I am.

Fierce determination tears through me, and I shove a branch out of my face.

A low growl rumbles from above me. Raising my head, my gaze meets the sharp, yellow glint of two eyes staring back at me. A choked scream escapes my throat.

The cat in the tree above me rises to its feet like fog coming off the lake. It's massive. At least twice the size of the one from earlier.

I stumble back, knocking into a tree trunk. The cat watches me, almost lazily. I inch away, eyes locked on it as it yawns, baring sharp yellow fangs and a long, pink tongue. I keep moving. It stretches, licks its paw, and begins to groom itself.

What is going on?

I back away faster, uncertainty fuelling my steps. The cat doesn't seem to notice or care. It just keeps licking its paw and running it over its head like a house cat. An enormous house cat that can crush me.

I stumble again, almost falling.

The cat yowls and leaps from the branch, landing with a

soft thud. It weaves in and out of the trees like a shadow, staring at me. Stalking me.

I take off through the forest, gasping for air, sweating in spite of the cold. Paws hit the ground in a soft, rhythmic thump. I glance back. The cat's close – too close.

I try to pick up speed, but there's nothing left in me. My steps become more of a stagger.

The beast slows with me. I gulp. It's playing a sick game of cat and mouse with me.

A cramp explodes in my side, and my heart pounds so hard I'm convinced it's going to give out. I can't do it. I can't run any more. Besides, where can I go that it can't catch me?

Gulping and gasping, I whirl around. 'Go away!'

It takes a few silent steps towards me.

'Leave!'

It crouches low, ready to pounce.

21

RAYA

A branch scrapes across my cheek. Brushing it away, my hand comes back with a smear of blood on it.

Great.

Everything in this place wants to kill me. But it's not going to win. Me, Bex and Zane are getting out of here – as soon as I find them, that is.

I shove a piece of hair out of my eyes, replaying the moment in my head. The wolves were chasing Zane while me and Bex kept running. We got to the trees, and I shoved Bex in. I'd hollered for her to keep going before racing back out to grab Zane – but how far did she get? And where the hell did Zane go?

I must've searched in the wrong place. It's not hard to do. The whole planet looks the same.

I slam my fist against a trunk, wincing – damn shuttle messed up my wrist. 'You think you won?' I yell into the empty air. 'You haven't won. You aren't going to win. I'm going to take you out, you piece of shit coward! This isn't over. It's never going to be over. I'll hunt you down and torture you till you wish you'd never heard of me!'

I give the sky the finger before pushing through the trees again, branches catching in my hair. Screw whoever thought this was a good idea. They're going to regret the day they decided I needed justice.

So let them come. Let them try and kill me with wolves and giant cats and bottomless pits and whatever else they thought they could beat me with. I'll show them what it means to mess with me. I march towards the red light, but then slow.

It's too obvious. Too easy.

I bet it's a trap.

Because whoever's running this thing is smart. Making us all believe it was Evie. Starting the whole thing with that poisoned burger, making it look like Greyson choked. Dropping Paloma off a cliff. Messing with Winston's suit. They've been planning this for a while now.

I swat another branch out of my way. There's no way that red light is the answer. But I bet that's where Bex is headed.

A snap echoes in the icy air. I pause, searching the trees. Nobody's there.

I creep forward – listening hard. Zane probably headed towards the light too ... if those dogs didn't crush him. I wrinkle my nose – what a horrible way to die. But it was a noble thing to do.

Too bad noble people die first.

A howl rips the air. I freeze, scanning the trees, waiting for I don't know how long. But nothing happens. Even the wind's stopped blowing.

A chill races up my spine in the eerie silence. I squeeze the handle of the knife, its grip familiar and reassuring. Screw the mind games, I'm not falling for them.

I sneak through the forest, staying in the shadows, listening for anyone or anything that might be following me. With each minute my heart races a little faster and my hands sweat a bit more.

It shouldn't be this quiet. It's not natural. I glance at the tiny bit of sky peeking through the trees. It's going to be dark soon. It's easier to get yourself killed in the dark.

Suddenly the ground starts trembling and shaking, tossing me to my hands and knees. A crack appears in front of me, getting super wide super fast.

'Shit!' Ignoring the pain in my wrist, I scoot back and scramble to my feet. But the dirt keeps on crumbling away, following me like it wants to swallow me up. I'm not going out this way either.

I run.

The ground moves and rolls around me. I dash around bushes and leap over gaps. Pieces of mud fly at me.

An unexpected pause and then it's quiet again.

I don't move, eyes darting all around, waiting for what's next. A roar shatters the silence, and a wave of mud and dirt and logs tumbles towards me. I leap over it and keep on going.

It changes directions, rumbling as it charges at me from the sides. Trees groan and sway, sliding down the back of the giant hill, standing tall, never falling.

What the hell's going on?

I back up, trying to watch both sides. The waves move slow now, as if they're watching me. But that isn't possible.

Unless it's one of those booby traps Zane and Bex were talking about?

Mountains rise around me, making a corridor with only one way out. It's herding me somewhere. Spinning round so I'm not walking backwards, I keep going in the direction it's leading, muscles tense, ready to fight.

I stray to the side a little and the wall moves in on me, pushing me back to the path, which is a lot narrower than it was. A few minutes later it slopes down, like it wants me to go faster.

I've got no choice but to follow.

22

ZANE

A flash of fire, an eruption of sound. I dive to the side, the bullet whistling over my head. Scrambling, I crouch behind a tree trunk, fear and dread coiling inside me. I've bought myself seconds; a minute if I'm lucky.

The gun cocks. 'Do you think hiding behind a holo-tree is going to make a difference?'

'Why are you doing this?' I scan the ground for a branch, a rock, anything to use as a weapon.

Footsteps scrape across the frost. 'You know why.'

'He was a bastard.' I run my shaking hands up the tree, its rough bark scratching my skin, but there aren't any branches this far down.

'I don't care.'

'He beat my mom.' I cringe at the desperation in my voice, but the footsteps stop. I seize my advantage. 'I was protecting her – protecting us. You can't judge something you never saw.'

'I'm not judging. You broke the law, regardless of the reason, and the penalty for murder is death.'

'Isn't that for a jury to decide?'

'You gave up that right when you lied to the Justice Seekers.'

I keep talking, stalling. There has to be a way out of this. 'What about you? You've killed far more people than I have.'

An unconcerned shrug. 'There's a difference between murder and exacting justice – the law recognizes that.'

'I'll turn myself in. I-I'll never tell anyone about what happened here.' My stomach twists and clenches as I switch tactics, hoping it works. 'I promise.'

'It's too late for promises.'

A twig snaps.

Damn. There has to be something – anything – I can use to fight back.

The gun appears around the trunk, followed by an arm.

With a wild yell, I throw myself at the body edging around the tree.

We slam to the ground. I grope for the gun mashed between us. It slips a fraction of an inch. My heartbeat echoes in my ears, thumping out a death beat as I grapple for the weapon.

I wrap my fingers around a gloved hand, struggling to prise their fingers loose, terror and determination permeating the cold air.

I cry out as a boot kicks my sprained ankle, my hold on the gun loosening.

I grit my teeth. It'll take more than that.

I tighten my grip.

A knee slams into my stomach.

Grunting, I curl inward, my hand slipping from the gun.

Then There Was One

I'm not losing this fight! I lurch upwards, grabbing for it with my other hand.

We start to tumble.

The gun goes off.

23

RAYA

The giant wall keeps me on the path it wants – curving and moving like some kind of living creature. It's gotten bigger, too, like it's afraid I'll take off and go where I'm not supposed to.

But I'm where I want to be. I adjust my grip on the knife, ignoring the small tremble caused by my wrist. I've got this.

'Bex?' Zane's voice comes from nowhere.

I swivel, but the only thing behind me is the wall of dirt.

'Raya?'

'Zane?' I whisper.

'Hello?' His voice shakes a little. Then, a little louder, 'What are you doing?' He sounds scared.

I'm about to holler back to see where he is but stop. What if it's a trap? I'm already in one, I don't want to walk into another. I creep forward, staying low, knife loose and ready.

The dirt wall shrinks and I break into a slow jog, muscles tense and ready. A bang like rock being blown apart cracks the silence.

I run faster, heart pounding like it never used to. The dirt wall's almost gone and now there's only two small slopes on my sides. Behind me it's disappeared – like it was never there.

I pause. I could turn round now. Find the switch. End the game.

A yell, a grunt and a thump. Whatever's going on can't be that far ahead. Forget going back. I'm not leaving anyone behind. I race towards the noise.

Two people in shiny brown suits wrestle a few metres away. I jerk to a stop. Why the hell are Bex and Zane fighting? It don't make sense.

Another bang.

One person crawls off the other.

Zane's lying on the ground, arms wrapped around his stomach, the sharp smell of iron invading the air. I stare, my mouth hanging open.

Why'd Bex kill him? Was Zane the killer all along?

Or, shit – is the killer Bex?

I sneak forward, weighing my options.

'I see you.' The other person turns and seems to look right at me, gun still raised.

It can't be . . . no . . . they wouldn't.

But all it takes is one little lie.

'Raya, you don't have to hide.'

I don't move. It may be a bluff.

'Come on out.'

The gun's pointed at my heart. I swallow, hard.

Bullets are faster than knives.

24

BEX

I grab a large stick and raise it high. The cat doesn't move. My chest heaves and my legs wobble as I wait, ready to strike the moment the cat leaps, hoping I trigger some sort of kill switch.

Its yellow eyes stare at me, cold and calculating.

I bend my knees, imitating Raya, branch held like a bat. The cat's shoulders undulate as it lowers a fraction of an inch. The wind stills and the trees stop swaying; it's as though the planet's holding its breath.

The cat leaps, claws outstretched, ready to flatten me.

I scream in rage and fear and race forward, swinging the branch with everything in me. It collides with the beast's leg. The cat tumbles to the ground, but it's back on its feet in seconds. We circle each other, slow and deliberate.

The cat growls, baring its fangs. I raise the branch higher.

It leaps.

I swing.

Its paw collides with my shoulder, bringing me down, the branch falling from my hand. The animal stalks towards me.

Sweat drips down my face and into my eyes as I inch to the side, groping for the branch. My fingers close around cold, hard bark. I will not be the victim any more. I am not this cat's prey.

I leap to my feet and charge, yelling and raising the branch high above my head.

The cat darts forward.

I swing the stick down.

It cracks against the beast's skull, sending reverberations up my arm. The cat stops, dazed. I hit it again and again. The branch cracks.

The cat lets out a soft, almost pitiful mewl and races away.

I slump to the ground, struggling to breathe, tears streaming down my face. Pain cuts through the shock of winning as my shoulder throbs. I pull back my suit and probe the spot, wincing at the pressure – I'm going to have another nasty bruise.

I climb unsteadily to my feet. No sign of the beast. But that doesn't mean much – it could be looking for another cat. Or maybe it's decided a surprise attack is a better choice. I'm not giving it a chance to do either.

Stumbling through the trees in the opposite direction, I search for Raya and Zane. I pause often, straining to hear any sound of the cat, or the wolves, or anything else that might be trying to kill me. I won't be an easy target.

Not any more.

I duck under a branch. Then again, if I'm being watched, there's no way not to be an easy target. But, if that's the case, why draw it out? Why not send a horde of giant cats and wolves to finish it? What kind of sick pleasure is this person getting from watching us all suffer?

Are Raya and Zane dead? I shudder. Maybe they abandoned me. I shove the words aside. It doesn't matter what's happened – I will find them.

A howl rends the air.

I jolt to a stop, scanning the forest and the bits of plain visible through the trees, poised to run when the grey mass materializes. Or climb. I survey a tree. I might be able to do it.

Blood pounds in my ears as I wait for the wolves, but none appear. After an eternity, I creep forward. Slower this time, quieter, making sure my boots don't crunch.

'Bex?'

I freeze. Did I hear my name? No. It's still and quiet – I'm hearing things.

'Raya?'

But I'm not. I jog in the direction of the voice.

'Hello?'

As I crest a small hill Zane comes into view.

Picking up speed, I lift my arms and wave, about to yell that I'm here when a figure emerges from the trees. I stumble, falling to my knees.

It can't be. It's not possible.

Winston's pointing a gun at Zane.

My hand flies to my mouth. This is wrong. This is all wrong. He died. I saw his body.

'Goodbye, Zane.'

I muffle a scream as the gun fires. Zane flies behind a tree.

I clamber to my feet as pieces of conversation float in the air. Winston advances on Zane. This can't be happening. Zane yells and hurls himself at Winston. They tumble to the ground.

Another gun shot. Winston crawling off Zane. Zane curled in a ball. Blood staining the ground.

'I see you,' Winston says.

My breath catches in my throat. He's not even looking in my direction. How does he know I'm here?

'Raya, you don't have to hide.'

My gaze darts to where the gun's pointing. Raya's standing there, staring at Winston. I take off across the frost.

'Come on out.'

She doesn't move.

'I am sorry to do this, you know. I did like you.'

An inhuman scream escapes from somewhere deep inside me. Winston swivels as I leap, smashing into him. We crash to the ground, the gun slipping from his hand. Before he can react, I jump to my feet and kick it away before lunging at Raya, grabbing her wrist, pulling her away. She cries out as we hurtle into the forest, but I don't stop.

Branches slap my face and body, failing to slow me down. Vaulting over bushes and fallen branches, I run as fast as I can.

'Go go go!' Raya yells from behind me.

I want to shout I'm going, but I can't speak through the massive cramp in my side. It hurts to move. Tears spring to my eyes.

A bang echoes behind us followed by the splintering of bark.

I keep running, panic chasing my steps.

Another bang.

Raya yells.

I whirl around. She's limping forward, blood blossoming on her thigh, a jagged hole in her leg.

'I got you!' I grab her hand. 'Come on.'

Another gunshot. Raya drops to the ground.

'No!' I yank her arm, and she yelps in pain. 'Get up.'

'Run!' she says through gritted teeth.

I shake my head. 'Not without you.'

Raya shoves me. 'Go!'

Winston's advancing on us, gun aimed at Raya.

I choke back tears. 'No.'

'You're hopeless, Rich Girl. Run! Now!'

Twisting, she lunges at Winston's feet. He topples to the ground, the gun falling from his hand. I dive for it, but they're in the way. Winston lets out a grunt and rolls to the side, Raya's knife buried deep in his thigh.

'Bitch,' he snarls. He fumbles for the gun. I leap over Raya, but my foot catches on her. I crash to the ground too.

BANG!

'No!' I scream. Raya falls back, a thin plume of smoke rising from a hole in her side.

I claw my way to him. 'Bastard!'

He points the gun at me, but I jam my fist on the knife hilt, and he howls. I grab the handle and twist, pushing the knife in deeper. He's going to pay.

'Casper,' he gasps. 'Casper, now!'

A low hiss fills the air. My eyes instantly water and my lungs sting. I cough, unable to breathe without pain. Winston pushes me off him and unzips his pressure suit, pulling a small gas mask out of his pocket. 'Sorry, Bex.' He fits it over his nose and mouth.

Coughing, I struggle to take a good breath.

'But, before you die . . .' He moves his hand to his waist.

I blink.

Winston's wavering in front of me, going in and out of focus, and then the illusion falls away, leaving behind a tall boy who's my age and dressed in a green Spectra Suit.

I stare at his handsome face. High cheekbones, dark blue eyes, auburn hair, a familiar sneer on his lips.

I know him.

25

REESE

Nine months ago

I lean against the doorframe, the sturdy wood oddly comforting, and study the once pristine white wall that's now covered in yarn, pins, pictures and scribbled notes. At its centre is a blown-up photograph of a girl with curly, black hair and a smudge of dirt on her cheek. She's oddly charming.

'Another one?' I make a conscious effort not to glance at the box of files sitting open next to Dad's desk, its contents spilling out, each one impatiently waiting for its turn.

He taps the picture, his smile more manic than happy. 'Yes, and it's a good one.'

I wind my way around the cluttered floor, careful not to knock over stacks that Dad swears are organized, and cross my arms, my burgundy sweater rough against my skin. 'So, what did this one do?'

'She killed a woman for a bag of food.' Dad traces his finger along a red piece of yarn to a smaller picture, the faint scent of alcohol caressing his words. 'A Ms Josephine Harris.'

'And why didn't she get caught?' My voice is even and methodical – this is always the first question.

Dad waves his hand erratically. 'Lots of reasons. Half the cameras on The Moons are broken so she's hard to track. No murder weapon, although I think I know where it is. The Justice Seekers hated Ms Harris so they aren't keen on helping . . .' His voice trails off as he stares blankly at the wall.

'Where's the murder weapon?'

Dad narrows his eyes, like he's struggling to understand what I've asked. His hobby of tracking down unsolved murders has a become an obsession – as though by bringing random strangers to justice he'll also find it for himself.

It's nothing more than a cruel joke.

He takes a swig from a silver flask engraved with his initials – a gift – his gaze never shifting, bloodshot eyes lost in a world only he inhabits.

'Dad?' I rest my hand on his arm – there's a brown stain on the sleeve. Coffee maybe. Or tea. 'Where did –' I squint at the small tag underneath the photo – 'Raya hide the weapon?'

A loud groan echoes through the room. 'Not this again.'

I swivel, glaring at Casper. But before I can say anything to him he says, 'I'm going to Mina's, our project's due in a few days.'

He doesn't wait for Dad to say goodbye – there's no point. Casper could drop off the face of the planet and Dad wouldn't notice. He used to be so proud of him, always bragging about how Casper would take programming to a whole new level that would revolutionize holo-technology.

But not any more.

The only people who matter to him now are in that file box.

I run my hand through my hair – I need to encourage Casper more. And to forge Dad's name on Casper's application for his school's programming camp, not to mention that we need groceries, and I haven't checked Dad's emails in a few days.

I glance at his tablet; the crack in the screen he meant to have fixed now cuts a jagged line down the entire left side. One more thing to do. One more task to ensure people don't notice just how bad things have gotten.

Sighing, I turn back to the wall, which will never feature the one person it should, because she's a Ryker.

26

BEX

'Reese?' I choke out between gasps for air. I saw his picture on the newsfeeds after the accident. Him and his dad and his brother . . . Casper. I'd printed it out, memorized their faces, apologized to them every day. I fall to my hands and knees, lungs aching, tears streaming from my eyes.

'This is the price you pay for killing my mom and Sam. For destroying my dad until he took his own life.'

'I'm . . . sorry,' I whisper.

'What was that?' He leans in closer.

I open my mouth, but I can't inhale enough oxygen to speak.

'Here.' He takes a quick breath before putting his mask over my nose and mouth. 'I want to hear you say it.' He coughs.

I breathe deeply, fresh oxygen filling my lungs. I exhale and take another deep breath. Reese snatches the mask away. 'Let's not get greedy. Now say you're sorry for killing my mom and my little brother.'

I stare at him, anger and guilt and remorse swirling through me. 'I'm sorry . . . about Sam,' I say so he can hear me. 'But not *her*.'

I close my eyes and slump to the ground.

27

REESE

Fury fills me as Bex tumbles to the floor – after everything, she's *still* not sorry my mom's dead? Fighting to reign in my rage, I nudge – kick – her on to her back with my boot, studying her for any signs of life. There's none. Grabbing a small mirror out of my pocket, I hold it up to her nose and mouth – no fog appears on the glass.

Overwhelming relief floods through me – it's over.

'Turn it off!' I yell.

The gas stops filling the holo-theatre, and a fan turns on. In a few minutes the air is clear. The trees flicker and disappear, replaced by a plain, green room.

I pull off my mask before clasping my hand over the knife. Gritting my teeth, I yank it out. Refusing to acknowledge the pain, I take a moment to study the wound before pressing my hand over it to stop the bleeding. It's deep, but thankfully Raya missed the artery.

'Do you need a doctor?' Casper clatters down the metal stairs from the control room, concern radiating from him.

'Probably. But I don't want to deal with any questions. Is there a first aid kit upstairs?'

'Yeah.'

'Get it.'

I press on the wound, wincing. It's a small price to pay, especially considering everything that could've gone wrong. I eye Bex's body and smile. It was all worth the risk.

Now, maybe, I can get on with life. Ensure Casper graduates high school. Go to university as I always planned. Become a lawyer like Dad. Make Mom proud. Live a life Sam wasn't given the chance to. A familiar ache squeezes my chest, making it hard to breathe even though the air is now clear. I miss them.

Casper hands me the kit. 'Here you go.'

I pull out sanitizing pads, gauze and medical tape along with a bottle of liquid InstaStitches, grateful to have something else to focus on. With a little effort, I wiggle out of my Spectra Suit and unstrap the bulletproof vest I've been wearing since I pretended to die as Winston – couldn't risk one of them grabbing the gun and shooting me instead.

Casper furrows his brow as he studies my leg. 'Do you think the InstaStitches will hold?'

I clench my teeth as I clean the wound and apply the liquid. 'They should, for now.'

'Were the boats delivered?' I ask once I'm done and dressed in normal clothes, ignoring the dull ache thrumming though my leg.

'Yup. One went straight to the harbour, and the other is on the loading dock along with our fake IDs, chains to weigh the bodies down, and supplies to sink the ship.'

I survey the corpses lined up against the wall, covered in green ColdSeal blankets to keep them from smelling. They'd been hidden in the trees, only metres from Zane, Raya and Bex, disguised by the holo-theatre as bushes.

'And you confirmed that we're still cleared to sail tonight?'

'Uh huh. I have us down for delivering one boat to Creor tonight and both of us returning on the other in the morning.'

'Perfect.' By midnight, all ten bodies will be at the bottom of the ocean and any trace of them gone. Except . . . I give Casper a sharp look. 'Did you delete the footage?'

'Yes. All of it. And I wiped the hard drive.' Casper hesitates before adding, 'I think Dad would be proud of us.'

'I know he would.' An eye for an eye, that's what Dad always said in his closing arguments to a jury. If they believed the defendant was guilty then the defendant deserved to pay the proper punishment, as dictated by the law, for their crime.

A ghost of a smile flits across my face. Of course, Dad and I often disagreed on what the proper punishment should be. I always took the view that if you robbed someone, then you should lose your possessions. Or, if you killed someone, you should be killed in return. A true eye for an eye. Dad argued that life was more nuanced than that, but it's not. It's quite simple.

I look at the blankets covering the bodies. All of them believed they had got away with murder, but it was just a matter of time. Dad had been gathering evidence on each person here when he died.

Because of Bex.

Because he couldn't stand the thought of a life without Mom and Sam.

Because he knew there would never be justice for them.

But I made sure there was.

Satisfaction settles deep within me. Everyone here got exactly what they deserved, and my family can finally rest in peace.

'I still can't believe you convinced Evie to open the shuttle doors.' Casper's also staring at the bodies.

'Her hatred for Raya overrode her common sense. But I *was* surprised it ended up killing her instead.' I glance around the room. 'Do we still have the holo-theatre rented for another two days?' It takes a full twenty-four hours for the venue's sanitization program to run, and I want to make sure there's time for a full cycle to ensure any evidence is destroyed.

'Yes. And the owners want to see the footage of the program we told them we were testing. Said they might buy it.'

'I'm sure they'd love that,' I say wryly. 'Too bad we'll be long gone by the time they figure out there is no program. Come on, let's get lunch. I haven't had anything decent to eat in ages.'

'What about . . . ?' Casper motions to the bodies. Oh yeah.

'I'll go grab something for both of us. You wait here.'

'But –'

'Look,' I snap. 'I know you don't want to be here with them, but they're dead, and someone has to make sure no one comes in. And I'm the one that's been trapped in that simulation for four days – I need to get out of here before I go mad.'

Casper raises his hands in mock surrender. 'Fair enough.'

'I'll be back soon.' I glance at my leg to make sure it hasn't started bleeding again before limping towards the exit, stomach growling in anticipation of a meal that isn't comprised of protein packs.

I'm halfway to the door when blinding pain shoots through me.

28

REESE

My hands fly to my stomach.

The holo-theatre flickers in and out of focus, darkness slowly overwhelming me.

Voices . . . a cacophony of voices. I'm running on a grassy knoll, a sparkling lake in the distance. The sun is hot, so hot . . .

*

Whoosh.

A grey blanket is being draped over a small, lifeless body. Next to it, a piece of floral fabric flutters from underneath a similar covering.

*

Drip. Drip. Drip.

The holo-theatre swims back into view. My hand is bleeding. No. The blood's coming from somewhere else. The room wavers, and the red droplets blur. They're not blood, but rain pinging off a matte, black coffin surrounded by mourners.

*

Knock. Knock.

'Is your dad home?' A tiny woman peers at me through even tinier spectacles, a navy-blue hat perched on her brown hair, her gold badge gleaming.

'Bexley Ryker won't be charged. I'm sorry, Judge.'

A mask of confusion and grief as the man topples forward, unsupported. My knees buckle, I can't hold the weight.

*

'Why, Reese?'

I turn to answer my brother. 'I'm sorry.'

*

'Where'd you find that?' Casper's standing in the doorway to Dad's office.

I look at the tan file in my hand, disorientated. 'In Dad's box of murderers.'

Casper raises an eyebrow. 'Seriously?'

'There are a lot of them.'

*

The bed springs squeak as I sit next to Casper. 'Do you know this book?' The cover shows a brilliant flower blooming against an emerald-green jungle.

Casper nods. 'Mina and I used it for our project. Why?'

'This is it. This is how we're going to do it.'

'Do what?'

'Make Bexley Ryker pay.'

*

I'm in a holo-theatre. I blink, confused.

Have we finished?

Or are we just getting started?

29

BEX

I circle round Reese so I'm facing him.

He's looking down, his hand moving in slow motion to the exit hole in his stomach, the shock on his face evident. Casper stares at him, mouth hanging open. I shift the gun, aiming it at Casper.

It's heavier than I thought it'd be – I meant to shoot Reese in the upper back. But I don't care where I shot him so long as he dies.

Reese's eyes land on me. Wide, angry, fearful. He opens his mouth as though he wants to say something, but nothing comes out. He drops to his knees, hands still clasped on his stomach, blood leaking through his fingers.

Casper's attention is fixed on the gun. 'Please,' he whimpers, raising his hands. 'Plea–'

I pull the trigger. The bang echoes throughout the theatre as Casper topples to the ground.

I smile with grim satisfaction. My aim was better that time.

Keeping the gun gripped in my hands, I stride over to Reese. He's struggling to stay upright, his breath coming out in raspy gasps. I squat next to him and press the gun to his temple. 'Did you think you were going to get away with it?'

He doesn't move, a single word escaping his lips. 'How?'

'I can hold my breath for seven minutes and thirty-three seconds, you stupid bastard . . .'

DAY SEVEN

DAY SEVEN

30

BEX

The coffee shop is as derelict and overlooked as the planet it's built on. Small and destitute, Ermos is an outer planet dedicated to manufacturing construction materials and, if not officially, a place people go to be forgotten.

'Welcome b-b-back! Today we've seen . . .'

I glance at the holographic woman flickering in and out of focus in the far corner, breath stuck in my throat.

'The price of . . . of . . . building matter . . . is –' Her static-y voice drones on about the rising costs of construction.

Releasing my breath, I settle on a hard, cracked plastic stool and open the cheap tablet I bought with the money I found among Reese's things. There wasn't much, but I was able to buy a transporter ticket to Ermos as well as a change of clothes and a couple of weeks in a run-down motel.

I peek over my shoulder as the tablet screen shudders to life – the holographic woman is still droning on. Have the Justice Seekers found the bodies yet? It seems like something that should've hit the newsfeeds after three days.

But so far, nothing.

Unsure if I'm relieved or worried, I take a sip of coffee and wrinkle my nose. It's stale. I should've asked Raya to teach me how to steal – that would've come in handy.

Raya . . .

I shift my focus to the tablet, each blink of the cursor a rebuke for not having contacted Mom yet. But I don't know what to tell her. Or how much. I wring my hands, stomach tight with dread.

Everything. I have to tell her everything.

Sighing, I lift my fingers to the keyboard, the movement slow and laborious, as though my hands weigh a ton. I allow them to hover for a moment before starting, giving myself a chance to change my mind, even though I won't. I'm done lying.

Mom,

I've written and deleted this letter a million times but have finally decided it's best to tell you the truth. It's a horrible and sad story, but you have the right to know what happened.

I brush my new fringe out of my eyes, its mousy colour in my peripheral vision still startling me. I haven't gotten used to having brown hair. Or a fringe. Now I know why people say not to get it done – but it does make for a good disguise. Not even Mom would recognize me. I hardly recognize myself.

With a sigh, I return to my letter.

It started over a year ago when I discovered Dad was having an affair. And not just any affair, but an affair with an outsider.

Fury bubbles inside me. Affairs with anyone not from the ruling class of Rikas are forbidden – can't risk someone from a lower class or another planet having access to our money or our jobs – but Dad didn't care.

Taking a deep breath in a futile effort to calm myself, I keep typing, hitting the keys a little too hard.

I kept tabs on Dad after I first saw them together, afraid someone would find out. It's crazy that you'd be the one ruined when he was the one who did wrong. That you'd be exiled from Rikas for not keeping him happy and I wouldn't be allowed to see you again. Crazy, stupid, backwards planet.

My finger strays to the backspace key, but I don't delete the rant – it's important she understands why I did what I did.

After a while, I was convinced the affair had ended, but then I found a letter from the woman threatening to blackmail Dad if he didn't leave you for her. The next day . . .

My hands begin to tremble, surprising me. What if Mom hates me for what I did? I stare at the stained white wall in front of me. But she'll understand. She knows what it means to protect those you love.

The next day I went out on Dad's solar yacht trying to figure out what to do when she sailed past me in this small motorboat that bounced happily on the water, not caring that she was about to ruin our lives – ruin you. I followed her, not knowing what I was going to do, and that's when her boat's motor died.

The words blur together as images of that day pierce my memory: the boat bobbing gently on the ripples; the sun reflecting on the water, turning it a brilliant blue; her white floral sundress fluttering in the wind as she tried to restart the engine.

She was only a few metres away from a concrete dock and, in an instant, I knew what had to be done. Before I could stop myself, I gunned the engine and rammed her, smashing her small boat between Dad's yacht and the dock.

Once I realized what I'd done, really realized it, I broke open the liquor cabinet, took a couple of drinks, and splashed tequila on my clothes to make sure everyone would believe I'd been drunk. That's what Dad told the Chief Justice Seeker when he slipped her an envelope stuffed with cash – even though I'm sure he guessed at the truth. But all he ever said to anyone who asked was that it'd been a mistake. Some mistake.

Tears streak down my cheeks, the small green dinosaur t-shirt clinging to Sam's lifeless body seared into my brain.

If I had known he was on board, I'd never have done it. If I'd never done it, Raya would still be alive. And Zane.

'Zane,' I whisper, his name a bittersweet memory. I still haven't figured out if I should contact his mom – tell her the truth. Or would that cause her more pain? Maybe I can send her some money anonymously, once I get some, enough to get her back on her feet. Or would that make things worse?

A long, grief-filled sigh escapes from somewhere deep inside me – there are no good answers. I run my fingers over the keys, doubt rippling through me once again.

Should I tell Mom about Reese – his motives, and everything that happened in the holo-theatre? Would she want me to reveal the truth to the authorities, even if it meant I was arrested? Or would she approve of my decision to set the sanitization program to run twice?

I scan the letter, uncertainty making it hard to focus.

I did what I had to do, and I'd do it again, albeit with Dad in the place of Sam. But maybe Mom doesn't need to know. Perhaps it's better if I protect her from the truth as well.

Taking another sip of coffee, I delete the letter and start over.

Dear Mom,

Well, I didn't win *The Pinnacle* – I didn't even make it past the preliminary rounds. Do you know they winnow down the competitors before the show even starts? At least you won't have to explain to Dad why I'm on it.

And I won't have to explain to her why I'm not.

Anyway, I'm not coming home. Or getting married. I hope you understand.

I pause, a crazy idea forming in my mind. It's worth a shot. A smile spreads across my face as I continue to type:

Would you send me some money? There's a promise I have to keep for a friend. And her dog.

With a new sense of purpose, I send the message, gulp down the rest of the coffee, and grab the tablet. With any luck, in a few hours I'll have enough money to get to The Moons. And from there, who knows.

I stride to the exit with a sense of freedom that's unfamiliar and glorious.

'This j-j-j-just in from the . . . the . . . Out . . . Planets!'

I whirl around – the holographic newswoman seems to be flickering in excitement as she beams at her unseen audience.

'. . . b-b-bodies have been . . . been . . . been discovered in a holo-th . . . eatre.'

I stare at the hologram, heart racing as she recites their names. 'C . . . Carson Be . . . Beckett . . . Maria . . . J . . . John . . . son . . .'

It takes an eternity for her to reach the end of the list.

But . . . the tablet slips from my fingers and clatters to the floor.

There's one name missing.

ACKNOWLEDGEMENTS

First and foremost, thank you to my amazing husband who has loved and supported me in innumerable ways. Without his dedication to me and my dream, this book would never have happened.

Thank you to my beautiful girls who have cheered me on and encouraged me over the years, and for showing me the video you made of this book – that will always be one of my favourite memories.

I will never be able to fully express my gratitude to Leslie Zampetti for believing in *Then There Was One*. She worked tirelessly on my behalf, always encouraged me and gave me great advice. A girl couldn't ask for a better agent!

A million thanks to my editors, Charlotte and Katie, for taking a chance on me and using their talents to improve my story. They challenge me to be a better writer and for that I am eternally grateful. Also, thank you Bella and Debbie for noticing where the story needed tweaking and making sure everything made sense.

I would like to thank Andrew French who has been immensely helpful, as well as a steadfast friend. Your advice has been invaluable. Also, I would not be where I am today without my friend Michelle. Thank you for reading every draft, loving my characters as much as I do, and for being there for me through it all. I will always be grateful we sat next to each other at that conference.

Beth and Colleen, you have encouraged me from my very first manuscript and continue to do so to this day. Your love and support have carried me through the tough times and I cannot thank you enough.

Kelly – my sister from another mister. You're the Raya to my Bex, and I love you for it.

To my parents, thank you for your love and support. Who knew the hours I spent reading on the couch and doing well in English would lead to this?

Thank you to the team at Penguin UK who worked so hard on the cover design, marketing, proofreading, and the million other steps it takes to publish a book.

And finally, thank you to my 10A English class – I told you I wouldn't forget.